"Wilson . . . does an incredible job of telling a compelling story while addressing important social issues. . . . Thought-provoking." —*Deep South Magazine*

"In light and lively prose that practically tap dances on the page, Wilson shrewdly probes the intricate tensions and machinations that lie at the core of this eccentric family unit. . . . A provocative and uplifting read." —*BookPage*

"Stellar. . . . Compelling . . . realer and wiser and sadder and eventually reassuring about human nature than dozens of other novels." —*Booklist* (starred review)

"Bittersweet. . . . Wilson delves into the drama and tensions inherent in this strange aquarium. . . . A moving and sincere reflection on what it truly means to become a family."
—*Kirkus Reviews* (starred review)

"Sweet and thoroughly satisfying. . . . Wilson grounds his premise in credible human motivations and behavior, resulting in a memorable cast of characters." —*Publishers Weekly*

"[A] moving novel about love, parenting, and the families we create for ourselves." —*Library Journal*

Baby, You're Gonna Be Mine

ALSO BY KEVIN WILSON

Tunneling to the Center of the Earth

The Family Fang

Perfect Little World

Baby, You're Gonna Be Mine

STORIES

KEVIN WILSON

ecco

An Imprint of HarperCollins*Publishers*

"Scroll Through the Weapons" (as "An Arc Welder, a Molotov Cocktail, a Bowie Knife") in *Ploughshares*

"Housewarming" in *South Carolina Review* and *New Stories from the South: 2010*

"A Visit" in *Missouri Review*

"A Signal to the Faithful" in *A Public Space*

"Sanders for a Night" in *Southwest Review*

"No Joke, This Is Going to Be Painful" in *Tin House* and *New Stories from the South: 2009*

"The Horror We Made" in *American Short Fiction*

BABY, YOU'RE GONNA BE MINE. Copyright © 2018 by Kevin Wilson. All rights reserved. Printed in the United States of America. No part of this book may be used or reproduced in any manner whatsoever without written permission except in the case of brief quotations embodied in critical articles and reviews. For information, address HarperCollins Publishers, 195 Broadway, New York, NY 10007.

HarperCollins books may be purchased for educational, business, or sales promotional use. For information, please e-mail the Special Markets Department at SPsales@harpercollins.com.

FIRST EDITION

Designed by Suet Chong

Library of Congress Cataloging-in-Publication Data

Names: Wilson, Kevin, 1978– author.
Title: Baby, you're gonna be mine : stories / by Kevin Wilson.
Other titles: Baby, you are gonna be mine
Description: First edition. | New York : Ecco, 2018.
Identifiers: LCCN 2017034160 (print) | LCCN 2017034600 (ebook) | ISBN 9780062450685 () | ISBN 9780062450524 | ISBN 9780062450678
Classification: LCC PS3623.I58546 (ebook) | LCC PS3623.I58546 A6 2018 (print) | DDC 813/.6—dc23
LC record available at https://lccn.loc.gov/2017034160

18 19 20 21 22   LSC   10 9 8 7 6 5 4 3 2 1

for Tony Earley and Colonel Padgett Powell

He's a child! It is hopeless! Hopeless! Hopeless!
—Carson McCullers, *A Member of the Wedding*

"We are the parents," Milton said. "We have to watch."
—Ann Patchett, *State of Wonder*

CONTENTS

Baby, You're Gonna Be Mine

Scroll Through the Weapons

It was almost midnight when my girlfriend got a call from her sister, who had been arrested for taking a kebab skewer at a cookout and stabbing her husband.

Even though it was over an hour away, I drove my girlfriend to their house so she could watch her nieces and nephews until their parents found a way to get back home. "If they end up killing each other," my girlfriend told me, "I think I'm the one who gets custody of the kids." I didn't have to say anything in response because she knew as well as I did that I would not be around if that scenario ever became a reality.

The kids were as close to feral as you can get, like animals dressed up in camouflage jumpsuits. Someone had dumped an entire box of frozen corn dogs onto a pan and was warming them on top of a kerosene heater in the living room. The younger boy, who was five, was dancing around his brother, eight, and sister, ten, who were tearing open packets of Pop-

Tarts even though there were already dozens of half-eaten Pop-Tarts all over the house. There were three or four kittens, their eyes oozing pus, running up and down the hallways, and my eyes burned from the smell of piss that saturated the air. In what was ostensibly the dining room, there were, I shit you not, six broken, outdated computers in plain sight.

The older girl, who I think was fourteen but looked older, lanky and petulant and tough, was playing a video game about the apocalypse, but all she kept doing was scrolling through the available weapons in her possession while the game was on pause. I couldn't stand still in the house because the toxins in the air would settle on me, so I kept pacing through the rooms, afraid to stop moving. In the kitchen, there was a person-sized puddle of grape soda that had turned solid, imprints of the kids' bare feet tracking it all over the vinyl floor.

My girlfriend took the middle siblings, who shared a room, into the bathroom and turned the shower on them and got them ready for bed. Then she made a bed on the sofa for the little boy and we watched him hump a pillow for nearly fifteen minutes before he finally fell into something that was barely sleep. The oldest kid just kept scrolling through all the weapons she could, if she wanted to, use on any number of irradiated mutants. My girlfriend went into the kitchen to clean up a little, and I watched the hypnotic clicking of the game as the girl went back and forth between items: brass knuckles, pieces of brick, a baseball bat with nails in it, a BB gun, a 9 mm pistol, a sniper rifle, a sawed-off shotgun, an arc welder, a Molotov cocktail, a Bowie knife, a sledgehammer, an empty two-liter bottle of Mountain Dew, a plasma rifle, and on and on and on. She had buzzed black hair and a lip ring, a complicated bird drawn on her left hand with permanent marker. She was wearing a ratty sports bra and sweatpants that seemed made for a giant.

Finally, without even looking at me, she said, "People always talk, but then, when you do something, they shut up."

I had no idea if she was threatening me or if this was connected to the paused game, but I did not, for one second, think about responding.

"Bitches are everywhere," she said without any emotion whatsoever.

"Okay," I said.

She finally unpaused the game, having selected a plasma rifle, and it was not more than five seconds before a zombie jumped from a tree overhead and ripped out her throat. She restarted the game, paused it, and scrolled again through the list of available weapons. The cat-piss smell was starting to settle on my clothes, particles of it like snowflakes on my eyelashes, and so I got up and did another round through the house.

I found a bone beside the toilet," my girlfriend said to me, holding up something white and hard; it was not a fragment of a bone, but an intact bone of unknown provenance. Human or animal, we did not know, and both seemed equally likely based on the other evidence in the house. We had to keep our voices down because the older girl was still in the living room, gnawing on the wooden corn-dog sticks until they splintered in her mouth, still trying to decide how best to kill something imaginary.

"He split her lip once," she said to me, like there wasn't a bone on the edge of the sink in front of us, like we were just going to table the unknown bone and talk about what we already knew, that her sister and brother-in-law were not going to re-solve anything anytime soon.

"Do you think the skewer is a direct, like, retaliation for get-ting her lip split?"

"I don't know," she said, seriously considering it. "It was, like, almost a year ago."

"You think your sister could take a split lip, hold on to that moment for almost a year, waiting for the right time and weapon, and stab him?"

"Yes," she replied, her eyes like a kaleidoscope with the real-ization of how right she was.

"Then it's just going to escalate, I think," I told her, as if this was the kind of shit I had any experience with.

"What do I do?" she asked me, and I was shocked to see her crying. She was crying about her fucked-up, always drunk, sarcastic sister. She was scared because her sister was in jail and she was probably going to have to pay the bail and her sis-ter would probably be released from jail at the same time her brother-in-law would be released from the hospital and they would probably just walk right back into this shitty house and fuck everything up again. My girlfriend was crying because her sister, who hated her, would need help, and my girlfriend would try to figure out how to give it.

I leaned across the sink to pull her close to me, and I knocked the bone into the sink and it made a clattering sound that made my teeth grind. But I held on to her and tried to calm her until I heard the little boy, moaning and half awake and needing some kind of assistance. She started to get up, but I set her on the edge of the bathtub, right next to a giant hole in the ceramic like someone dropped a bowling ball on it, and told her I would take care of it.

Before I had even completely knelt down to look at the boy, he had his arms around my neck. "Are you having a bad dream, buddy?" I asked, and he whimpered and nodded. "It's okay," I said, and I am not lying when I say that I was suppressing my gag reflex the entire time I was holding him, this sweet little boy who was in no way responsible for all the awful shit that swirled around him on a daily basis. I thought back to what my girlfriend had said about custody if the parents killed each other and I thought, *Fuck it, maybe I'll take this one and light out for parts unknown.* I'd never held a baby, a toddler, or any child really, but I was getting used to being needed by something powerless. The boy had snot running down his nose and I didn't even think about it when I took the sleeve of my shirt and cleaned up his face. I lowered him back onto the sofa and he, like he was a black belt in jujitsu, snatched my hand and pulled my entire left arm underneath his body, right up against his crotch, and he humped my arm for what felt like a long time until the battery inside of him wore out and he was asleep again. I looked over at the teenage girl, still scrolling, still obsessed with finding some kind of A-bomb of a weapon that automatically ended the game in her favor, and she was smirking, shaking her head like I'd just been punk'd, like she'd set this all in motion and now I had done something embarrassing for her.

"You ever kill a fucking thing in this game?" I asked her, my face hot with embarrassment.

"More than you ever could," she said.

My hand was tingling, like it had some kind of special power that the little kid had imparted in the course of his humping.

"In real life," I said, "I don't think you can just pause the action until you find the right weapon."

"That's why I'm practicing with this game," she said. "When I go into the Marines, I'll be ready."

"You're going to be a marine," I said, my voice lacking the slightest bit of surprise or suspicion.

"I'm gonna be a sniper," she replied, "or a light machine gunner, or on the back of a fifty cal, and I'm gonna be the best." I noticed that she'd duct-taped a butterfly knife to one of her boots.

"Fair enough," I said.

I went back into the bathroom to find my girlfriend now on her knees, scrubbing the tub with scouring agents that had not been utilized once in the house's history. I told her that it was too late to even think about cleaning this place. She replied that she was going to sleep in the bathtub, its surface offering the quickest possibility of cleanliness. "The sheets," she said, shuddering, "require more than I can handle right now." I asked her what about me. I could not fit in the tub with her. She suggested that, it being summer, I could sleep on the front porch. Now that the tub had been scraped clean and disinfected, she settled into it and twisted her body into the shape of sleep. I leaned over and kissed her. "We'll figure this out," I told her, and I hoped that she noticed that I had said *we*. I wanted her to know that, despite her questionable genetics, whatever hidden DNA contributed to the inhabitants of this house, I was a part of this now. I wanted her to know that, if we ever combined our genes, the good would outweigh the bad. But she was already snoring, so who knows if my intentions were understood.

Back in the living room, the oldest kid was asleep, her gums bleeding from the corn-dog sticks, her hand in some state of rigor mortis, her thumb depressing the controller so that, all night long, she would be scrolling through her weapons. I walked out of the house, across the lawn, and slept in my car, the windows rolled up, already reeking of my new circumstances.

I woke the next morning to find the two middle kids sitting in the passenger-side front seat. One of them had twisted off the stereo knobs and the other one was trying, and failing, to get the car's electric cigarette lighter to ignite. The girl, her teeth a crooked mess that, at her age, seemed sweet enough, said, "Are you going to marry Sassy?" I asked her if my girlfriend was Sassy. They said yes, and I said yes in reply without hesitation. They asked what they could call me. "Just call me Cam for now," I told them. "We're hungry, Cam," the boy said. I looked around the car but I kept it clean so there wasn't any food around. I said we should go inside and find something, but they said they were out of food and that Sassy wanted me to drive them to the Creekside Market and get some food. They were in their underwear, or maybe it was their pajamas. "Fine," I said, and I sped off without telling them to put on seat belts. They shared the front seat and leaned out of the window. If a car crash could have maimed them, I would have been shocked into a coma.

At the market, I handcuffed my hands around their wrists and led them up and down the tight aisles of the market. The air in that building was humid and smelled of crickets and worms from the bait boxes near the register. We got some cans of Vienna sausages and some more Pop-Tarts and gallon jugs of fruit punch. I did not trust the eggs or milk in this place, where the refrigerated section was humming smoke and rot. The girl asked for some boxes of macaroni and cheese and so we got four of them. The boy asked for some kind of powder candy that turned their mouths shocking shades of blue. Fine with me. I bought whatever they asked for. The total was more than I had expected, but that's what life is like with four kids, I supposed. It seemed like anything more than two kids was resigning your-self to a life of food in bulk and lack of funds. I figured, now that I was so sure I was going to marry my girlfriend, when the previous night I imagined the ease of leaving her, that if we did come into custody of the kids, we could choose two of them to keep and send the other two into foster care. I knew this was wrong, but I also knew the rest of my time with these kids was going to be a silent audition for my grace. We bagged up the goods and sped home, their mouths toxic with the candy they had not saved for their siblings.

Back at the house, I found the oldest girl removed from the couch for the first time in our short history together. She was standing in the utility room and holding a garbage bag while my girlfriend, her nostrils plugged with tissue paper, shoved her gloved hand into the dryer. "What's going on?" I asked. The girl just shrugged and, when she saw her brother and sister skipping into the kitchen with the food, dropped the garbage bag and shuffled, her body getting closer to the kitchen without any apparent ambulation, toward them. My girlfriend gagged and turned quickly away from the dryer. "Where the fuck did she go?" she said. I motioned toward the kitchen without moving my gaze from the dryer. "What's going on?" I asked again.

"All of their clothes smell like . . . like this house," she said. "So I told them we needed to wash their clothes, and they said the washing machine was broken. And it is, I think, or maybe a fuse is blown. But when I looked in the dryer, which does work by the way, there was . . . this thing in it."

I picked up the garbage bag and held it out for her. She gathered her courage, took a sharp intake of breath, and then retrieved a dead squirrel from the mouth of the dryer with her thumb and index finger. Half of the squirrel was fur and half of the squirrel was bone. It was flattened. She weakly tossed it toward me, toward the garbage bag I realized too late, and it fell to the floor, right at my feet. We both danced out of the room, into the hallway, and stared at the corpse.

"Do you think it died in there?" she asked.

"Or what?" I asked.

"Or do you think someone put it in there?" she said.

One of the kittens started to paw at the squirrel. Its claws got caught in the fur and it shook its paw to disengage itself. My girlfriend picked up the squirrel and dropped it like a grenade into the bag. I twirled the bag shut and took it into the backyard. The less said about the backyard, the better. Rusted tractor. Burned-up motorcycle parts. Elaborate pet cemetery.

"Okay," my girlfriend said to the kids, who were eating, of course, every last one of the Pop-Tarts. "I want each one of you to pick three outfits: shirts, pants, socks, underwear, plus one pair of pajamas, and your bedsheets. We're going to the Laundromat."

The little boy cheered, the frosting and fruit filling between his teeth like something caught in a bear trap.

I played Old Maid with the kids while my girlfriend got the washing machines whirring into the early stages of shocking all the death out of those tainted fabrics. She had a plastic bag filled with quarters from the change machine and they were rapidly declining. I shuffled the cards and discovered the pattern of play; they cheated. Without hesitation or attempt to hide it. I dealt the cards. The child who received the Old Maid card would quickly pretend that it was one of a pair and place it, facedown, on the table. After about fifteen minutes of the game, with only one card, a two of clubs or a jack of hearts, left, we would realize that someone had lied. I then had to flip everyone's cards over until the cheater was discovered. Only then did someone lose and someone else win. At first, I was pissed off. I would explain how receiving the Old Maid card would not mean that you ended up with it at the end. But the kids did not want to take this chance. They wanted to cheat their way to freedom as quickly as possible. After a few hands, I simply gave up. I took cards and then let someone else take them from me. I let the kids sort it out on their own and the game became nothing more than an incredibly inefficient way to shuffle cards. "Are you guys having fun?" I asked them. The little boy cheered, excited to be doing anything. The other kids didn't answer, trying to figure out who had already lost and who would lose again.

I emptied a snack machine and let the kids fight over the contents. I sat with my girlfriend while she watched the dryers flash-fry the clothes. "I don't know if I can walk back into that house," she said. I asked her why we needed to go back at all.

"Let's just take them back to our place," I said.

"It's an hour away, for starters," she replied. "And it's a one-bedroom apartment."

"It doesn't smell like cat piss and dead squirrels, though," I offered.

"I just . . ." she said. "I don't want them to do to our place what they did to that house."

"They can't possibly. Not in a day or two," I said.

"I think they can," she said, staring at the kids, who had sug-ared themselves into what looked zombie enough to be called resting. Their internal batteries, leaking fluid and electrons, were simply recharging themselves for another backbreaking surge.

"What do we do, then?" I said. "We can't clean that whole house. It's not possible. It needs government assistance."

"We do the best we can," she finally said. "We do just enough to keep them alive."

"If we could get rid of the cats," I offered.

"That would help," she agreed.

We got the kids to fold their own clothes, which had the same effect as if we'd asked them to turn their clothes into origami tumbleweeds. It was hypnotic, to watch their folding, somehow, become unfolding. But my girlfriend walked them through the steps, as if she was in a training video for the Gap, and the kids got it mostly right and we placed them all in some garbage bags and I felt like Santa Claus, carrying a sack of things that, though maybe not what they'd explicitly asked for, would make their lives happier than it was before.

Their father was at the house when we returned. One of his friends was sitting in an idling truck and the kids seemed happy to see their dad, who was shoving some of his clothes, and a twelve-pack of beer, into yet another garbage bag. The house, I determined, was 30 percent garbage bags. The kids wanted to hug him, but he turned slightly away. "I'm injured," he told them. "No heavy lifting for a good long while, kiddies."

I didn't want to look full on, but I was curious as to the exact state of his incapacitation. He looked sheepish and a little peeved, but that might easily be his default state. He was a tiny man, skinny to the point of breaking in half, and his teeth had that brown rot of chewing tobacco.

"I have to recuperate," he told us. "I'm staying with Jerry for a few days, until I can get back to work."

"What about Cindy?" my girlfriend asked.

"She's still in jail, I think," he told her.

"Could we maybe talk about this on the porch," I said, trying to be a grown-up. "Away from the kids?"

"They've heard so much worse," he said.

"I believe it," I told him.

"But are you going to press charges?" she asked him.

"Not up to me," he replied.

"Really?"

"Well," he continued, "I don't pretend to be a lawyer. I don't think it's up to me, though. She brought this all on herself, so she's got to clean it up by herself."

"And what about the kids?" my girlfriend asked him.

"Can't you just keep watching them?"

"Until when?" I asked.

"Until Cindy comes back," he said, getting irritated.

"Fine," my girlfriend said. "Fine, go get drunk and have fun."

"This is all your sister's fault," he said, and then he pushed past us and hobbled outside. He turned, noticed the garbage bags I was holding, and asked, "What's in those?"

"We washed some clothes for the kids," I said.

"Did you do any of my laundry?" he asked.

We shook our heads. If there had been a kebab skewer anywhere in reach, my girlfriend would have stabbed him with it.

"Well, thanks a lot," he said, and eased into the truck before they drove off, leaving us alone, again, with the kids.

The kids fought. They shared the same spaces, made paths in each other's footprints. It was necessary, to keep your space singular, to place an elbow in someone's mouth, teeth on an ankle, knuckles digging into someone's back like rough stones. After twenty or thirty attempts to keep the magnets of their feet and fists from attracting another's, I gave up and let the ruin come down on top of me. I noticed that this happened without much resistance on my part. This was life, I imagined. Or, rather, this was a terrible life, the way you slowly gave in to your surroundings and let it wash over you. I did not completely notice the smell of the house by this point, honestly.

Finally, what we had been expecting since the moment we entered the house happened; my girlfriend's sister called from jail. I kept the kids away from the phone, left my girlfriend to her pained privacy. One of the cats peed on a magazine that was lying on the floor and the younger girl picked up the magazine and simply moved it to the coffee table. I noticed that not a single toy of theirs was intact. This was, I began to understand, by design. If you ruined your own toys enough, no one else would try to steal them.

"Okay," my girlfriend said when she returned only a few minutes later. "It's complicated."

I walked into the bathroom with her and she discussed the basics, which was all she could get out of her sister. Bail was set, and the charges weren't as bad as they could have been, mostly regarding the shit she gave the police who arrested her. My girlfriend needed to come up with five hundred bucks for bail. It was a lot of money for us. I do tattoos and my girlfriend does piercings at the same shop; we're not rich. But we are not in a single dollar of debt, and the reason for this was that we didn't put up bail for every idiot we knew who got locked up. Then I thought about the four kids, all of them in our apartment, all the breakfast cereal they would inhale, and it seemed like five hundred was a fair price for our freedom.

"What about the kids?" I asked.

"I imagine she'll get to keep them for now," she said. "Maybe child services will be involved at some point, but who knows. I think they get to keep the kids as long as the kids don't get hurt."

"I'm happy," I admitted, "but it still seems kind of fucked-up. It seems like a stabbing should invite some sort of inquiry into your fitness as a parent."

"The deeper you get into this shit," my girlfriend said, "the more you realize that nobody is keeping anyone else from fucking things up."

I bought a boatload of pizzas and brought them back to the house, where I found the kids helping to straighten up the living room. There were eight garbage bags filled with detritus and old food and what may or may not have been actual shit. There was a landfill of cheese curl dust between the cushions of the sofa. Heavy objects like broken furniture and boxes of rain-diseased textbooks had been moved from the middle of the room, like hostages in a negotiation, and pushed against the walls as if to keep the house propped up. It gave space to the room and allowed some measure of air to circulate. My girlfriend emptied the remains of a can of Febreze into the air and the room just swallowed it whole.

In their newly laundered clothes with their hair combed, the children merely looked like freaks in a carnival show instead of wild animals. They were on the floor, huddled around the stack of pizza boxes like it was a campfire, and the youngest one said a short blessing that started off as a prayer and ended as a death metal intonation, the other kids simply kneeling on the floor as if expecting benediction, against all signs that suggested the opposite. We ate and it felt, for the first time, like an actual family and not adventurers in an inhospitable, unstable region. We smiled and our teeth were not scary. They were just the quickest way to show happiness. I imagined my girlfriend and me ten years down the line, the faces of the children replaced with those of our own design. It made me long for the future, which I never, ever, did in real life.

The same routine as the night before, my girlfriend got the middle kids ready for bed. They lined up and gave me a hug. They smelled like kids, powdered sugar and belly lint, and it made me tender toward them. They scrambled into their bedroom and it wasn't long before they were asleep. I rocked the little boy against my chest until his head lolled to the side and I transferred him awkwardly to one of the sofas. He twitched like his foot was keeping a kick drum time to his own unsteady heartbeat. His dreams, I could not imagine.

My girlfriend and I sat on the floor and watched the oldest do her thing with the video game, finding no weapon to her liking, eventually giving in to her inevitable and quick death. She wanted, I now understood, to be stronger than anything evil. But she never would.

Eventually, my girlfriend yawned and retired to the bathtub. I kissed her and continued to watch the oldest kid nervously scroll through the weapons for the millionth time: an arc welder, a Molotov cocktail, a Bowie knife. It would never end, the possibilities for ruination. She eventually chose the Bowie knife and tried to hack a zombie into bite sizes, but it got the jump on her and it was game over.

"Fuck," she finally said.

"This is a hard board," I said without conviction.

"No duh," she responded. "It's the hardest board in all video games. I got the cheat code off the Internet just to get here. I used some of my own money to buy all the weapons that don't even come with the actual game. I've done all the shit I'm supposed to and I just keep getting ass-killed like some chump. Nobody on the message boards will even talk about this board."

"What are you supposed to do?" I asked.

"Not get killed."

"That's it?" I asked.

"I guess so."

It made sense enough to me. Surrounded by death and decay and no hope of anything getting better, all you could hope for was not to fall into the same fate.

"Just run," I finally said.

"Yeah, okay," she said, making a wanking motion with her free hand.

"I'm serious," I said. "Don't fight them. Just run as fast as you can."

She considered this, wondered if she was being mocked. "I do have some boots somewhere in this game that make me run really fast."

"Use them. Just run and don't stop running."

She got the boots from the inventory and restarted the game. Before the zombie dropped out of the tree, she was already digging into the earth and pushing herself forward. The zombie fell out of the frame.

"Shit," the kid said, alive for as long as she'd ever been alive. "Fucking shit."

"Keep running," I said. On the little map in the upper left-hand corner, I could see a swarm of red dots forming behind her. They moved not quickly but with singular purpose.

"I'm running," she said. She ran and ran and ran, and the territory evaporated under her feet. She jumped over any non-living impediment. Anytime her route was cut off, she changed directions and kept running. It was like the Pied Piper, trailing an unending line of zombies. She ran and ran and scorched the earth behind her until, finally, nearly an hour later, there was nothing left.

"Fucking shit," she said, looking over at me. The game suddenly shut down and the screen had returned to the title. "I beat that shit," she said. For the first time, I could see a radiance inside of her.

I offered her my extended hand for a high five, but she just smirked and shook her head. She restarted the game and went back into her inventory. I knew what was coming. Even when you've smashed through the people who want to fuck you over, you still want to keep tabs on the things that might keep you safe. I stood up, my bones popping. "Good night," I said, and she nodded, her eyes that blue glaze of reflected screens.

I walked into the bathroom and knelt over the tub. My girlfriend was asleep but just barely. It was easy enough, just with my presence, to bring her back to me.

"It'll be fine tomorrow," she said, still half asleep.

"Not for them," I said.

"I guess not," she replied.

After a few moments of silence, she said, "I asked my sister and she said that they had never finished the paperwork for custody."

"So what does that mean?"

"The kids don't go to me. They go somewhere, and I guess it could maybe be me, but it's not the law."

She adjusted her body, pulling tighter into herself, and I kicked off my shoes and squeezed into what was left of the tub. We were jammed into each other, sharing a foxhole, and we held each other tight against the constant presence of unhappiness that infiltrated the air around us. We would tear out our fingernails digging our way to something good. The world would try to fuck us and we would stab it with whatever weapon was available to us. We would make every object a weapon that would protect us from anything that tried to convince us that we would not live forever in happiness.

Housewarming

Mackie's son needed help with the deer. "It's in our pond," Jackson said to his father, "and we've got a housewarming party tomorrow afternoon and this damn deer is in our pond. It's dead, by the way. I don't remember if I told you that."

"I assumed that," Mackie said. "This is the first I've heard of a housewarming."

"It's just some people from work," his son said without pausing. "It's no one you would want to be around."

"How did it die?" he asked.

"Well, it drowned, I guess. It's floating in our pond. I don't know what else to tell you."

"You want me to come up there?" Mackie asked.

"Why do you think I'm calling?" his son replied, and both of them hung up the phone without saying another word.

Mackie had driven the route from his own house to Jackson's cabin over a dozen times in the last month. Since Jackson and his wife, Cindy, had bought the house in November, Mackie had been coming by to help renovate, make it livable.

Two weeks after closing, his son called during his break at the factory and told him, "Cindy says we should put new tile in the kitchen before we move in, since we're doing all these other projects at the same time." Mackie showed up at the empty cabin—Cindy was staying with her sister until the repairs were finished—and found the boxes of tile waiting in the kitchen, the old linoleum pulled up and curled in the corner of the room. He started mixing mortar, snapped on his knee pads, and got started. The house smelled of new paint and wood chips, and Mackie wished he'd brought a mask for his face. When his son got off work, his truck winding down the long driveway, headlights flickering through the trees, Mackie was cutting tile with a wet saw he'd brought from his own house. With each cut, the water shot into his face like sparks, his eyebrows dripping wet. "We're making good progress," Jackson said, peering inside the house at the kitchen floor. "We are," Mackie replied, drying the re-formed tile with a towel, touching the new shape along the smooth edges.

Mackie's knees ached from the constant kneeling, fitting the tile into place. His son was standing over him, his pockets filled with foam dividers to place between the tiles. It was good to work together, Mackie feeling his son's eyes on his hands, learning how to make things work. Another piece had to be cut and he did not want to stand again, to walk to the front porch and lean against the saw. "Jackson," he said, "hand me a tile." Jackson walked gingerly to the box and brought one back. Mackie took out his red pencil and marked off the section, handing the tile back to his son. "Make that cut," he said. Jackson went outside and Mackie listened to the whine of the saw as it started, the sound of metal touching ceramic, and then he heard his son shouting, "Goddamn it all." Mackie shot up, immediately blaming himself for not doing it to begin with. He was already hoping for the best of the worst, just a finger, not his thumb.

"Motherfucking, son of a bitch," his son was screaming, down on one knee, facing away from Mackie. The wet saw was turned over, the dull gray water pooling around it. When Mackie knelt by his son, Jackson stood up and pushed past his father, back into the house. Mackie looked around for a digit, blood, but he didn't see anything. He ran back to the house and found Jackson in the bathroom, water running, examining his face. "A goddamned piece of tile popped up and hit me in the face." Mackie looked at his son's reflection in the mirror; a small cut was bubbling blood just under his right eye. "I could've been blinded," Jackson said, staring angrily at Mackie. "Don't we have any son of a bitching goggles?" Mackie shook his head. Jackson turned off the water, took out his handkerchief, and pressed it against the cut. "Well, I'm driving to the Walmart to get some, then." His son was out of the house, into his truck, and pulling out of the driveway, while Mackie stood on the porch, lifting the wet saw upright. He worked until midnight, waiting for Jackson to return, and finally gave up. He rolled out his sleeping bag and slept in his clothes, waiting for morning, listening to the house settle around him.

The next day, Jackson showed up with a bandage covering the wound, a pair of goggles resting on top of his head. "Got to

be safe," he said. "We can't get hurt anymore." Mackie nodded
and they worked into the evening, finishing the job.

When he got to the house, Cindy was waiting on the porch. "He's
waiting for you," she said. "It's awful, that deer. You can see it
from the house, just floating in the water. Its eyes are open." She
hugged him and then pointed toward the trail, which led down
to the pond. "Don't let him get too angry," she said. "He takes
everything so personally. This isn't his fault, of course." Mackie
nodded. "I know," he said.

Jackson was throwing rocks at the deer, which was floating
about ten or fifteen feet from the shore, its swollen belly rising
above the surface of the water, a small island. Mackie stood and
watched his son for a few seconds without making his presence
known. His son had surprisingly good aim, the rocks cutting
through the cold air and thumping against the belly of the deer.
"Fucking deer," his son said to no one. Mackie wondered if Jackson was trying to sink the deer, trying to get it fully underwater
and hidden. He stepped out from the trees and waved to his
son. Jackson nodded, then threw another rock. "This isn't going
to be pleasant," Jackson said. "I know," Mackie responded.

Jackson had come back to Tennessee last year, to stay, Mackie
hoped. After high school, Jackson had left to work as a me-
chanic in Huntsville, and then moved around the southeast for
the next eight years, never staying long in any one place, Mackie's letters to him bouncing back with no known forwarding address. He would wait until Jackson's next phone call, locating

his son for the time being. Sometimes he would get calls from jail, Jackson asking his father to post bail and Mackie would be in the car, driving for hours to Louisville or Mobile or Daytona Beach to retrieve his son. This particular time, Jackson had shot out the tires of his neighbor's car. "He'd cut me off a few days before," Jackson had told his father on the drive back from the police station. "Cut me off and nearly made me slam into him. I yelled at him and the son of a bitch smiled. Smiled." Mackie could feel his son's anger vibrate within the car, as if the event was happening all over again. "Well," Mackie said, "he probably don't remember that." Jackson smiled, his face white from an oncoming car's headlights. "I know that," he said. "That's why I shot his tires. To remind him."

We need a boat," Jackson said. Mackie agreed with him, but they didn't have a boat. He walked toward the edge of the woods and dragged a fairly long branch back to the shore, something to work with, a tool. He sat down on the ground, which was wet from the melting frost, and took off his shoes and socks, rolling up his pant legs. Jackson was still staring out at the deer, as if waiting for it to show signs of life, to swim to the shore and jump into the woods. "Okay," said Mackie, but Jackson still didn't move. "Okay," he said again, "here's what we'll do." Jackson turned and saw Mackie, barefooted. "Good lord, Dad, it's thirty degrees out here."

"We have to get in there, Jackson. We have to wade out there and get that deer. Then we'll take it somewhere else. Hell, we'll just toss it on the side of the road if it comes to that, but we need to get it out of your pond. That's why you called me."

Jackson looked at Mackie's feet again, then back at the deer. "Maybe we should call animal services or something," he offered. "It might be diseased. We should get an expert out here."

"Son, they're not going to come on a weekend. This housewarming you're having for your friends? It's tomorrow. If you don't want them to see this deer in your pond, we're going to just get in the water and fish it out. Now take your shoes off, so they don't get wet."

Jackson kicked at the ground. "Let me hear the rest of the plan first."

"It's pretty simple. We'll wade into the pond, and I'll take this stick and move away from you. Then I'll direct the deer toward the shore and you get ahold of it and then you drag it in. Then we'll both pull it onto land and get rid of it."

"Maybe I should be the one with the stick," Jackson said.

"Son," Mackie said quickly, a flash of irritation striking his voice, "just take off your shoes and let's go get the damn deer."

Jackson had last been in Raleigh, painting houses or working at a guitar store. Mackie had received a postcard. *Got a job and a girl,* it read, *and my probation for the dog thing is done.* A few weeks later, his son called. Mackie had been slightly shocked to hear his son's voice, "Hey, Dad," without the usual mechanized voice intoning the particular jail where he'd been locked up, which usually opened any phone call he received from Jackson. "You okay, son?" Mackie asked. "Better than okay," Jackson answered. "Much better than that." Mackie was glad to hear it, but he still would not allow himself to believe it was true.

"Amy's pregnant," Jackson said.

"Who?" Mackie asked, worried again.

"Amy. The girl I told you about in the postcard," Jackson said, his voice rising. "She's pregnant. We're going to have a baby."

"Did you marry her? Are you already married?"

"You don't have to be married to have a baby," Jackson answered, the connection fading and then coming back.

"I know that," Mackie said, feeling stupid for having asked, complicating things. "I just wanted to know if I'd missed anything. Congratulations."

"If it's a girl, we're going to name it Carla, after Mom."

"That's a nice name," Mackie said, remembering his wife. His son was just a boy when she died, and it made him happy to hear that he still thought of her. "What about a boy?"

"Jackson Junior," Jackson said. "Jackson Junior for sure."

Mackie asked to speak to Jackson's girlfriend, but she was taking a nap. "I'll wake her," Jackson said, and before Mackie could stop him, the phone was set down and there was silence, humming. Less than a minute later, a voice, barely a whisper, a sore throat, answered. "Jackson said you wanted to speak with me?"

"I just wanted to say hello and to tell you congratulations."

"Thank you," the woman said, her voice still quiet. When she didn't offer anything, Mackie continued, "And I want you to call me if you need anything. If you need anything at all, you give me a call, okay?"

"I'll do that," she said, and then hung up.

It wasn't working. The branch he'd found, substantial enough to steer the animal toward Jackson, was too heavy and Mackie couldn't control it, the water up to his armpits, the shock of the cold taking away every other breath. Jackson was shivering, waist deep in the water. "I'm gonna have to get out of the water soon," he shouted, and Mackie understood that he hadn't planned this well. He felt the situation falling out of his control, into a place where Jackson's anger would surface and take over. Mackie tossed the stick into the water and began swimming toward the deer, kicking his legs under the water, his clothes weighing him down. "I'm going to push it toward you," he shouted to his son over the sound of the water splashing around him. "Wade out a little farther and grab it." He finally reached the deer and touched its fur, which was unexpectedly colder than the water. It was heavy, but he'd anticipated the weight of this dead animal. The bad things he'd carried in his life had always been just as heavy as he'd expected, always measuring up to his worst expectations.

"Keep swimming," his son instructed. "Just swim a little farther to me and we'll be done. C'mon, Dad."

Jackson's girlfriend called Mackie three weeks later, at two in the morning. When Mackie answered, he immediately said, "Jackson?" anticipating another phone call from jail, another thing to fix. "It's Amy," the soft voice replied. "Jackson's girlfriend?" she offered helpfully. "What's wrong?" Mackie asked. "I lost it," she said, crying. "I lost the baby."

"Oh God," Mackie said. "I'm sorry, honey."

"And Jackson," she continued, "he thinks I did it on purpose. He says I did something wrong. He keeps hitting me."

Mackie sat up in bed, felt his neck stiffen and jerk to the left, a tic he'd had since childhood, as if the danger was just over his left shoulder. "He hit you?" he asked, to be certain.

"He hits me," she answered.

"Put him on the phone."

"He won't talk to you. He doesn't want to talk to anybody."

"Amy, you need to go to a motel, or go to a friend's house. We'll figure this out, but you cannot have him hitting you. That's got to stop."

"I don't want to call the police, but I might have to."

"Amy, call them if you need to. Let me think and I'll call you back."

"I don't want him here anymore," she said. "I don't love him now."

Mackie hung up the phone and was already out of bed, putting on his clothes, grabbing his keys off the dresser. Before he knew it, he was in the car, on the interstate, going to see his son.

I've got it," his son announced, the weight of the dead animal shifting from father to son. He watched Jackson tug the deer by its legs toward the shore, a tiny wake trailing behind it. He watched the white tail of the deer and then saw a jerk in the movement, a hesitation, and then there was a splash. Jackson was under the water, flailing, the deer spinning just slightly, and Mackie waded through the water to reach his son.

Jackson was thrashing around in the water, his feet and arms surfacing and then submerging, splashing water everywhere. When he realized how shallow it was, he stood up again, soaking wet, the leg of the deer in his hand. "The fucking leg fell off," he screamed. "You told me to just drag it in," he said, staring at Mackie, "but it's decayed."

"Let's get it to the shore," Mackie said. "Then we can get angry at each other." Jackson stared at his father a little longer and then turned and threw the detached leg onto the shore. "I'm grabbing the antlers this time," Jackson said. "Pull his damn head off." Mackie pushed the hind end of the deer toward the shore. "Let's just get it out of here," he whispered.

Eight hours and he was in North Carolina, staring at his son's house, the car idling on the street in front. He saw his son look through a window and then quickly close the blinds. A few seconds later, Amy looked out the window, shaking her head. Mackie thought about what he would say to his son, how he could fix the situation. He felt foolish for driving this far without having a plan, some way to help. His son was now coming down the steps of the porch, pointing at him. Mackie still couldn't think of anything to say. He got out of the car.

"Go home, Dad," Jackson said. "I'm sorry Amy called you and that you had to drive all this way, but go home."

"Could I talk to Amy?" he asked. He could see her in the window, but her hand was shading her eyes.

"Go home, Dad. Please go home."

"Did you hit her, Jackson?"

"She lost the baby, Dad."

"Did you hit her?"

"Please go home"

Mackie punched his son in the mouth and then placed his intertwined fingers behind his son's head, pushing Jackson's face into his own knee. Jackson fell to the street, and Mackie was already pulling him into the car, placing his body across the backseat. His son was unconscious, his mouth bleeding, and Mackie slammed the door and walked up to the house. He knocked on the door and Amy opened it.

"I need some rope," Mackie said.

"He really did hit me," Amy said. Her throat showed pale purple fingerprints where he had grabbed her, and there was a deep cut above one eye. She looked so young, barely out of her teens, and Mackie felt sick all over again.

"I know," Mackie finally said. "I'm going to take him back to Tennessee. Is that okay with you? He won't come back here and bother you."

She thought about this and then nodded. "I'll get you some rope," she said.

He drove ten miles above the speed limit, his son tied up in the backseat, groggy, shouting obscenities. He stopped only for gas, pissing in a bottle, letting his son wet himself rather than untie him. His son kept struggling against the ropes, lying on his stomach, his ankles tied to his bound wrists, but Mackie had fashioned the knots well, the added pressure only cinching the knots tighter. "Well, I'm gonna shit in my pants, you asshole," his son yelled from the backseat. "I'm your son and you're going to let me shit in my pants." He let his son shit in his pants.

After five hours, his son fell asleep and Mackie had the rest of the drive to think about what he'd done. He thought about it for five minutes and then focused on the road, counting billboards, watching for highway patrol cars. He knew when they reached Tennessee, he couldn't keep his son there. He couldn't keep fighting his son, knocking him out and hoping he'd awaken a better person. He'd do what he could, help him find a job, get him an apartment. He'd fix his son and then hope it stuck.

Back home, in the garage, when he dragged his son out of the car, reeking of sweat and piss and shit, Mackie told him about his plan. "You stay here and we find something for you to do and you get yourself straight." His son fell into a corner of the garage. "I don't do drugs," he said. "It's not like that." Mackie shook his head. "I know that. I wish it were that easy. You're a good boy, Jackson; you just get too angry. You need to understand that things happen and they're usually bad, and you just figure out how to deal with it without beating somebody up or killing their dog or setting their tree on fire. Do you understand?" Jackson slid a finger into his mouth and spit blood. "One of my teeth is loose."

"Will you try?" Mackie asked his son. Jackson nodded and went inside to take a shower while Mackie climbed back into the car, pressed his face against the steering wheel, and kept himself from crying.

Fucking deer," Jackson kept saying. "Fucking dead, three-legged, no-account deer." They were on dry land now, both cold, getting colder in the wind. They had stripped out of their wet clothes, father and son now in their wet boxer shorts, shivering, their hair dripping cold water down their bodies. Neither had thought to bring a change of clothes. "This," Jackson said, "is getting worse."

The deer, sans leg, was still beautiful. It was an eight-point buck, the cold having preserved the skin except for a small wound at its chest and the exit wound near its right back leg. A hunter must have shot it and chased it into the pond, then decided it wasn't worth the effort, or perhaps never even found it. Either way, it was here now, dead, glassy-eyed, lying in the grass between Mackie and Jackson.

"We should bury it," Jackson said. "Cindy said to bury it." It was a nice idea, but the ground was too cold for that. The county dump was closed until Monday. "Well, we can't leave it here," Jackson shouted. "Fucking deer." Mackie thought if they could get a tarp under the deer, they could drag it to Jackson's truck and dump it on the side of the highway. "Someone from the city will come get it," Mackie told his son. Jackson seemed reluctant to agree. "Fucking deer." He finally nodded and Mackie went to find a tarp, to wrap up this deer, and to get through the day, freezing cold, soaked to the bone, but otherwise undamaged.

Two months after he brought Jackson back home, his son now servicing and setting up video poker machines at strip clubs and gas stations, the phone rang again in the middle of the night. It was Amy, her voice as soft as the first time he'd talked to her.

"Is he okay?" she asked.

"Are you okay?" he asked her. "I want to know that first, because if you aren't, I'll go make him worse."

She started to cry. "I'm okay, I think," she said. "I'm better without him here."

He told her that Jackson was trying harder to be a good person.

"I had hoped that he would turn out to be a good person," she said, "but I couldn't stay with him long enough to find out."

Mackie couldn't think of a response that would help anything and so he stayed silent.

"I wanted to thank you," she said, still whispering, as if concerned that Jackson might be listening to them. "You helped me and I wanted to thank you for that."

Before he could answer, she hung up the phone. He kept the receiver against his ear, listening to the dial tone, waiting for her to come back on the line.

Mackie was in the shed, nearly naked, looking for a tarp, when Cindy nudged the door open. "This must not be going well," she said, avoiding eye contact with Mackie.

"Do you have a tarp?" Mackie asked.

"We have extra clothes," Cindy said. "You don't have to use a tarp for that."

"No, I need a tarp to wrap up the deer. Extra clothes would be nice, though."

"You can't bury the deer?"

"No." He felt unable to explain any further and she didn't push the issue. He found himself liking Cindy more and more.

After he located an orange tarp, wrapped up like a sleeping bag, Cindy waved him into the house, and he stepped into the warmth, a fire going. She handed him some clothes for both himself and Jackson and he put on an ill-fitting shirt, pants that were too tight and left unzipped, and squeezed his feet into shoes two sizes too small for him. "How is he doing?" she asked him.

"He's doing fine. We just got a little wet trying to get the deer."

"Anything could set him off, I've learned," she said. "The smallest thing; you never know."

"He's fine," he said. "I'll take him the clothes and he'll be fine."

* * *

At his son's wedding, waiting off to the side of the altar, groom and best man, Mackie rehearsed his toast in his head. Jackson put his hand on Mackie's shoulder and said, "Thank you for all this. You made this happen." Mackie shrugged. "I didn't do much," he said. "You knocked me out, tied me up, brought me back here, and helped me get a job. You did a lot." Mackie told him that he didn't want any thanks, that he was just happy he'd cleaned himself up, had found a nice woman, was settling down.

"You saved me from that woman," Jackson said.

"You mean Amy?" Mackie asked.

"Yeah, she was a bad influence. She made me think things would always be happy, nothing but good times, but that's not reality. She really had me off the rails, and you came and got me away from all that, and I want to thank you."

"I don't want any thanks for that."

Jackson pulled the flask out of Mackie's coat pocket, his gift to his father for being the best man. He took a swig of whiskey. "I filled it before I gave it to you," Jackson told his father. "So that's two gifts I gave you."

When Mackie got back to the pond, Jackson was beating the deer with his raised boot, shouting curses, now totally naked, his strikes stripping wet chunks of fur from the animal's body. Mackie dropped the tarp and the clothes and charged after his son. "Stop," he shouted. "Jackson, that don't help a goddamned thing. Just stop." Jackson pushed his father and kept hitting the deer with the boot. "A perfect day before this fucking deer showed up," he screamed. Water was dribbling from the deer's mouth, its eyes wide open. "Calm down, Jackson," Mackie shouted again, pulling his son away from the deer. Yanking his arm free, Jackson whirled around and punched Mackie, catching his right cheekbone, which caused Mackie to wince and release his son. Jackson ran away from Mackie and the deer, through the woods, making sounds that seemed like sobbing.

Mackie lay out the tarp and rolled the deer onto it, the water still deep in the deer's body. He knew better than to wait for his son to return. He pulled the corners of the tarp together and dragged the deer as best he could through the woods, stopping every few minutes when his hands got too sore. He thought to leave the deer on his son's front lawn, but realized it would be cruel to the deer, the further abuse Jackson would inflict upon it. Mackie knew he would just have to take responsibility for this dead thing, until he could find a way to put it to rest.

He could see Cindy through the window of the house. She was frowning, continually looking over her shoulder at what Mackie imagined was Jackson, hiding until he was gone. He lifted the deer into the backseat of his car, shoving it into the spaces that it would go, trying to make it fit. The passenger seat was now folded forward to accommodate the head and neck of the animal, the mouth of the deer now peeking out from the tarp. There was still frost on the deer's whiskers. He waved to Cindy, who did not wave back, and drove down the mountain, the air conditioner on to keep the deer from thawing out too much, to keep the smell of decay away from his senses.

Back home, in the garage, Mackie tried to think of what to do about the deer. The options were just as limited as they were at Jackson's house. He did not want to bury this deer, the hours upon hours of breaking through the frozen earth, no matter how much better he thought it would make him feel. It wouldn't change anything. He would dig a hole and fill it back, and everything would be the same.

His teeth were chattering. His nose wouldn't stop running. He checked the rearview mirror and noticed the skin under his right eye was starting to swell from where Jackson had punched him. He opened the tarp and stared at the deer's dead eyes. He rubbed the condensation from its snout. He knew he had to get out of the car, to get the deer out of the car, but he couldn't do it, not just yet. He sat in his garage, the deer beside him, and tried to catch his breath. He waited for the muscles of his heart to send blood throughout his body, to make him warm again.

Wildfire Johnny

Trey was seventeen, smoking weed, his body sprawled across the top of a jungle gym in the playground of the old abandoned elementary school. It was two in the afternoon and he had been delinquent since lunch from the private school where he, according to the guidance counselor, "Resisted Challenges." Now, taking deep hits from the ill-made joint, he listened to the sound of the world around him, the gnats hovering just beyond the smoke that swirled in front of his face. He heard a bird calling, insistent, and then he heard the sound of cars driving on the highway. And then he heard the sound of a tomcat hissing and he turned to watch the animal, its fur electric, as it zigzagged for a few seconds and then made a beautiful, arcing leap through a window and into the school.

From Trey's stoned perspective, it looked like the cat had suddenly been possessed by the devil. It was a satanic cat. He was so high. Had he imagined the cat entirely? He wanted that cat; he thought it would make a good pet. So Trey, grunting as he stripped himself off the playground equipment, strolled over to the window, long ago shattered by idiot kids much like Trey, and stared at the tomcat, orange and black, its left eye missing. "Good kitty," Trey said and then started clicking his tongue. He took off his jacket to use as a means of capturing the cat, which was now hissing, pacing in a tight circle. Trey pulled himself through the window, landing in a heap, and the cat immediately turned away from him and dove into a closet, disappearing through the cracked opening of the door. Trey tried to imagine a name for it, Beelzebub, maybe just "Bub" for short, and slowly opened the door of the closet to find that the cat had vanished. He checked every creepy cubby that had once held children's boots and lunch boxes, but there was no sign of the cat. He felt the loss as keenly as if the animal had been his childhood pet and not some disease-ridden hell spawn of his imagination.

He then noticed a small tin box in the last cubby, dusted with rust. Hoping for rare coins or a handful of uncut diamonds, he reached for the box and clicked it open. Inside was a straight razor, folded up, its handle made of ivory. There was scrimshaw on the handle and Trey took the razor and the box out of the closet and into the light that was pouring in through the window. In curling, ornate script, the words *Property of Wildfire Johnny* had been etched into the ivory. Framing it on either side were a cutlass and a rifle, crossing to make an *X*. *Wildfire Johnny*. If the cat had been real and he had managed to catch it, he would have named it Wildfire Johnny.

He flipped open the blade, which was dazzlingly polished. He touched the edge and instantly saw a thin line of blood appear on his fingertip. He sucked on his finger, carefully closing the blade. Inside the box, there was a piece of paper, yellowed, brittle. He unfolded the paper and had to squint to make out the tiny writing.

> *Whoever possesses this blade will gain access to its particular magic. As long as you have the razor, you will be able to travel through time.*

Holy fucking shit. Trey had a magic razor. He could go back in time. He was too stoned to work out the particulars of what he might do in the past. Still, it seemed like a good power to have. He kept reading.

> *You may travel twenty-four hours into the past. To do so, simply take the blade and cut open your throat. With one expertly executed slash, you will find yourself twenty-four hours in the past, bearing no signs of the injury, able to undo any forthcoming misfortune. You may travel as many days into the past as you wish, as long as you cut open your throat for each twenty-four-hour interval.*

Trey felt like maybe it would have been better to find some rare coins. He'd just plunk those coins down at some antique dealer, walk out with a few thousand dollars, and buy a really nice MacBook. He was thinking that even the cat, if he could domesticate it and teach it a few tricks, would be better than some sinister, magical razor blade.

There was one last paragraph, and Trey reluctantly scanned it.

> *The razor blade holds no moral power over you; the magic may be used for good or evil. Use it wisely and you will find yourself at an advantage over any and all humans and spirits.*

Had Wildfire Johnny written this? Was someone with such a fucking badass name to be trusted or was it too good to be true? Was this some weird prank that was popular in the Roaring Twenties, flapper girls getting old assholes to slit their throats in the hopes of staying young forever? He got out his phone and searched for "Wildfire Johnny" but nothing came up that made any sense. He looked up "magic razors that grant time traveling powers if you slash open your throat" and the search results were even more useless. He looked up "Wildfire Johnny urban legend razor blade" and found no news articles about kids in the '60s dying in grotesque ways.

He put the razor to his neck. Either it worked or it didn't. The only way he'd find out was to slash open his throat and gurgle on his blood until he either died or woke up a day earlier. It seemed like maybe not a fair trade-off. He felt that it was better to wait until it was a true emergency, when it was a life-or-death situation that required time travel, and then he would find out the true extent of Wildfire Johnny's gift. He folded the razor and put it back in the box. Then he climbed out the window and walked back to his car. He looked in the rearview mirror and styled his hair for about ten minutes, almost forgetting about Wildfire Johnny and the razor blade.

That night at dinner, when his parents asked him about his day, he asked them what the words *Wildfire Johnny* might mean to them. "Are you high, Trey?" his dad asked. He never mentioned it again.

Eventually, because he was a teenager and, even more importantly, because he had trouble really maintaining his focus on any single topic of interest, he kind of forgot about the razor blade, kept it in his sock drawer in his bedroom. At the heart of it, having led a charmed and easy life, he could not imagine what would be so bad that the prospect of slashing your own throat was preferable.

So he didn't slash his throat. Not when he got caught smoking pot in his car in the parking lot at school and was suspended for ten days. Not when he backed his car into his dad's new lawn mower and his dad had called him a "major-league disappointment fuckup." Not when he scored in his team's own goal during the district championships and lost the game for his high school's soccer team. A few times, he sat on his bed after these awful moments and held the straight razor to his throat. But he couldn't do it. He had watched a horror movie where the killer slashes his victim's throat and the blood had sprayed in such a forceful way that it covered the walls of the room. He figured that this was an exaggeration for the purposes of the movie, but it still filled him with intense dread. He always assumed that the next time something awful happened, he would finally do it. He imagined Wildfire Johnny shaking his head, disappointed in Trey for wasting his gift.

Then, after the senior prom, he was so damn close to losing his virginity to Donna Frododio, but he couldn't get his dick hard. He was sitting on the edge of the pullout sofa in the guest room of Donna's older sister's apartment. He was tugging on himself furiously while Donna lay back on the bed, waiting for him, smoking a cigarette in a way that later made Trey think of contemporary novels about marriage and ennui. "Just a second more," he said, frantic, but Donna said she was too drunk to stay awake and she just handled her desire on her own and went to sleep, Trey still looking at his limp dick. After she was snoring, he covered her up with a blanket and all he could think about was Wildfire Johnny's straight razor, sitting there in his sock drawer, completely ineffectual. Could life get worse than this? How could it be worse? He looked at Donna. He imagined her telling her girlfriends about how he couldn't get it up. A dick that doesn't work seemed to Trey at this moment to be just about the saddest thing in the world.

He knew with certainty that if he had the razor right now, he would drag it slowly across his throat; at that moment, he was willing to gamble on whether or not he would wake up a full day earlier. But what else could he do tonight? Trey simply curled himself around Donna Frododio and promised himself that, from that day forward, he would always have the razor with him, would never again be caught in a moment where he could not slash his throat wide open and be saved from his own stupidity.

And then, a most marvelous piece of luck, life became easy. Even though his grades had been attained through sheer inattention, he got into a well-respected liberal arts university. He didn't get any merit scholarships, his grades had not been that good, but his parents could afford to send him, and he settled into life away from them. He made mostly B's and sometimes A's when the subject really appealed to him. He started writing silly humor pieces for the student magazine, and it brought him a kind of nerdy fame at the small school. Everyone there seemed to be just like him, curious about the world but not entirely sure what to do with that curiosity, hoping that it would simply be enough to have it at all. He partied right up to the point that he could keep himself from getting sick and then he would stop drinking for the night. The summer after his sophomore year, his father got him an internship with a magazine in New York, and he fact-checked articles that seemed really unimportant to him, but helped him understand that this kind of story could be an asset to the world at large.

In his junior year, he hit it off with a really drunk freshman who made out with him for thirty minutes on the ratty sofa of some filthy fraternity house. They went back to her dorm room, and they both got naked, and then she said that she was having second thoughts. So he said that was fine and he went back to his own dorm room. He felt the razor in his pocket but didn't feel any real need to use it. It was just nice to have it, to know it was there.

Two weeks later, the same girl said that she'd really been impressed that he'd not, how could she phrase it, made her do something that she didn't want to do, and they ended up having sex that same night and it was really nice, and, lying beside her afterward, he felt the confidence of a life that rewards you for good decisions.

He graduated with a B average, and he found a good job in Nashville with a website called the Gentleman Caller, a kind of lifestyle magazine that mostly reviewed incredibly expensive clothing and kept its readers abreast of the latest news about men's grooming. It was slightly ridiculous and sometimes the tone of the website spoke to a kind of affluent white dude that Trey was just slightly below in terms of wealth and status. But the editor, a man the same age as Trey, liked his funny pieces about the difficulty of making a proper mint julep or about how sweatpants were becoming really fashionable or why it was cool to shave with a straight razor. They drew a lot of traffic to the site, and after two years he was given his own column, "Man

Manners," where dudes asked him about issues of navigating the modern world and he made up his answers on the spot. Another website interviewed him. He was Internet famous. It felt both entirely unearned and yet completely his due.

And then he was driving home from a bar, where he'd had two whiskey smashes but wasn't nearly drunk, and he tried to turn left across traffic and didn't see a car coming in the opposite direction. He smashed into the car, totaling both of them. He was stunned from the air bag and he felt like he'd broken his ribs. Trey had to kick the passenger door open by putting both feet against the door and pushing it until it bent enough for him to get out.

In the other car, a man was staggering from the driver's side to the backseat, and he pulled a young girl, maybe twelve years old, from the smashed car. She was bleeding profusely from the head and her entire body was limp, her neck at a weird angle.

"Oh, God," the man screamed. "Help."

"Oh, shit," Trey said. "Oh . . . oh, shit."

"She's dead," the man wailed. He placed the girl flat on her back and listened to her chest, put his ear against her mouth. "She's dead."

Trey instinctually moved toward the man, to verify that the girl was indeed dead, and the man jumped up and grabbed Trey's shirt.

"I'm sorry," Trey said.

"I'm not going to let you go," the man said. "Not until the cops get here. You're not going to run away." He was screaming and crying at the same time.

"I'm not going to run away," Trey said.

"You're drunk," the man said. "You drunk-driving son of a bitch."

"I'm not," Trey insisted. A police cruiser pulled up, and a cop ran over to them.

"He killed my daughter," the man said, pointing at Trey.

"It was an accident," Trey said.

"I need you to stand over there," the cop said to Trey, and Trey walked back over to his car. The cop radioed for more help. The man returned to his daughter on the ground.

Trey felt the razor in his pocket. He imagined what was waiting for him. He'd killed someone. He might go to jail. Possibly for a long time. He'd lose his job. The guilt of it all.

He pulled out the razor and opened it. He considered the blade, could not quite convince himself to go through with it. Maybe he was wrong. Maybe they would prove that he wasn't at fault and nothing would happen to him. But he had killed the girl, that was certain. No matter what, he'd have to live with that. His hand tightened on the blade, and then the father shouted, "He's got a fucking knife!"

The cop instantly turned to face Trey. "Put that down, sir."

"Oh, shit, no. Okay, it's not a weapon or anything. Wildfire Johnny gave it to me. It's a kind of magical implement."

"Put it down, sir." The officer now reached for his weapon.

Two more police cruisers pulled up. The cops had their weapons drawn as they exited the vehicles.

Trey closed his eyes, brought the razor to his throat, and slashed it in one motion. He heard screams, and a mist of blood sputtered from his neck, covering his hands, and then he passed out, collapsed on the asphalt. People were rushing toward him, but then everything was black and quiet and safe.

When Trey came to, he was sitting at home, watching a TV show while he held a bag of pork rinds. He slowly came to awareness. He was watching an animated show about really stupid people that he was embarrassed to admit that he liked. He looked around the room. He was alone. He gingerly touched his neck with his fingertip. Nothing. No blood. He checked his phone. It was eleven o'clock at night, the day before the accident.

He stood up on unsteady legs and walked into the bathroom to look at himself in the mirror. There was no mark, no evidence of the violence that he had done to himself. In the pocket of his sweatpants was the razor, folded shut, humming with intent. Though there was no mark on his skin, Trey could recall in great detail the extreme pain of the action, the sensation of drowning coming right on the heels of the feeling of his own throat opening up. It made him shudder to remember it. He did not want to experience it again. And yet, here he was, in designer sweatpants, his belly full of artisanal pork rinds, instead of standing over the body of a dead girl. It was a fair trade-off, he decided.

Trey walked back into the living room of his apartment and turned off the TV. He felt groggy, hungover, and he slipped under the sheets of his bed, interested in and slightly terrified of what would await him in the morning.

Instead of driving to work the next morning, a morning he had already experienced once in his lifetime, Trey went into the guest bedroom and wheeled out the expensive bicycle that his parents had bought him for his twenty-third birthday and that he had never once ridden. He searched the closet for the helmet they had included, which still had a bow on it. After he had awkwardly carried it down the stairs of his apartment, Trey wobbled his way through traffic for the five miles it took to get to the offices of the Gentleman Caller. He had nearly crashed on three occasions and could not entirely remember the rules of the road and was a full forty-five minutes late for work, but it was all in service of changing the outcome of this day.

His boss came to his cubicle and said, "You were late today, man, and we're leaving early for drinks for Trevor's birthday. So get to it, okay?"

Trey nodded and got to work on an article about the strange similarities between the characters of a popular fantasy TV show and the characters on *Seinfeld*. Then he answered some "Man Manners" questions, one of which wanted to know about tipping your weed delivery guy. How was he so good at this? he wondered. Was it embarrassing or worthy of pride?

He wished that he knew the identity of the father and daughter that he had hit this evening, could look them up online. He tried to remember that, in addition to preserving his own future, he had saved a girl's life. He thought about how he could become a kind of international time wizard, slashing his throat right after a terrorist event, and then warning officials about it when he woke up a day earlier. It seemed like the best way to use his power, but it also seemed like it could lead to intense scrutiny of his actions, perhaps make him a target of the terrorists. And who would believe him, anyway? If he told the authorities about a horrible event that was going to happen, how would he not also be implicated in their eyes?

Instead, he started thinking about writing a TV show about a guy who was an international time wizard, but Trey immediately understood that he would have to change the particulars of it, that slicing your own throat would not make for a very cool protagonist. By the time he had outlined the pilot in his head, he was already bored with the idea and the workday was over.

Trey declined the invite to the party at the bar and instead rode his bike home, feeling slightly more at ease, noticing that his way home was a few degrees downhill and a little easier to maneuver. He felt grateful for Wildfire Johnny, for the way he had calmed the disturbance in his life, and he looked up briefly at the sky, which was hazy with streetlights and lacked stars, but he felt an overwhelming sense of oneness with the world. Half a block from his apartment, he crashed his bike trying to hop onto the sidewalk, but it wasn't very painful and it wasn't worth changing the outcome by going back in time. He limped home, pushing the bike, still so very happy.

About five months later, Trey wrote a "Man Manners" column where he made a joke about affirmative action, and it blew up in a big way. A woman on Twitter named @dee_light82 tweeted:

> Look at this bullshit about affirmative action that this guy wrote.
> Typical white privilege. People wonder why I'm so upset all the time.

It got retweeted too many times to count and his boss called Trey into his office. "The article is going viral, dude," his boss said. "In the worst possible way."

"I'm so sorry," Trey said, somewhat mystified by how this had gotten so intense so quickly. "It was just a joke."

"Well, I didn't really get it, and it doesn't seem like anyone else did, either."

"It was just one line in the column," Trey said, feeling helpless.

"I think we might have to suspend you," his boss then said. "Just so people understand that we're not racist."

"I'm not racist, either," Trey said, nearly shouting.

"Well," his boss said, "some people think you are. And we can't have them thinking that GC is racist, too. That would be real bad for us."

"Could we ask Jayson to write something to say it's all a misunderstanding?" Trey asked, desperate. Jayson was the only black guy at the Gentleman Caller, and though Trey did not know him well, had never really clicked with him, he thought maybe Jayson could vouch for him.

"I'm not going to ask Jayson to do that," his boss said. "That seems like a bad move."

"I guess so," Trey said. "How long will I be suspended?"

"A week or two," his boss said, looking at his Google Calendar. "That should be enough for people to kind of forget."

"Do you think they'll forget?" Trey asked hopefully.

"Well, they'll forget where they read it. They might not forget that you wrote it."

His boss put out a post saying that the Gentleman Caller was committed to diversity and equality and that this particular column was a gross example of how important it is to remain aware of how words can affect those around us. Trey was not mentioned by name, but the post did say that the writer of the offending column had been immediately suspended and would undergo sensitivity training.

Trey timidly walked back to his boss's office and asked about the sensitivity training.

"That's just for show," the boss said. "I don't have time to look into that and set it up. Just don't do it again, man."

"And I'm suspended right now?" Trey asked.

"I guess so," his boss said, looking at his watch.

"Can I go home, then?" Trey asked, and his boss nodded. Trey walked out of the office; no one would look at him, especially not Jayson, and he got his bike and rode the long way back to his apartment, feeling the wind against his face, wanting to drive right into an oncoming car.

He spent the rest of the afternoon googling his name. He had already shut down his Twitter and Facebook accounts when it became too much to handle. The first page of the search was still populated with his articles for GC, but it didn't take long before the newer articles about his racist column were coming up. He had such a unique name, Trey Beauregard, that nothing came up but his own information; there was no way to hide among other Trey Beauregards.

He called his mom and she assured him that he wasn't racist. "We didn't raise you like that," she said.

"What can I do?" he asked her.

"Continue to be the person that I know you are, and people will come to understand that you're good."

He thought about writing to one of his college girlfriends, who was Hispanic, to ask her what she thought, but he hadn't talked to her in a while, and he was afraid of what she would say.

If you now searched his name on Twitter, it was impossible to keep up with it. He took out the razor blade and opened it up. This seemed like an emergency to him. Trey felt intense anxiety about the pain that would come, but he assured himself that it was temporary. He had to trust Wildfire Johnny's promise that this was an unlimited power, that he hadn't used it all up already. He checked the Internet one more time and then dragged the razor across his throat so quickly that he surprised himself when the blood spurted out of him. He felt the blood rise up in his throat, could taste it on his tongue, and it dribbled out of his mouth. He fell forward onto his laptop and shuddered a few times.

When he woke up, twenty-four hours in the past, he was just about to leave the office, having finished his column, which would run the next morning. It took him a few seconds to orient himself, for the realization of what had already happened to fully hit him. He went back onto his computer, took out the offending joke, and sent the new draft to his boss to okay. He took the deepest breath he had ever taken, could feel his life solidify around him again, his identity preserved. He looked around the room at the few people still at work. They had no idea what had transpired. Again, he thought about it in terms of selfishness. Yes, he had prevented himself from being labeled as a racist, but he had also saved the magazine from embarrassment and helped preserve its integrity, whatever that might be. He had done the right thing. He did not feel racist. Trey was certain about this. He would be more careful in the future. He would be a little more aware of his actions. It shouldn't be too hard, he assured himself.

The next day, he did some Internet searching and found some information about a writer who was going to be reading in town the following week. His name was Gordon Gibbs, a sixty-three-year-old African American writer who had built a small but dedicated following for his novels about African American life in Detroit, dealing with family and race and identity. His novels rarely sold more than a few thousand, but his newest book, a huge departure, was a fantastical, sprawling novel about a group of African Americans who discover and decide to re-populate the lost city of Atlantis. It was getting big reviews, was steadily rising on the bestseller list, and there was talk of a film option in the works.

Trey pitched the interview to his boss, who okayed it because he was intrigued by the "underwater stuff," and Trey met with Gibbs in the back room of the local bookstore an hour before the reading.

Gibbs was six feet nine inches tall, bald, with hoop earrings. He wore an olive green corduroy suit with sneakers. He was holding an unlit cigarette and expertly flipping it around his fingers. He looked furiously bored. Trey instantly wished that he were more than sixty pages into the novel.

Trey asked him questions about his career, about the novel, and Gibbs spoke in a measured voice, with great patience. Trey asked him about why he had decided to move away from Detroit and write about this mythical landscape.

Gibbs asked Trey if he would come outside with him, and they stood and walked outside and stood on the sidewalk in front of the bookstore, where Gibbs lit his cigarette and began to smoke.

"So I've been writing these books, and they're very good books, but nobody was reading them. They were complicated novels about race and about being black in the twentieth and twenty-first centuries, and most people don't have time for that, or don't want to have to think about it too much. I wasn't making much money. So I thought I'd take the same issues that I always write about but hide them in this fantasy about Atlantis. And it worked."

"That's brilliant," Trey remarked.

"Well, I don't know how well it worked," Gibbs continued. "I think most people might miss what I'm really trying to say."

He looked at Trey for a few seconds, took a long drag on his cigarette. "I think maybe you might miss it," he said to Trey.

"I'll try not to miss it," Trey promised, and Gibbs nodded, finished with his cigarette.

"I guess all I can ask is that you try," Gibbs replied, but he wasn't looking at Trey any longer.

After the post went up, Jayson came over to Trey's desk. "I had wanted to write about Gordon Gibbs," he said flatly.

"I had no idea," Trey admitted. "I'm sorry."

"Have you read any of Gibbs's books?" Jayson asked.

"Well, I'm almost done with the new one," Trey said, smiling.

"I see," Jayson said. He started to walk away and then turned back to Trey. "Why did you want to write about Gibbs, anyway?"

"He seems important, like people should know about him. Race is important, right?"

"It is," Jayson said, looking at Trey like he couldn't quite figure him out or perhaps that he had him figured out and was hoping to be proved wrong. Trey just smiled.

"Sorry again," he told Jayson, who nodded and held up a hand in acceptance of the apology. Trey thought he should invite Jayson out for a drink that evening, but the longer the day went on, the less it seemed like a good idea.

Six months later, the media company that owned the Gentleman Caller decided to start a similar website for women, called the Hatbox. One of the ways to cross-promote the sites was to start a new column that would run on both websites called "Mr. and Mrs. Lonelyhearts," where Trey and a new advice columnist would respond to the same question about relationships and love to highlight and try to navigate the complications between men and women. The company set up a lunch date for Trey and the new columnist, a woman named Ashley Taylor.

When he got to the restaurant, an upscale version of authentic Texas barbecue where the waiters came by often to replenish your stack of warm, damp cotton napkins and refill huge jars of jalapeño-infused iced tea, he saw Ashley waiting at a table. She was black, which he noticed right away, and he was happy that this was not surprising to him or cause for him to be nervous.

She waved to him, and he waved back and walked over to the table. "Mr. Lonelyhearts," she said, smiling.

"That's me," he said.

"I like your work. It seems just barely aware of how silly it is. I liked your advice column. And I liked that Gordon Gibbs profile that you did; he's one of my favorite writers."

"Mine, too," he replied; though he'd only read the most recent book, he'd meant to check out his other books. He wished now that he had read some of Ashley's own work; why had he not done this? Jesus.

"I really love your stuff, too," he ventured, hoping not to be questioned too deeply. "I think we'll be a good match."

"I hope so," Ashley said. She had a southern drawl that sounded similar to a kind of sorority girl from big southern schools, like a girl from Texas who went to the University of Alabama. A girl who wore pink but had handled a dead deer.

She was light-skinned, had a smattering of freckles that covered her face. She had a gap between her two front teeth. Her hair was in a bob, straightened, and dyed blond at the edges. She had thick-framed glasses, but he wondered if they were prescription.

"Where are you from?" he asked her.

"Mobile, Alabama," she said. "But I've been in New York since I graduated from college and went to grad school. I'm not sure about coming back, if I'm being honest." She looked around at the restaurant. "But Nashville feels kind of like a Disney version of the South. I don't know if that's good or bad. Probably bad."

"It's okay," he said.

"So are you ready to work together?" she asked.

"I think so. I think it'll be fun," he answered.

"What do you know about relationships?" she asked him.

"Not much," he admitted. "Not enough to be an expert."

"Are you dating someone now?" she asked.

"No," he said. "Not for a while, actually."

"I left somebody back in New York," she admitted. "I actually moved here to get away from the fallout from that relationship. So I guess we're just two lonely hearts, telling people how to get other people to fuck them."

"I guess so," he said.

"Do you think it's better if we agree with each other, or if we have different viewpoints?" she asked him.

"I think it's good if we're just honest and see how it lines up," he said.

"I'm pretty sure that we're going to have different viewpoints," she said, smiling. He smiled back, but his lips stuck to his teeth and it looked like he was having a stroke. He blushed.

"Your ears are bright red right now," she said.

"I'm nervous," he said.

"Don't be falling in love with me, Mr. Lonelyhearts," she said.

"I'll try," he said.

The column was an immediate success. It struck the right balance between irreverence at even doing an advice column in this day and age while also treating the questions with some degree of seriousness. People liked it. Ashley and Trey would simply get on GChat and go over the questions for that week, and they would publish the chat, with edits to remove the moments where they simply talked about TV shows or music, which happened more and more as they got comfortable with each other over the computer. They met up once a week at that same Texas barbecue restaurant to pick the questions for that week. Ashley drank Palomas through a paper straw, and Trey drank smoked mescal that burned the shit out of his throat.

With the questions, Trey favored loyalty while Ashley always encouraged those who wrote in to leave before it got worse. Trey wasn't sure that true love existed and so thought it was nice to simply accept what you had in the moment in order to give tangible meaning to your life. Ashley thought everything should be predicated on good sex and good communication and that life was too short to live without these things. Trey thought most of the questions revealed weird hang-ups on the part of the writer, while Ashley thought people weren't as fucked-up as she'd anticipated.

"So," she asked him over GChat one night, "are you using my good advice to find a girlfriend?"

"I'm compiling it," he responded. "I'm studying it. But no luck yet."

"Have you ever dated a black girl?" she then wrote, and Trey felt his heart do that weird hiccup thing where you knew that your life could change if you did everything just right.

Before he could write back, she added, "I bet you haven't."

"No," he wrote. Then he added, "I dated a Hispanic girl in college." There was no response from Ashley, so he then added, "Maybe she was half Hispanic."

"Good lord, Trey," she finally wrote back after an agonizingly long time.

"What?" he typed.

"Good night, Mr. Lonelyhearts," she said, and she left the chat.

He thought about slashing his throat, but what would it accomplish? He would still have the same answer for her when the moment came around again. Perhaps he could slash his throat enough times that he would be far enough in the past that he could date a black girl, then come back to this very moment and reply to Ashley that indeed he had dated a black girl before, indeed he had.

It was an interesting hiccup in Wildfire Johnny's gift that he hadn't considered. If he slashed his throat to go back twenty-four hours in the past, if he did it again, right away, he'd go back another twenty-four hours. As long as he could keep doing it, he could go back as far into his past as he wanted. All he'd have to do then was live his life again, which seemed like it would either be very exciting or very boring. His head hurt. He didn't even bother reaching into his pocket for the razor. It wasn't worth it.

The following week, he met with Ashley at the restaurant, and after they talked about the questions for the week, he asked her out on a date.

"You don't think these are dates?" she asked him, smiling.

"Oh," Trey said, confused. "I guess I haven't thought that."

"Maybe they're more like pre-dates, practice dates," Ashley said.

"So would you be interested in an actual, real date with me?" he asked her again.

She considered the question, looked at him. He wondered what she saw. "Yeah," she finally said. "Okay."

Trey was as happy as he'd ever been, in a life that had been mostly easy, mostly happy.

Ashley was still staring at him, which made him self-conscious. "You won't regret it," he said.

"We'll see," she said.

They went bowling at a restaurant that had its own alley, as well as an outdoor pool, a shuffleboard. Reese Witherspoon was right next to them. Ashley took a picture of her with her phone.

They drank beer out of cans. They ate fried avocado. Trey nearly bowled a perfect game, only fucked it up at the last possible moment. Reese Witherspoon had cheered for him. Ashley had rubbed his shoulders for good luck before each frame. In the car on the way back to Ashley's apartment, she told him that she didn't realize that bowling could be sexy.

When they had sex, Trey was so nervous that he asked for her advice before he did anything. "You're lucky," she said, when he was going down on her, as she shifted his head to the place that she wanted him to be. "Some girls wouldn't like a dude who didn't know what he was doing, but it's better this way. I get exactly what I want."

After they had fucked, Ashley said he could either stay the night or go back home. Trey said that he wanted to stay. They couldn't sleep, so they drank some whiskey and answered questions for the "Lonelyhearts" column. "Go for it," they both instructed the sad people seeking love. "Fall in love. Do it."

In the morning, as Trey collected his clothes from the night before, the razor blade fell out of his pocket.

"What the fuck is that?" Ashley said.

"Oh, it's just a good luck charm," Trey replied, putting it back in his pocket.

"'Cause it looks like a fucking razor," Ashley said. She grabbed his arm and made him show her the razor. "What are you doing with this?"

"I carry it everywhere I go," he said.

"That's kind of creepy, Trey," she replied.

"It's just. It's silly," he said, and when she simply stared at him, he continued. "It belonged to . . . my grandfather. We were really close. I, um, I used to watch him shave with it and it was just a good memory, the smell of his shaving cream. He died when I was young and I got to keep it."

"Okay, I guess," she finally said. "I wish he'd left you a pocket watch. When you fuck a guy and a pocket watch falls out of his pants, you don't feel like you're about to get murdered."

She took the razor from his hand and opened it. "Your grandfather's name was 'Wildfire Johnny'?"

"It was his stage name. He was, like, a performer."

"This could do some real damage," she said, pointing it at him. "If shit goes down, I guess you'll be ready."

"I hope so," he said, and then he took the razor back and put it safely into his pocket.

After three months of dating, they announced their relationship to their editors, who said it would be interesting to make it known to their readers. It caused a huge flurry of activity, people on Twitter freaking out that Mr. and Mrs. Lonelyhearts had fallen in love. The *New York Times* did a profile of them, the two of them photographed at the barbecue restaurant, Ashley resting her head on Trey's shoulder. As they read about their relationship online, Ashley turned to Trey and said, "I never said *love,* just so you know. It's too early for that."

"I'm in love with you," he said. "I think."

"Good," Ashley said. "That's good information for me to have."

Trey started to use the razor more liberally. One night, after he ate some leftover Thai food, he got food poisoning, and the vomiting was so intense that he took the razor and, almost without thinking, slashed his throat. When it came time to eat the Thai food, he threw it into the garbage, whistling a happy tune.

He got caught up in an eBay auction over a rare punk rock record and ended up winning with a bid of six hundred and seventy-five dollars. He logged into his bank account and looked at his balance and then slashed his throat. All day long, repeating it, he simply listened to a YouTube clip of the song and felt like it was just as good.

He backed his car into a utility pole, and a throat slash later, the car was fine, not a mark on it.

The weirdest part of going back in time wasn't the disorientation of jumping back, it was the boredom of going through the same twenty-four hours again. What he figured out was that, if you simply shut your mind down, as if you were meditating, you could just allow your previous actions to replay, as if you were being carried away by the tide. Then, when you needed to act, to change the past, you woke up, took control of your body, and did what needed to be done.

After Ashley and Trey had been dating for a year, his parents wanted to meet her, were driving up to Nashville to have dinner with them. "Are your parents cool?" Ashley asked.

"Not especially," Trey said.

"I mean, are they cool with the two of us being together?" Ashley then said.

"Oh . . . sure." Trey had not thought about it. "They're cool."

"They know that I'm black?" she asked.

"Oh, yeah. They saw the photo in the *Times*," Trey said, trying to think back. He didn't talk to his parents all that much, honestly.

"Well, good," Ashley said.

When they walked into the restaurant, his parents were already sitting at the table. They stood up to greet them, and Trey said, "Hey, Mom and Dad, this is my black girlfriend, Ashley."

Ashley turned to look at Trey with a look of complete bewilderment.

His mother's ears turned red. "Honey," she said to Trey.

"Oh, God, I'm sorry. I'm just nervous," he said, looking at his parents and then back at Ashley.

"Jesus, Trey," Ashley said.

Trey felt for the razor in his pocket. "If you guys will excuse me for just one second, I need to go to the bathroom."

"Trey," Ashley said, holding on to his arm, but he pulled away and rushed to the restroom, leaving Ashley and his parents standing there, staring at one another.

There was another guy in the bathroom, washing his hands, and Trey went into the stall, slashed his throat, gurgling, blood spray. Just before he passed out, he heard the man shout, "Holy shit!"

When dinner came around again, everyone got along so well. Afterward, his mother took him aside for a second and said, "We really like her, sweetie."

"So do I," he said, smiling.

Most of Ashley's friends were black, professors at Vanderbilt or visual artists, some of whom had started their own gallery. But she had white friends, too, Asian friends, Hispanic friends. Trey thought back and tried to remember if he had ever had anything other than white friends. There was James, a black kid, with whom he'd been best friends in junior high, but they'd drifted apart and then gone to different high schools. There was an Asian kid, Paul, that he'd been friends with in college, though he could not remember his last name. At work, sometimes he got drinks with Marco, but he couldn't remember if he was Mexican or from South America.

"I don't have any black friends," Trey once said to Ashley.

"You don't actually have that many white friends, either," she told him.

"I'm serious, okay?" Trey said. "Do you think it's a problem?"

"If you think it's a problem," Ashley replied, "then you should try to change it."

"How?" Trey asked.

"God, Trey, you're a writer. Read writers of color and reach out to them to talk about their work. There's Jayson at your work. Go out with him for drinks."

"I don't think Jayson likes me," Trey said.

"Just open yourself up. Be deliberate. Don't force it, but get over the fact that it makes you uncomfortable to be around black people."

"I'm not uncomfortable," he said.

"You know what I mean," she said.

"I'm comfortable with you," he said, and she sighed.

"You're a good boyfriend, Trey," she said.

"If we had kids, they'd be mixed race," he said.

She kissed him. "Let's watch some TV, okay?"

Trey did a profile of Will Ferrell for *Esquire,* his first big celebrity profile, and it went really well. "You're a good interviewer," Ferrell had said to Trey, who blushed.

"It's good," Ashley said after she'd read his draft. "It's really good."

"Thanks," he replied. It was good, he thought.

"Do you think you'll do more celebrity profiles?" she asked.

"If they let me," he said. "It's fun."

"What else do you want to write?" she asked.

"Silly things," he said. "Weird stuff."

"You'd be a good reporter," she said. "You have a kind of blank slate thing going on that would make people confide in you. You could get people to admit that they'd murdered someone."

"I don't want to write about murder," he said.

Ashley had gotten her MFA in fiction at Columbia, and she was writing a collection of stories, one of which had been published in *Tin House.* She was also interested in long-form journalism, but that didn't really appeal to Trey. He wanted to look at something, say a few things about it, then move on.

"You should try to write a novel," she said. "A comic novel."

"Maybe," he said.

"We can't do the Lonelyhearts forever," she said.

"We can't?" he asked.

"I can't," she said.

In Maryland, a fourteen-year-old African American boy was shot in the parking lot of a Walmart. He'd bought a toy gun from the store and was playing with it in the parking lot when somebody called the police. When he didn't put the gun down immediately, terrified of the lights and the police officers, they shot him.

"This is such fucking bullshit," Ashley said.

"It really is," Trey said.

"It's murder, plain and simple," she said. "And it's happening all the fucking time."

Trey wondered if it was actually murder. It seemed more like manslaughter, accidental, the police losing control.

"How realistic was the gun?" he asked her, looking over her shoulder at the computer.

She turned to look at him. "If we had kids," she said, "and they played with a toy gun, the police would shoot them."

"The world is fucked-up," he said.

"You have no idea," she said.

Ashley got an assignment for *The New Yorker,* a big break, to write an article about her father's half brother, who had been convicted twenty-five years ago for the rape of a white woman. Just last year, he had been exonerated thanks to DNA evidence. She was going to Birmingham, Alabama, to meet with him for the first time. She would study the case, talk to people involved, write about all of it.

"Can I stay with you?" Trey asked.

"You can come see me," she said. "But you can't stay. I want to talk to him by myself."

"But you don't even know this guy," Trey said. "He could be dangerous."

Ashley just stared at him. He both loved and hated it when she stared at him. He understood that she was probably trying to figure out what it was that she loved about him, but it also meant that he had her attention.

"You can drive down with me. My brother lives in Birmingham, too; you can meet him."

Ashley and her parents did not talk; they were evangelical Christians, fanatical, and she had grown tired of fighting with them. But she still talked to her brother, who was six years younger. His name was Freddie and he was a producer. Ashley had shown Trey her brother's SoundCloud page, heavy bass and weird metallic beats, swirling sounds. It sounded like what an alien would rap over. Apparently he was blowing up, was becoming well known among Atlanta rappers, was making good money. Trey looked at Freddie's Instagram, lots of clips of him making beats, always smoking huge blunts. A few photos showed him standing around with dudes who were brandishing guns. It felt entirely foreign to Trey, but he found himself listening to Freddie's beats all the time when he was writing.

They drove in separate cars to Birmingham, pulled up to the parking lot for Freddie's apartment in downtown Birmingham, a few miles away from where things were respectable and expensive. There was a massive dog in the stairwell and he eyed them as they walked up.

When he opened the door, Freddie was wearing sunglasses, velour sweatpants, and a Japanese T-shirt that Trey, thanks to the Gentleman Caller, knew for a fact cost more than two hundred dollars. Freddie smiled and gave Ashley a huge hug. She giggled. Without acknowledging Trey, he took Ashley's hand and pulled her into the living room. Trey walked in, awkward, not sure where to stand.

"You look great," Freddie said to his sister. "It's good to see you."

"You, too," she said, and then Ashley gestured for Trey to come closer. "This is my boyfriend, Trey."

"Hi," Trey said, and Freddie simply nodded. "I like your music," Trey offered.

"You like rap?" Freddie asked, looking interested for the first time in Trey.

"Oh, yeah," Trey said.

"Who do you like?" Freddie asked.

"Oh, just, you know, everyone," Trey replied, flailing. He could not remember the name of a single rapper at this moment.

"Eminem?" Freddie asked, nodding.

"Among others," Trey said, and Freddie was done with him.

Freddie and Ashley sat on the sofa and talked about people they knew, minutiae about Mobile, frustrations about their crazy-ass parents. Trey sat in a recliner and tried to think of a rapper who would impress Freddie. He knew nothing that he said would be good enough.

A few hours later, it was time for Trey to go back to Nashville, and Ashley would spend the night with her brother before starting her work the next day. Trey shook Freddie's hand. Freddie said, "My sister likes you a lot."

"Freddie," Ashley said, shaking her head.

"Do right by her, okay?" he said. "She's a real unique person."

"I will," Trey said, "I know." He felt like he had received a blessing, that he could now marry Ashley.

"Bye, sweetie," Ashley said, kissing him, and then she closed the door when he walked into the hallway.

The month turned into two, and Ashley was still working. "It's insane," she said. "This place is so blatantly up-front about its racism that they don't even think to not tell you the truth. I can't get over it. My dad's brother doesn't even seem entirely surprised by any of it. He's just accepted it, like, what else could he have done. He's a really interesting guy, the exact opposite of my dad."

"Do you think you'll be back soon?" Trey asked.

"I really don't know," she replied. "There's so much to figure out."

"Maybe I could come see you," he said.

"I don't think that's a great idea," she said. "I need to stay focused."

"I miss you," he said.

"Well, fuck, I miss you, too," Ashley said, sounding frustrated. "But this is important to me, Trey. It means a lot to me, to my career, to my family."

"I understand," Trey said, but he wasn't sure that he did. He felt like she was becoming so frustrated with the racism of the justice system that she couldn't stand to be around him, that he was responsible for it.

Ashley had asked him to write her half of the "Lonelyhearts" column. "You know my voice as well as I do," she said. "You're a good writer."

He told the woman who was concerned that her boyfriend

was becoming too obsessed with his job that she needed to give him an ultimatum, that she was more important than work. Ashley agreed. "Nothing's more important than your relationship. Ask him how much he'll like his career if there's no one there for him when the workday is over."

I'm just frustrated," Ashley said one night after they'd been arguing for a solid hour. She was crying. "It's not about you, really."

"It sure feels like it's about me," Trey said, annoyed.

"That's fair. I guess it is you, a little bit. I feel like maybe this time away has made me think more about what our relationship is. I think maybe we should take some time to—"

Trey already had the razor to his throat, a quick slash.

As soon as he came to, he went online and found a first edition copy of Gordon Gibbs's first novel, nearly five hundred dollars. He ordered it and had it overnighted to Ashley. When the phone rang that night, Ashley wanting to talk, he simply let it go to voice mail.

The next night, she called him. "Oh my God, Trey," she said. "The book! It's amazing. Thank you."

"I love you," he said.

"Well, I love you, too," she said.

"People are going to love your first book," Trey said. "I'll sell first editions online for thousands of dollars."

"I'll even autograph them," she said.

Two weeks later, he got a call from Ashley, who was frantic, nearly sobbing.

"The police arrested Freddie," she said.

"What?" Trey said. "When?"

"Last night," she told him. "He was sitting on the steps in front of his apartment, and they just pulled up and started harassing him. They said that he smelled of weed, but he didn't have anything on him. They pushed him against the wall, and when he tried to get them to tell him what was going on, one of the cops hit him. Then they hit him some more. They said that he had a gun on him, which he obviously didn't. They planted it, Trey."

Trey thought about those Instagram photos of Freddie's friends with their guns. He thought of all the photos of him smoking weed.

"This is fucked-up," he said.

"I feel like they're punishing him because I'm writing this story about my uncle and how racist the justice system is here."

"What can I do?" he said.

"He hasn't even seen a judge yet, but I'll need to pay his bail when it's set," she said. "But I don't have hardly anything in my account right now."

"I'll get it," he said.

"Come as soon as you can," she said.

He got there that night, went straight to Ashley's motel room, a run-down place off the highway, not many cars in the parking lot.

Ashley was in her underwear, smoking a joint.

"Where did you get that?" he asked.

"From a drug dealer, Trey," she said. "Jesus."

"Tell me what's going on," he said.

"I haven't been able to talk to Freddie since he first called," she replied. She was agitated, pulling at her eyelashes, a nervous habit of hers when she was really stressed. "I don't know what's going on."

"We'll get him out," he said. "We'll get him a good lawyer. It'll be okay."

"I don't think so, Trey," she said. She looked up at him. "I think it's fucked-up and it's going to stay that way. I'm just so tired of this shit. I don't think I can live in the South any longer. I need to go back to New York."

"Oh, like the New York City Police Department is any better," Trey said, and he could tell that this was the wrong thing to say.

"Don't do that, Trey," she said. "As soon as I get things sorted with Freddie, I'm moving back to New York."

"What about me?" he asked.

"Come with me," she said.

"I like Nashville," he said, but then he quickly said, "but I like you more."

"Come here," she said.

He held her, felt her body ease into his embrace. They made their way to the bed and had sex; he came so fast, but then he worked on her with his hand until she shuddered against him.

They fell asleep and then woke the next morning. All day they waited to hear about Freddie. There was nothing. Ashley kept writing, and Trey surfed the Internet in the tiny motel room. He went out and got Chinese food and brought it back for them to eat. Ashley let Trey read her article, which was amazing. It was the kind of thing that was so far beyond Trey's own ability that he knew it would get her a lot of attention.

"It's amazing," he said.

"Thanks," she replied, smiling.

"It's going to be a big deal," he told her.

"And right after this, I'm going to write about what's happening to Freddie. I'll just write about every single injustice that I'm one degree apart from. I'll write forever."

The next day, they finally heard that Freddie's bail was $15,000, and Trey thought about the dent in his bank account, which he'd already fucked up by purchasing that Gordon Gibbs first edition.

"I'm still so fucking angry about this," she said. "I'm going to have a hard time not punching every fucking cop that I see in that place."

"I'll bail you out," Trey said, and she laughed out loud. As they got dressed, brushed their teeth, Trey said, not really thinking much of it, "Where do you think they got that gun that they planted on Freddie?"

"Who knows?" Ashley replied. "They probably have a box of guns in the trunk of their cruiser to plant on black guys."

"But couldn't it be traced?" Trey said. "Why would they risk it?"

"What do you mean?" Ashley said.

"It just seems excessive," he said, shrugging.

"Do you think it's his?" she finally asked him, her hands now on her hips, like she was ready for a fight.

"I don't know," he said.

"Fuck you, Trey," she said.

"I said that I didn't know," he shouted. "I've never had to deal with somebody getting arrested. It's all new to me."

"Keep your money," she now said. "I'm going to call my parents."

"Fuck, don't do that," Trey said. "I said I'd pay for it. I believe you."

"You think the world is so perfect that if something bad happens to a person, you think there's a reason for it. You think they deserved it."

"That's not fair, Ashley, really," he said. He could feel everything slipping away.

"Sometimes I feel like we're a hundred miles apart from each other," she said. "I feel like there's things that you'll never understand about me."

"I'm trying," he replied. It was over. He could feel it ending, the way things went away and never came back.

"I don't think that's enough," she said. "I think you should go back to Nashville. I think you should stay there."

"You're angry," Trey said. "We should talk about it."

"I don't want to talk," she said.

Trey opened his wallet and pulled out the hundred bucks that he had. "Take it," he said. "Anything you want, I'll give it to you."

"Go home, Trey," she said.

Trey stared at her for a few seconds, unsure of what to do. She turned away from him, reached for her cell phone, and walked into the bathroom. Trey took out the razor, held it to his throat, and started to drag it across the skin. Just then, Ashley walked back into the room. "Trey!" she shouted. "What the fuc—"

Twenty-four hours earlier, Trey was lying in bed, staring at his computer. He looked around. Ashley was sitting at the wobbly desk against the window. She was turned around in her chair, staring at him.

"What the fuck did you just do?" she asked him.

"What do you mean?" he replied, still trying to come out of the haze, of feeling his blood pulsing inside his body.

"I saw you, Trey. You cut your fucking throat open. Right in front of me."

"No," Trey said, confused. He tried to get up, but the sheets were stuck to his legs, and he couldn't get free. Ashley was now standing, backing away from him, pressing herself against the wall.

"I saw you. It was fucking horrifying. I told you we were over, and you cut your throat, and now here we are. What's going on?" she asked him.

"It's complicated," he said. "I'm not sure why you remembered."

"I'm scared of you, Trey," she said.

"Let me explain," he said.

"I think you better leave," she said, and Trey once again, nothing to lose, slashed his throat, fell against the headboard of the bed, and woke up twenty-four hours earlier.

He was in his own apartment in Nashville. Immediately, the phone rang. He looked at the screen and saw that it was Ashley. He answered.

"What are you doing?" she said. "What's going on?"

He slashed his throat again. He didn't know what else to do, how to fix anything. He woke up twenty-four hours earlier and, without hesitation, slashed his throat again. The pain was excruciating, not enough time passing between the act to help him forget the sensation. He took a few minutes to think it over.

His phone was ringing again, Ashley on the line. He let it go to voice mail, but the phone just rang again. She remembered what had happened. Somehow she was caught up in the time warp, he guessed. The phone rang again, and he moved to answer it, no way to avoid what was coming. But then he stopped. There was a way, he realized. If he just kept going, slashing his throat every day for three years, until he found himself before he had met Ashley, maybe she wouldn't remember. The memory wouldn't be connected to anything.

He took the razor and slashed his throat again; as he bled out, he heard the phone still ringing.

Time had no shape or feeling. He was in a tunnel, moving backward, with no control over his body. After thirty days, he felt like he'd been running a nonstop marathon. The phone kept ringing, but he wouldn't answer it. Soon he'd be back to when Ashley was back in Nashville, when she would be in his apartment. He had to move quickly. His throat opened up and it felt like he didn't even need the razor to do it anymore, that he could just touch his skin and the blood would come.

"Why are you doing this?" she asked him once, when they were sitting on his sofa.

"I promise it'll be okay," he told her.

"I don't believe you," she said, but he was already drowning in his own blood.

He was two years back in time, always checking the calendar on his phone whenever he woke up again.

"Just talk to me," she said.

"I love you," he said.

"I love you, too, you stupid fucking idiot," she said.

He slashed his throat.

When he finally made it to the day that he had first met her, he didn't even hesitate. He slashed his throat again. And again. He went back an extra thirty days, just to be safe. He waited for the phone to ring. He looked her up online, read her articles again. What would happen when they met? Would she remember? How could she believe it was anything other than a strange dream?

What he really wanted to know was whether he could start over with her. So much of their relationship had been pure joy. He had fucked up some, but he felt like he could, if given the chance, smooth over those things. He would stop writing silly shit about sweatpants. He would get involved in real issues. They would team up for social justice. He would open himself up to the world.

He went to the library and checked out Gordon Gibbs's first novel, *Soldier's Joy,* about a black man who returns to Detroit after two tours in Vietnam. He's now addicted to heroin, but he doesn't feel entirely out of place back in Detroit. Trey read it in a single day. He would talk about it with Ashley when they met again.

What else could he do? Was it enough to live the last three years of his life differently? He moved through the thirty days in a kind of haze. He simply let his body go through the motions of living. The closer he got to the day when he would walk into the restaurant, see her at their table, the more he felt like it could work.

At night, he started to think about the things he had done. He thought, for the first time in many years, about the reason why he and James, his friend from junior high, stopped being friends. They had been playing basketball at the park when two redneck boys who were sophomores in high school challenged them to a game. James was good, played on the junior high team, so good that he could carry Trey to a win over these two boys, no matter how dirty they played. When they were two points away from winning, James spotted up for a shot, and one of the boys said, "Miss it, you dumb nigger." The shot clanged off the rim. James looked over at Trey and then back at the boy. "What the hell did you call me?" James asked. The boy and his friend moved closer to James. "You heard what I called you," he said. James again looked at Trey, who had gone to retrieve the ball.

"Let's just finish the game, man," Trey said to the two boys, who were now smiling.

Trey passed the ball to James, who stared at the two boys, who did not make a move. James spotted up, shot the ball, which fell effortlessly through the hoop, and the game was over.

"Good game," Trey said to the boys, who still were staring at James. He was watching them carefully, waiting for what came next. Finally, the boys spit right at James's feet and walked away. Trey heard them say the n-word again, then laughter.

"Good shot," Trey said to James, and he offered his hand for a high five, but James pushed it away.

"Why didn't you do anything, man?" James asked him as they went to get the basketball, which had rolled to the edge of the court.

"What could I do?" Trey asked.

"You could have helped me beat the shit out of them," James said.

"They're older than us," Trey said.

"Still, man," James said.

"Forget those guys, man," Trey said to his friend. "Don't let it get to you."

"Yeah," James said, looking toward the distance where the boys had been walking.

Trey felt ugly, like his skin was blistered and angry. He held the razor. Could he go back that far, to that moment with James? Could he run over to that boy, right after he'd said what he'd said to James, and punch him square in the mouth? The two boys would then kick Trey and James until their teeth loosened and their ribs bruised. Would he and James still be friends?

He thought about when he was four years old, one of his earliest memories, when he'd told a black girl that he'd just met at the park that she looked kind of like a monkey. His mother had heard and taken him to the bathroom and spanked him for the first time in his life, so hard that he had wailed for an hour afterward. He thought about the only Korean girl at his elementary school, when he told her that her lunch that she'd brought from home smelled awful, and how the girl had cried until the teacher had let her call her mother and go home. He thought about how she never brought lunch from home again. He could not remember her name.

What did he want exactly, to go back in time and remove every moment that he had hurt someone? To be worthy of whatever came to him? All he wanted at the moment was Ashley, to be worthy of her. He knew that he wasn't, not yet.

But the day was here, when he was to finally meet her. Trey dressed, combed his hair. He drove to the restaurant. He walked inside and saw Ashley, sitting at the table. She waved to him. He waved back. He took a step forward. He checked his pocket for the razor. It was there. It was there like it always was, like it always would be, for as long as he needed such things.

A Visit

Missy heard that her mom was in the hospital, had been assaulted in her own home, from a second cousin who had listened to the whole thing on her police scanner. "As soon as I heard the name June Weaver, I figured I should tell somebody. It sounds bad, Missy."

Missy was in bed, just asleep enough that this phone call felt like an anxiety dream, but she slowly worked her way through the facts. Her husband was snoring like a drugged elk, and she shoved him until he rolled onto his stomach and his breathing normalized. From what she could understand, the bare essentials that came over the police scanner, someone had broken into her mother's home, where she lived alone, demanded money, assaulted her, and then run off, still at large. They had taken her mother to the hospital over in Custer. Missy thanked the second cousin, a woman she had no memory of ever meeting, not fully awake enough to wonder how the woman had her phone number, and sat in bed, unable to do anything other than think about her options.

She knew she would have to go to her mother in Slidell, a four-hour drive from her apartment in Atlanta, and take care of things. Her only sibling, Tommy, was a bartender in Las Vegas; she didn't even have a phone number for him any longer, hadn't seen him in a couple of years. She'd have to take some personal days from the travel agency, her boss surely pissed about it, and her husband and their daughter, Kayla, would have to fend for themselves for a few days. This was easy enough to figure out; the hard part was the uncertainty that awaited her. Her mother, eighty-two years old, had been beaten up, probably by some meth addict, and Missy only knew that there were so many outcomes that were untenable for her, as coldhearted as that seemed.

Their apartment was too small to accommodate her mother. If her mother needed help once she got back from the hospital, there was no money to pay for it. A nursing home was out of the question, too expensive, and her mother would never consent to it anyways. If her mother died—and Missy could not prevent her mind from going to these dark places—she had no idea how to even go about untangling all her mother's affairs, whatever they might be. She saw her mother on Christmas and Easter, occasionally answered phone calls to help her figure out some tricky website or how to program the satellite TV. Now, as she quickly packed a bag and explained to her groggy husband what was happening, her mother had become the world entire. All the details of how she cared for herself and spent her days, which had become hazy and easy for Missy to ignore over the years, crystallized into a solid and definable sadness.

Before she left, she kissed Kayla, who, even in her sleep, reached out and hugged Missy, and then she was in the car, navigating by memory the turns and highways that led back to her childhood home, her mind unable to settle on any real thought. The interior of the car was dark and silent, and she realized that, though she should be exhausted, her body was rumbling with adrenaline, her hands gripping the steering wheel so tightly that it made her teeth ache.

Four hours later, as she drove down strange highways, past houses that seemed to have exploded, all their contents now on the front lawn, every five miles seeing yet another fireworks store that was just a run-down trailer strung up with Christmas lights, she arrived in Custer. She pulled into the parking lot of the hospital and suddenly realized that she should have called ahead; why had she never thought to phone the hospital to check on her mother's status? Everything had happened so fast, she supposed, though that didn't account for the four hours in the car, listening to talk radio and smooth jazz; besides, whatever the outcome, she would still need to come here. No situation would have allowed her to stay in Atlanta.

She walked inside, the lighting so bright, and found a nurses' station. "My mom came here earlier tonight," she said to the disinterested nurse who was playing with her cell phone. "June Weaver?"

"You family?" the nurse asked, suddenly suspicious.

"I'm her daughter," Missy answered. "Can you tell me anything about how she's doing? Can I see her?"

"She ain't here," the nurse finally replied.

"What?" Missy said, the accumulation of exhaustion now settling on her frame. She felt her knees slowly buckle, and she steadied herself against the counter.

"Well, she was here. They brought her in and the cops were here, but she left about thirty minutes ago."

"You let her go?"

"We told her that she should stay, but she didn't want to. We couldn't keep her."

"She went back home?" Missy asked. "But why would they let her go back home? Somebody broke into her house and beat her up, right? How can she just go back there?"

"Well, they caught the guy, so I guess it's okay," the woman said. She had clearly moved on to other business, with Missy still standing in front of her.

"Is she okay?" Missy asked, and then, the questions building like a wave, one after the other, she interrupted herself. "Who even drove her home? She lives by herself."

"Let me ask Janie," the woman said, and she pushed her chair away from Missy and walked over to another nurse. They consulted for a few seconds and then the nurse came back, shrugging. "Some man picked her up."

"Jesus," Missy said. Her nerves were so raw that she knew that she needed to punch someone, but she couldn't figure out who it should be. She walked back to the parking lot and called her mother on her cell phone, but it went to the answering machine. "Mom?" Missy said into the phone, almost shouting. "It's Missy. Are you home? I'm real worried, Mom. Pick up, please."

The machine clicked off, and Missy heard her mother's soft southern drawl. "Hi, Missy."

"Mom, what in the hell is going on? Are you okay?"

"I'm fine, honey. I got some stitches on my cheek, but they gave me some medicine at the hospital, and I feel real fine."

Missy started crying, unsure of the emotion she was experiencing. "I'm coming to see you, Mom," she said.

"Honey, don't worry about me. It's such a long drive. I'm fine, I told you."

"I'm here," Missy shouted. "I'm at the hospital right now. I drove here as soon as I heard."

"Who told you? Why did they tell you?"

"Junie's daughter called me," Missy said.

"Honey, Junie doesn't have a daughter. She's got four boys."

"Jesus, Mom, I don't know. One of those cousins called me. And she called me because you're my mom and you got assaulted and you were in the hospital. You should still be in the hospital."

"I'm fine, honey," her mother said, as if this explained everything. "But come on home. I'll make you some breakfast. Do you want some biscuits? I think I have some granola from the last time you were here, that kind that you like."

"Don't you dare make breakfast, Mom," Missy said. "Just rest, and I'll be there in a few minutes."

"What about coffee? You must be tired."

"Mom," Missy said but couldn't find the strength to continue. She took a deep breath, knowing her mother was still waiting for her to answer, calmly waiting as if nothing was wrong and Missy was just in the area and had decided to visit. "We'll make breakfast together when I get there."

"Okay, honey," her mother said, and then hung up the phone before Missy could say anything else.

When Missy pulled into her mother's driveway, she noticed that her mother's Cadillac was parked in the grass, leaving the carport open for Missy to park her own car. This was one of her mother's habits, moving her car out of the way whenever Missy and her family visited, as if they deserved the covered parking, and Missy now realized that her mother had probably come out here to move the car before Missy arrived. She immediately felt a burning frustration for her mother's constant selflessness, but that quickly gave way to sadness, the idea of her mother hobbling into the driveway in order to move her own car.

In the house—Jesus Christ, the door left unlocked so that Missy (or another intruder) could just walk right in—she found her mother sitting in her easy chair, listening to talk radio. Missy shuddered at the sight of her mother's injury, an angry line of stitches that ran from temple to midcheek. The entire right side of her face was bruised and puffy with swelling. Missy put a hand to her mouth to stifle any sound of alarm, and her mother smiled when she saw Missy in the doorway. "Honey," she said, rising unsteadily to her feet. "How are you?"

"Mom," Missy said, rushing over to her. "Sit back down. Are you okay? What happened?"

Her mother fell back into her chair and then took a sip of water before answering. "It's just awful, honey," her mother began. "I was cleaning up in the kitchen last night and someone knocked on the door. It was Leland King, one of Duncan's boys."

Leland had gone to school with Missy; he'd been a few years younger than she was, a skinny, weasel-like boy, his little frame always supporting layer upon layer of camouflage. His brother, Donnie, had been one of Missy's best friends, and Leland had often hung out with them, but he was so quiet, always sitting at a remove from them, nervous and twitchy like a feral cat.

"He asked if he could come in, said he needed to ask me something, so I let him in and made him a cup of coffee. I thought about calling Duncan, because it was strange that Leland was here at that time of night. I don't think I'd seen him since you were kids. But he wasn't acting strange, just sipped his coffee and made small talk with me about his family and what he was doing now; turns out he married some girl from Charleston and they had just moved back here to live with his brother while he looked for work. Finally, he said he needed to borrow some money, about three hundred dollars, and he had run out of people to ask. Now, you know I don't keep that kind of money in the house, and I told him as much, and he got real agitated and was crying a little, and that scared me. But I couldn't do a thing about it at that point."

Missy wanted to tell her mother that she should never have let Leland in the house, but she knew it was pointless. Everyone knew everyone else in Slidell, and it would have been impolite to turn someone away. She remembered that when she was a child ladies would come in and out of each other's houses to borrow ingredients for dinner, random children would take up space in the living room, no boundaries that kept one house separate from another.

"He asked if I maybe could loan him some jewelry that he could pawn, and then when he had money he could get it back and return it to me. I knew he was in a bad way, but I wasn't going to give him any of my jewelry. Some of that stuff has been in our family for generations. I want to pass that on to you and Kayla."

"Mom," Missy said, moving her mother along.

"Well, he got real quiet for a few seconds; he was still crying, though. Then he told me that when he was in high school, he was here at the house with you and a few other friends and you were all going to the Dairy Queen in Custer, but he said he couldn't go because he didn't have any money. Do you remember this, honey?"

Missy shook her head. On any given night, she and her friends were driving to the Dairy Queen to hang out.

"He said I gave him five dollars and told him to go with the rest of you. He said it was the nicest thing anyone had done for him up to that point, maybe ever. Now, I have no memory of this at all, but I imagine I did it. I tried to help out all you kids when I could. Anyway, I thought he better go back to his brother's house. I said I should call his brother to come get him, and then, honey, it was so fast, he jumped up and tried to grab me. I don't know what he thought he was going to get out of it, since I didn't have the money and that jewelry is hidden in my closet in a lockbox. I don't think he even knew what he was doing, but he knocked me off balance, and I fell and hit the edge of the table. I guess I passed out for a second or two, but when I woke up, he was gone, and I managed to call 911 and they took me to the hospital."

Missy leaned over her mother and embraced her, which her mother accepted without comment. "I'm so glad you're okay," Missy said.

"I'm tough," her mother said, but, to Missy's ears, there was no emotion or genuine belief behind it, even though it was most certainly true.

"They caught Leland, I think," Missy said. "They said something about it at the hospital."

"Yes, I told the police, and they picked him up at his brother's house. This all happened while I was at the hospital, but they said Leland's been in trouble before, all mixed up with drugs, and that he confessed almost immediately when they picked him up. I almost feel bad for him, if I'm being honest."

"Don't feel bad, Mom, for crying out loud. He beat you up. He's an awful person."

"I said I *almost* felt bad for him, honey," her mother replied.

"And who drove you home? The nurse said some man picked you up."

"It was Willy. I called him and he was there in no time," her mother said.

Willy was the man who cut her mother's lawn and had done so for as long as Missy could remember. He was nearly eighty himself, Missy guessed. He was probably the person who interacted with Missy's mother the most, doing odd jobs around the house whenever something needed fixing, occasionally eating lunch with her, watching TV. Missy felt happy to know that someone in Slidell was watching over her mother.

"Have you slept at all, Mom?" Missy asked.

"Off and on. Not really."

"Do you want to sleep now? I'm here, so you'll be fine."

"It'll mess up my schedule; it's almost morning anyway. I should just get on with the day. You should sleep, though. You drove all this way."

"Mom, I can't sleep if my eighty-two-year-old mother who just got out of the hospital is going to stay up."

"Do you want breakfast, then?" her mother asked.

It was useless to resist. Breakfast would be prepared no matter what she said. Her mother was already reaching into the refrigerator for a package of bacon. Missy nodded her assent, and the two of them made biscuits and gravy and bacon and a pot of coffee. They ate at the table, the same table where her mother had sat with Leland King the night before, and they watched the hummingbird feeders that were strung along the window move in the breeze. Her mother winced with each bite, the way it irritated the stitches, but she seemed to be genuinely okay. Missy had expected the worst, to be bathing her mother and wheeling her from doctor to doctor, but she was hours past getting assaulted by some meth head and she was reading the newspaper as if nothing had happened. It was this matter-of-factness that had always disconcerted Missy. It seemed impossible to complain about anything because her mother dealt with more, and without any visible complication.

Missy and her husband could barely pay their bills on time; the apartment was back to being a complete wreck a day after it was cleaned; she had been trying to read a single novel for the past eight months without making it past page fifty. But her mother had cleaned up her own blood off the kitchen linoleum the minute she had come home from the hospital, not even a trace of what must have been a terrifying experience left behind.

While they were washing dishes from breakfast, Missy's husband called to check on her. "How long do you think you'll be there?" he asked the minute it was established that her mother was not dead or incapacitated. "A few days at least," Missy replied, and she noticed her mother shaking her head and gesturing to her that she could leave anytime. "Just to be safe."

"Kayla is mad that you didn't take her with you," he told her.

"I'll be back soon," Missy replied.

After Missy hung up the phone, her mother said, "You don't have to stay on my account, honey."

"Just a few days, Mom. I'm here, so I might as well get to visit."

"What about work? You can't just miss work and expect them to be okay with that," her mother said. Missy had worked as a receptionist for the travel agency for ten years now, but her mother was constantly worried that she was going to be fired. It had always interested Missy that her mother believed she was a fingernail away from losing her job.

"It's fine. I can stay for a few days," she said, ending the conversation, and the two of them returned to the rest of the day, taking out the garbage, paying bills, watching a game show that Missy did not understand on even the most basic level but which seemed to greatly interest her mother.

"This is nice," her mother said, "just the two of us."

Right after lunch, someone rang the doorbell. Missy made her mother stay seated while she answered the door to find Leland's brother, Donnie, shuffling awkwardly on the welcome mat. When he saw Missy, his face burned red with embarrassment.

"Shit, Missy," he said, shaking his head. "I'm so sorry."

She had seen Donnie from time to time when she was visiting her mother, but it was always a shock to see how much he had changed since they were in high school. As a teenager, he'd been skinny like Leland, pasty and freckled. Over the years, he had gained a ton of weight, which had turned his proportions to a boulder with arms and legs. He had a beard that wasn't yet at ZZ Top levels but was certainly long enough to suggest an insane backwoods survivalist. Now he was standing in front of Missy, who could not imagine letting him inside.

"I just wanted to check on your mom," he said, still shuffling as if he had created a brand-new dance. "I feel like shit about this. My brother is a fuckup, but he generally only fucks himself up."

"She's okay, I think," Missy finally said, taking pity on Donnie's awkwardness at having to make this visit. "She got roughed up pretty bad, Donnie. She had to get stitches, and her face looks awful."

"I know; the cops told me all about it. Well, I just wanted to tell her that I was sorry and that as soon as Leland gets out of jail, whenever that is, I'm sending him and his wife on their way. He won't stay in Slidell. He should never have come back in the first place."

"Okay," Missy said, sensing that she needed to get back to her mother, to spare her this scene.

"Are you staying with her?" Donnie asked her.

"For a few days," Missy replied. "Until she feels better."

"Well, maybe I'll see you around," he said, the slightest smile forming under that thick beard.

"Okay, then, Donnie," Missy said. She closed the door softly and locked both locks, Donnie still standing in the doorway.

"Who was that?" her mother asked. "Was it Willy?"

"It was Donnie," Missy said, deciding for honesty. "He wanted to apologize for Leland."

"Donnie was always the sweetest boy. He's done right by his mom and dad, running the lumberyard for them and whatnot."

They watched more TV until her mother finally sank deeper into her easy chair and began to breathe in rapid, shallow bursts before settling into sleep. Missy took an afghan off the couch and draped it over her mother. The swelling on her face had gone down, and the angry red line of the cut had started to fade back into her skin, replaced by a deep purple bruise. Her mother's mortality, inevitable, growing more and more likely, still seemed impossible to Missy. Her father had died so early, when Missy was only ten, and it had always seemed to her that those lost years had transferred to her mother, that she had gained another forty or fifty years tacked onto her own life. But it was hard to be immortal when twitchy fuckers like Leland King were busting into your house and beating you up. Missy thought they should install a security system but realized the complication of it would dumbfound her mother; plus, those systems only worked if you didn't open your door voluntarily and let intruders into the house.

Just then, Missy heard a knock on the screen door, and she found Willy on the steps, holding a paper bag. Missy opened the door to let him in, and he carefully scraped his work boots over the welcome mat for what seemed like twenty minutes before he came inside.

"How is she?" he asked.

"Sleeping right now," Missy said. "But she seems okay."

"Good," he said, his deep voice like a proclamation from God.

"Thank you so much for taking care of her yesterday, Willy," Missy said, giving him a hug. She could smell the familiar scent of pipe tobacco on his overalls as he embraced her. Sometimes, when she had come to visit for the holidays, she could smell that smoke on her mother's clothes. She had often wondered if Willy and her mother were a secret couple—the sly intimacy they maintained with each other and had for years. When Missy was younger, she had hoped her mother and Willy would marry and that she would have another father, but she knew a black man and a white woman, especially when that woman was her mother, would never happen here in Slidell.

"I told her she needed to stay at the hospital," he responded, looking sheepish, "but I think June honestly felt like she was inconveniencing everyone in the hospital just by being there. Sometimes she's too polite for her own good."

"What's in the bag?" Missy asked.

Willy looked confused for a second and then seemed to remember the paper bag he was holding. "Medicine," he said. "The doctor at the hospital gave her a prescription for pain pills, and I picked them up this morning."

Missy took the bag from him, and the two of them stood awkwardly in the hallway, unable to think of more to say.

"It's good that you're here," Willy finally said.

"Just a few days," Missy said.

"Still good," Willy said, before he nodded, as if affirming something he'd only been thinking about. "Tell her I came by to check on her," he said, and then he clomped back to his truck and drove off.

When Missy returned to the living room, her mother was slowly waking up, her eyes unfocused, and she seemed shocked to find her daughter in her house.

"It's me, Mom," Missy said.

"I know it's you," she said. "Who was that at the door?"

"Willy. He brought you some pain pills."

"Well," her mother said, lightly touching her stitches and wincing. "Let's have some of them."

One hydrocodone knocked her mother into a comalike sleep, and Missy was left to wander the house, trying to figure out what to do with her time. She checked her e-mail and made some phone calls to her husband and work, and only thirty minutes had passed. It was less than a day since she'd arrived to help her mother, and she was already thinking of when she could leave, could return to the routine of her life. As evening arrived, her mother awoke, and Missy forced her to stay in bed, bringing her water in a giant plastic mug and giving her back issues of *TV Guide* to read. For dinner, Missy made grilled cheese and a chocolate milk shake, which her mother ate without complaint. The medicine seemed to have worn off; her mother had shaken off the cloudiness of the drugs, but she kept asking for her pocketbook so she could give Missy a hundred dollars to give Kayla.

"This house is yours when I die, honey," her mother said suddenly, in between sips of milk shake.

"Let's not worry about that right now," Missy said.

"The house and everything inside it," she said. "That's why I wouldn't give Leland King that jewelry."

"If someone comes to the house again, Momma," Missy said, "and they ask for the jewelry, just give it to them."

"I'm going to get your father's shotgun from the attic and keep it by the door," her mother said, smiling as if remembering something wonderful from long ago.

"Let's see what's on the TV," Missy said, flipping the channels until she found a cooking show featuring a caricature of a southern cook, a show she knew her mother hated. She took the dirty dishes into the kitchen, and even after the entire kitchen was cleaned, she stayed away from her mother, checking her e-mail on her phone, flipping through coupons in the newspaper, until her mother called her back to the bedroom.

"I'm going to bed, honey," her mother informed her. "Your room is all made up and ready for you."

"Call me if you need anything, Mom," Missy said. "That's what I'm here for."

"You're so good to me," her mother said, and Missy walked back into the kitchen, the entire night ahead of her.

Missy wished she'd brought that novel from home, now that she finally had time to read it. She briefly examined the books on the shelves in her mother's living room, a strange assortment that looked like they'd never even been opened: a biography of Hitler, some Sidney Sheldon novels, three books on typewriter repair, *Roots,* and Agatha Christie's autobiography. Instead, she took a long bath and drank one of the Michelob Lights that her mother kept for Willy when he came to visit. She kept willing herself to get tired, to let the warm water and the alcohol seep into her and put her to sleep, but she was wide awake. Her body seemed to understand that she was free of her daily responsibilities to her husband and daughter and wanted to do something fun. Among the very limited options, the house creaking softly around her, she decided to drink another beer.

After she changed into her pajamas, she grabbed another bottle of beer and then when she went to lock all the doors, she noticed Donnie's truck in the driveway. She opened the door and found Donnie sitting on the steps, smoking a cigarette. She almost cried out when she saw him, shocked to find him. How long had he been there? What was he doing?

He jumped up and immediately apologized.

"Sorry, sorry, sorry," he said, his huge body unaccustomed to sudden movements. He stubbed out the cigarette.

"What the fuck are you doing, Donnie?" she asked. "You scared the shit out of me."

"I don't know what I'm doing," he admitted. "I just feel so awful about what happened to your mom. And then I felt bad that you had to come back here to take care of her. I thought, I don't know, you might want to talk or something."

"I don't," Missy said.

"That's fine," Donnie said. "Leland's wife is still at my house, and I don't really feel like being there. I've just been driving around, and I saw the lights on here and thought I'd drop in. I'm sorry, though. I'll leave."

Missy thought about the rest of the night, the boredom of being alone, and she walked outside and handed Donnie the bottle of Michelob Light. "I'll be right back," she said, and she went back to the fridge for another beer.

They sat in Donnie's truck for privacy, and they drank their beers in silence, still getting used to the weirdness of the situation. The truck was an absolute disaster, the upholstery ripped up and leaking foam. The floorboards were littered with dozens of Trivial Pursuit cards, and Missy finally picked one up and read the first question aloud: "What does it say on the bottom of New Jersey license plates?"

"Garden State," Donnie answered, his voice robotic and emotionless. Missy looked over at him, and he shrugged. "I read the questions when I'm driving," he said. "I just toss the cards after I answer them. I've gone through boxes of them."

"You were always a scholar," Missy said. Donnie had been salutatorian at their high school but hadn't even entertained the idea of college, going straight into the lumber business with his father.

Donnie blushed, but his beard covered up most of his embarrassment.

"Do you wanna smoke some pot?" he asked suddenly.

"Sure," Missy answered just as suddenly.

Donnie produced a joint from the front pocket of his work shirt and lit it up, taking a deep hit. He passed it to Missy, who did the same. She smoked pot if someone at a party had it, did coke or pills on rare occasions when her husband was too drunk to notice. This strain was weak enough that it merely rounded off her anxiety and let her settle down. They passed the joint back and forth until it crumbled into ashes. Missy leaned out the open window of the truck and looked up at the clear sky.

"How are things in Atlanta?" Donnie asked her.

"Fine, I guess," she replied, not sure she really wanted to get into it. She was just high enough to be happy, and she didn't want to ruin it.

"Don't you miss Slidell?" he asked, and she shook her head.

"No offense," she said, quickly realizing this was Donnie's life.

"I hate it here, too," he admitted. "I figure I'll stay here until Mom and Dad pass and then I'll sell the business and move to Florida and just become a beach bum. Or I'll finally meet somebody and get married, and I'll be here forever."

"That sounds depressing, Donnie," she said.

"Most things are." He shook the empty beer bottle as if the action could refill it.

They talked about high school and caught up on people Missy

only faintly remembered. Most of them were still in Slidell, and Missy felt the slightest sense of pride that she had made it to Atlanta, even though she barely made more than minimum wage and lived in a run-down apartment, even though her husband had become little more than a buzzing irritation and her daughter was just getting old enough to put distance between her and Missy. She imagined a life in Slidell, where very little was different except the fact that they could afford a house. She thought about her mom's offer of the house when she died, and it didn't seem like the worst outcome, all of a sudden.

"I had such a huge crush on you," Donnie admitted, which Missy knew. It had been obvious all through high school, and Missy had always appreciated that Donnie was smart enough to not push her on it, since she didn't feel the same for him.

"Ancient history," Missy said, wondering if there was more pot around.

"Still do," Donnie said.

Missy knew the polite thing would be to smile and nod in a knowing way to Donnie and then talk for a little longer and then go back inside and go to bed. But she was so tired from the events of the past day and she was at least somewhat high and she was on her own and sitting in the truck of a man who was in love with her, which was, despite his overall bearishness, the most flattering thing she'd experienced in at least several years. And so she made the bad decision because it was easy and there was no one to stop her. She leaned into Donnie and started kissing him. His beard did not tickle; it fucking scratched her face like crazy. But she kept at it because she had initiated this bad idea and she had to stick with it. Donnie, for his part, seemed fairly shocked and very grateful for the way things had played out. She kissed him and kissed him and started to press her body against his. Fucking up, she now remembered, was so easy and so comforting; she had spent a good portion of her adult life trying not to fuck everything up, every ounce of herself put toward the effort, and all it had gotten her was a life just slightly below happiness. Donnie wanted her, had wanted her for years, and it had taken the assault of Missy's mother by Donnie's brother to facilitate it. It wasn't fate; she understood this, but it would do for the moment.

"Are you sure about this?" Donnie said, and Missy didn't even try to respond to this stupid-ass question. She just kept kissing him and then, without looking, did her best with her hands to unbuckle his belt and get his pants off. His body was so huge, took up so much space in the truck that it was nearly impossible to get his pants down, but she managed it without the slightest amount of grace or sexiness. It was pure doggedness in the pursuit of a shitty idea. He pushed the seat back as far as it would go, and she went down on him, which she hated doing under the best of situations. A few minutes later, it was over. She pressed herself as far from him as possible, her back flat against the passenger-side door, as if she could distance herself from what she'd just done.

"Can I do something for you?" he asked, and even if he had not had that beard, she would have said no. She shook her head and then Donnie said, "I love you, Missy."

"I better get back inside," she replied. "If my mom wakes up, she'll wonder where I am."

"What are we gonna do?" Donnie asked, pulling his pants back on and buckling up.

"I can't think about any of that right now. I'm sorry, Donnie, I just can't talk about it now."

"I understand," Donnie said. "I'll come by tomorrow night, same time, and we can talk about it."

"Fine," Missy said. "I have to go now."

She stumbled out of the car and went back inside the house, not bothering to turn around or acknowledge Donnie. She stood in the hallway, the lights off, until she heard his truck pull out of the driveway and head down the street. She crouched on the floor, her face touching the linoleum, as if praying, and did her best to accept what had just happened.

Two years ago, her husband had slept with the mom of one of Kayla's friends, and he had immediately told Missy about it and how much he regretted it. At the time, Missy had wondered why he hadn't just kept his mouth shut and what he'd gained by telling her. Now, having done the same thing, she knew for certain that it was best to never tell anyone when you fucked around.

She was beginning to feel delirious from the events of the night, coupled with an intense realization of how little sleep she'd had in the last day, but her body's engine would not slow down. She paced the hallway, then wandered around the kitchen, hoping that motion would lead her to some kind of answer on how to proceed. She could not see Donnie tomorrow night; that much was certain. You could live with a mistake only if you made it once. But he would be back the next night, waiting for her. Her one option, she determined, would be to leave, to pretend this entire trip was a dream, and get back to Atlanta.

She crept into her mother's bedroom and clicked on the bedside lamp. Her mother opened her eyes and seemed unsurprised to find Missy hovering over her. "What's wrong, honey?" she asked.

"Mom, I just got an e-mail from my boss. She says I need to

get back to work because the other secretary is going to be out sick and they really need me. I don't know what else to do."

"Well, you need to get back there. I'm fine. Don't worry about me."

"I am worried, though, Mom. I hate leaving you so soon after I got here, but I have to get back to Atlanta."

"Are you okay to drive, honey?"

"I'll be fine."

"You were so sweet to come to me. It means so much."

Missy was so close to crying that, in order to prevent it, she grabbed her mother and hugged her tightly.

"Watch my stitches now, honey," her mother said.

"I want you to come live with us in Atlanta, Mom," Missy said.

"I can't do that. I'm fine here, really."

"I wish you were closer to me," Missy said, meaning it.

"I do, too," her mother said, squeezing Missy one last time before they released each other.

"I'll call you tomorrow morning to check on you," Missy said, already moving out of the room.

"Be careful, honey," her mother replied, now sitting up in bed, wide awake.

Missy packed up what little she had brought with her and then, on her way out, took two of the beers from the fridge and carried them into her car, pulling out onto the empty street. When she passed Donnie's house, his lights were still on, but she just kept driving, setting her life back in motion.

Two hours into her drive, replaying the night's events over and over in her head, she understood that she would not be going home. The thought of returning to the apartment, to her job, to her family was suddenly impossible to imagine. Again, she felt the ease of further ruining her life, of sliding down the slope without resistance. She pulled off at the next exit and drove to the closest motel, a Super 8, and pulled into the parking lot. A gang of men with the builds and uniforms of construction workers were standing around a truck drinking beer, and they watched her in silence until she walked inside and approached the front desk. She got a room and used her emergency credit card; she paid all the bills in the house, so she knew her husband wouldn't see the charge. She walked out of the office, key in hand, bag over her shoulder, the two beers clinking together inside the duffel bag, and again passed the men.

"Care to join us?" one of the men said, which made a couple of the other men laugh quietly.

"No, thanks," Missy said, wondering if she should have said anything.

"We'll be here most of the night," he said, and Missy realized how strange it was that these men were in the parking lot at nearly one in the morning, as if they were some sort of club that held monthly meetings. She was proud of herself for resisting their offer to join them, having at least enough sense to keep herself safe while she was making bad decisions.

The room was terrifying in its level of upkeep. The carpet crackled like cellophane when she walked on it, and the bedsheets, when she turned them down, had the texture of flypaper. She wanted to get ice from the machine outside, to cool down the two beers, but she didn't want to risk seeing the men again. So she sat on the only chair in the room, as uncomfortable as it was rickety, and drank both beers as quickly as possible, trying to gain back some of the low-key buzz from earlier in the night. She closed her eyes, imagined her mother alone in her house, her family waiting for her in the apartment in Atlanta. Here she was, somewhere between these two places, her whereabouts unknown by everyone but her. With the slightest bit of luck, there would be no ramifications for her actions over the past day. Her mother would be fine; Donnie would get the message; and her husband would never know anything. Missy could drop herself back into her regular life and, if she proceeded with caution, everything would be okay.

Even considering the state of the motel room, Missy felt its pull on her, the desire to live here forever, the crowd of men both protecting and menacing her. She closed her eyes and felt the ease of how quickly she separated herself from the waking world.

She thought of Kayla, who was so complicated and yet inherently good, a kind person. How had that happened? Suddenly, she remembered a moment from her own childhood. A new grocery store had opened in Custer, and her mother had taken her for the grand opening. When they walked in, an employee handed Missy a balloon and even though she was too old for it, she held it as she and her mother wandered around the store. "We're not buying anything," her mother had told her in the car. "I cannot imagine the prices at a store like that. But we can look."

To avoid being conspicuous, her mother had taken a shopping cart and they looked at the brightly lit aisles, everything looking so new and clean. Everything at the Shop-Rite in Slidell had dust on it, be it can or box or fruit. "It's nice, I'll say that much," her mother said.

At the end of one aisle, a woman in an apron was handing out samples of some kind of cracker with a cream cheese spread. People were lined up, a few people actually pushing to move the line forward. "Stay here," her mother told Missy. "I'll get us one cracker to share." Missy watched as her mother walked toward the line and then froze. Her mother gestured for a young man to go ahead and get in line and she stepped back a few paces. And as the line moved and more people joined the line, Missy's mother simply stood there, holding her purse close to her chest. After a few seconds, she walked back to the empty cart, her shoulders slumped. "We don't need that cracker," she told Missy, and they pushed the cart out of the store, where they left it on the sidewalk. On the drive back to Slidell, Missy held on to that image of her mother. There was a tinge of pity, but she mostly felt an intense love for this woman, her mother, who had made her. She resolved, in that exact moment, to always love her mother, to always be kind to her.

Missy stood up and paced around the hotel room. She thought about going back to Slidell, making breakfast for her mother, spending the rest of the week there. But she could not make herself do it. She could not go back. Instead, she thought of Kayla. She wondered if there had been a moment yet where Missy had revealed her own vulnerability to Kayla; how could she have not noticed it?

She gathered up her belongings, throwing them together. She left the key on the table and stepped out into the night. The men were still there. "Leaving so soon?" one of the men said. Missy opened her car and, just before she closed the door, she said, "Go fuck yourself." As she started the car and quickly pulled out, she could hear the other men hooting. She got back on the interstate, following the lights of the trucks rumbling ahead of her. If she drove fast enough, she'd be there as Kayla woke. She would slip into her daughter's twin bed, wrap her arms around her, and she would hold on to her just long enough to convince herself that nothing would ever change.

A Signal to the Faithful

The first time Edwin passed out during Mass, he could not determine whether the act made him more or less holy. An altar boy, he was kneeling at the side of the altar, his hand resting on the bells, as Father Naylon began the consecration of the bread and wine. Edwin felt something electric run up his arms, his head swimming with the sound of the bells that were not yet ringing. He could not hear Father Naylon speak the words *Do this in memory of me,* though he saw his mouth shape those sounds. Edwin could hear nothing and he thought that perhaps no one in the congregation could hear anything, either, and it was his job, as the priest raised the host aloft, to ring the altar bells so they would know that a miracle was occurring. Something that was once one thing was becoming another, better thing. He tried to grip the handle of the bells and felt the world go dark.

When he came to, Father Naylon was cradling him, the service halted, Edwin slowly realizing that he was responsible for something. For Edwin, being responsible for anything, good or bad, was a source of terror. His goal in life, clearly defined at ten years old, was to pass through this world into heaven without leaving any trace of his presence. And, now, here he was, none of the parishioners having partaken of the host, deprived of the miraculous, and Father Naylon was lightly slapping his cheek until the feeling returned to his body. He had not left his body. He had receded deeper into it.

"I'm sorry," was all Edwin could offer to the priest.

"The spirit moved you," Father Naylon replied, a sheepish smile, his nicotine-brown teeth barely exposed. "At an inconvenient time, unfortunately."

Edwin's mother was now at his side, helping him to his feet. Edwin felt his body sway, his mother and the priest holding on to him, and he looked down at his waist, where the ends of the white rope that served to cinch his gown moved back and forth like the pendulum of a grandfather clock. The priest, apparently assured that Edwin was recovered, returned to the altar and Edwin followed his mother to a pew, where he rested his head on her lap. He closed his eyes, his face heating up as he realized the extent to which he had embarrassed himself. He scrunched his face as tightly as he could, trying to erase the still-forming memory of his accident, when he heard the sound of the altar bells ringing, alerting him to the fact that something important was happening just a few feet from him. He felt the urge to weep but resisted.

After Mass, after what felt like every member of the congregation had checked on his health, Edwin shuffled back to the sacristy to remove his alb, resisting the urge to pull the hood over his head as he walked. The other altar boy had already left, and Edwin found Father Naylon sitting on a chair, facing his open cabinet, which held his vestments. He was smoking a cigarette, a habit in which he indulged practically at all times other than during services. His brown hair was swept back in a manner that made him look like Elvis Presley. His hands were large and often bruised or bandaged from keeping the rectory in livable condition. When the priest made the sign of the cross, his hand tapped against his body with such heavy force that it seemed as if he were trying to quiet a misbehaving child.

Father Naylon had come to Saint Rose of Lima in the spring of 1985 from Nashville, having only recently been ordained. He was young for a priest, late thirties, which Edwin's mother mentioned often, how lucky they were to have someone so young in this tiny congregation in the Deep South, where most of the parishioners were either northern transplants or the rare breed of southern Catholics or Mexican laborers and their families who had begun to fill up Coalfield, working on the farms that made up most of the town.

"A handsome priest," Edwin's mother said, "makes Mass easier." With Edwin's father out of the picture since Edwin was three, Edwin's mother liked to mention that other men were handsome and how this handsomeness made life more tolerable. Edwin was not yet sure if he wanted to be handsome or ugly or merely unmemorable. All the options seemed to have their own specific problems.

Edwin yanked the cincture loose from his body and then tried to shimmy out of the alb, pulling it over his head. He found that the temporary darkness so closely resembled the easy way that he earlier fell out of consciousness that he felt the panic swirl around him again. His arms twisted in the gown and then he felt a sharp tug as the alb was pulled free from his body. Father Naylon, cigarette dangling from his cinched-tight lips, snapped the alb free of creases and folded it over his arm. With his other hand, he removed the cigarette and blew a holy ghost of smoke toward the ceiling. Edwin watched it dissipate, his face again burning with embarrassment. Was this life, Edwin wondered, the constant betrayal by your body, the ceaseless withstanding of embarrassment?

"Don't worry about today, Edwin," Father Naylon said, his voice soft and gentle. At all times, Father Naylon's voice sounded as if he was reciting scripture.

"I'm sorry, Father," Edwin replied.

"Not your fault at all, of course," Father Naylon said, handing the robe to Edwin, who placed the alb and cincture on a coat hanger before placing it in the cabinet.

"I got dizzy up there," Edwin said. He knew he should be returning to his mother, who was waiting in the car by now. He did not want to bother Father Naylon with anything as trivial as his constant fears of the future. "I hope I don't feel it ever again."

Father Naylon held out his hand and tapped the ashes from his cigarette into his open palm. He then spit into his palm and pestled the mixture into a paste, which he quickly, without warning, dabbed onto Edwin's cheeks.

"This," the priest promised, "will ward off dizziness, I believe." The priest smiled, which made Edwin close his eyes. "Keep it on your face for three hours and you'll be protected from fainting spells."

"Is this a rite?" Edwin asked.

"It's a different kind of magic," the priest assured him.

Edwin nodded and then walked out of the room. As he made

his way to the car, he could feel the light coat of ashes on his cheeks, as if he had walked through dust kicked up by a team of horses. He imagined that he was a cavalryman facing down an oncoming horde of Indians, a temporary shift into make-believe, which happened often to Edwin. His mother, of course, would draw attention to the marks, wanting to know their provenance. She would ask questions and, right now, Edwin wanted a silent ride back home, time to rest and recover, to analyze the precise moment that he sunk out of the world for that brief instant. And yet, he needed the protection of these marks. With each step, he felt the window shrinking, the sharp pain of needing to make a decision. Right after the stinging sensation of indecision, he had a white flash of understanding that perhaps the fainting had been, itself, miraculous. That someone, perhaps God, was trying to tell him something important. That he had come back to the world too early to learn the mystery that his unconscious could deliver to him. He thought that maybe, though he hated to consider it, something special had happened to him.

He quickly licked his fingers and removed the ash from his face. Perhaps he did not want to be protected from whatever danger might be waiting for him. He slipped into the backseat of the car and rested his face against the window, watching the clouds hover in the air, the car now turned homeward, and he felt the small, but noticeable warmth of the sun on his face and he thought, *This is a miracle,* without knowing exactly what *this* was.

Two weeks later, again during the consecration, Edwin passed out for the second time. He was ready for it this time, the ringing in his ears like there was a phone hidden deep inside his body that he was unsure of how to answer. Just before his sight dimmed, he tensed his body, straining to hear whatever message could reach him in this dark part of his brain. He slumped to the side, as if he was inspecting a speck of something on the carpeted floor, but, almost instantly, found himself snap awake. He jerked his body upright, the flash of unconsciousness so quick that he hoped that no one else had noticed. Father Naylon was holding the host heavenward, without the necessary accompaniment. Edwin quickly rang the altar bells with a Pentecostal vigor, with such abandon that Father Naylon had to finally turn to him and nod in acknowledgment, which calmed Edwin's hand. Edwin rang the bells again, with great composure, when the wine turned into the blood of Christ. When his mother came to the front for Communion, she touched Edwin's arm and gave him a questioning look. As she received the host on her tongue, Edwin smiled to reassure her. She nodded and then lowered her head as she walked back to the pew. He made it through the rest of Mass, processed down the aisles when it had ended.

After they performed their post-Mass duties and were changing out of their albs, Jeremy, the other altar boy, who was fourteen years old and sometimes drank the wine in the sacristy when Father Naylon wasn't around, said, "You looked like Mike Tyson punched you out up there." He laughed and mimed Edwin slumping over. Then Jeremy pretended to use Edwin's head as a punching bag before Father Naylon returned to the sacristy, having finished meeting with the parishioners. He quickly lit a cigarette. Jeremy stopped his boxing routine and shoved Edwin as he walked away. Father Naylon placed the cigarette on the counter and removed his vestments. When he was finished, he continued to smoke the cigarette and motioned for Edwin to come to him. Edwin walked over, bowing his head, prepared for either punishment or benediction.

"Are you okay, Edwin?" Father Naylon asked.

"I'm sorry again, Father," Edwin replied.

"But are you feeling better?"

"Yes, Father. I'm sorry."

"Edwin," Father Naylon said, pausing to take a slow drag of the cigarette. "You don't need to constantly say that you're sorry when you haven't done anything wrong."

"I'm sorry, Father," Edwin said before he could catch himself. He brightened with embarrassment, his skin prickly. "I'll stop doing it."

"Unless," Father Naylon continued, as if he hadn't even heard Edwin, "you have done something that requires forgiveness." He took another drag, the cigarette more ash than tobacco now, and then said, "What I'm asking, Edwin, is if you are, perhaps, doing this on purpose. For attention."

That anyone would believe he wanted more attention, that he wanted anyone to witness him in a position of weakness, so flummoxed Edwin that he started to stutter. He turned an even brighter shade of red, his pale skin like a fever-threatened thermometer. He imagined his actions looked like guilt, but he could not stop himself.

"Maybe you want to get out of school on Monday, so you pass out on Sunday."

"No, Father. No, I promise."

Father Naylon stared at Edwin for nearly five seconds, his face impassive. Then he leaned toward the sink and dropped the spent cigarette into it. "I believe you, Edwin. I'm sorry I suggested it."

"I'm sorry," Edwin said.

"You're a good boy, Edwin. You are kind and you are serious and I believe you are very much invested in this faith. Sometimes, sensitive people like you and me, we are prone to moments when we are overcome by the immensity of the mysteries of our religion. We understand that these are important and beautiful things—transubstantiation, heaven, saints, miracles—everything that makes Catholicism so necessary. But, Edwin?"

Edwin merely nodded, shocked that Father Naylon would mention him as being in any group that included the priest.

"Mania is not the aspect of religion that we should emulate," he continued. "There's such a fine line between sainthood and mania. It's best not to try for either and simply do the best you can."

Edwin did not entirely understand what Father Naylon was telling him, probably because Father Naylon did not entirely understand what Edwin was actually feeling. The fainting was not, he had decided, from his own desire to talk to God. Perhaps—Edwin was still formulating this theory in his mind—something (and perhaps that something was God) wanted to talk to Edwin.

The priest turned away, his lesson imparted, and lit another cigarette. Edwin stared at the cracked nail on the priest's right thumb, the dark blood bruise at the center of the nail. It made him think of stigmata, and he suddenly felt the urge to run out of the church, knowing that, once he returned home, he would find so little evidence of God that he could make it another week without too much worry.

Edwin's mother kept him out of school the next day. "Once seems like something any kid could do," she told him on the way to the doctor's office. "Twice seems like it should be checked out." Edwin did not resist the trip; he was not against the idea of a pill or shot that could be administered to prevent future fainting spells. That way, if the medicine failed him, he would be certain of the miracle-related possibilities. This seemed like the best way to proceed, Edwin decided: to treat the miracle with science and see how it responded.

Dr. Cameron did some preliminary work: stethoscope, blood pressure, tongue depressor, eyes and ears, a tender examination of lymph nodes. During all of this, the doctor kept up a steady conversation with Edwin and his mother, his voice unworried and tender. Finally, everything as it should be, Dr. Cameron sat on a rolling chair and wheeled himself close to Edwin.

"So you're passing out at church?" he asked. Edwin merely nodded. It felt good to establish this fact, to set forth the essential problem and wait for it to be solved.

"Forgive me because I don't know much about Catholics. I'm a Methodist myself, but I imagine there are enough similarities that I can understand the basics. So you've been passing out during a pretty important part of the service?"

Edwin nodded.

"Well, everything checks out. You're in good health. You're a healthy young man. The next step would be blood tests and maybe a heart monitor. But I don't think we need it. You guys kneel and stand up during church, right?"

Edwin again nodded.

"Take it easy when you stand up or kneel down. Go slow. The main thing, I think, is to make sure you keep breathing. See, in exciting moments, sometimes our brain forgets to keep breathing. We hold our breath, waiting for something good to happen, and then we get dizzy, and then, if you're not careful, you'll pass out. Since you aren't passing out at home or school, I think this is probably the case. Just keep breathing. Tell yourself to keep breathing."

Even at this young age, Edwin believed that every doctor's visit that didn't end with medicine was a failure. He wanted something that would assure his good health, which his own body could apparently not guarantee. To simply keep breathing seemed like ridiculous advice, but, even as he considered the mechanics, he found it incredibly difficult to enact. "Keep breathing," he whispered to his body, but he was not sure his body understood the command. Already Edwin was figuring out that it would take vigilance to keep himself out of harm's way.

Edwin and his mother walked back to the car. His mother shook her head. "You have so much going on in that head, Edwin," she said. "Only a kid like you would have to be reminded to keep breathing." The tone of her voice was such that Edwin could not entirely decide if she was pleased or annoyed by him.

On the way to McDonald's, she told him that he would need to take a few weeks off from serving Mass, which made Edwin, for the first time all day, feel a little dizzy. The task of being an altar boy had never entirely appealed to him, with its possibilities for mistakes. The only reason he had done it in the first place, and continued to do it, was the simple fact that the congregation of Saint Rose of Lima was predominantly made up of old people. There were fewer than a dozen boys who were of age to serve Mass. There were some Sundays when there was only one altar boy. Edwin had felt that he was among the last of a dying breed, that there was something noble in the dwindling numbers, that he was a part of something special that might not exist much longer. This was one of his main fascinations, the way in which some people held out against the inevitability of life for as long as possible.

When Edwin expressed his worry about his importance to the mass, his mother shook her head. "I think Father Naylon would rather have only one altar boy up there if the other one was constantly passing out during the service," and Edwin found that he could not argue with this logic.

Now that he was back home, the entire afternoon open to him, Edwin retired to his room and harnessed his imagination to quickly establish the particulars of his favorite game. The room became a fort, while everything outside the room became an invading army. He grabbed his toy rifle, which had a bolt action that made a pleasing *schkkk-tunk* sound as he reloaded, and then stripped to his underwear and socks. Edwin had decided that, if he didn't have an exact replica of the necessary costume for his games, it was better to not be clothed at all.

For the past six months, he had been obsessed with this scenario, a small battalion against an overwhelming army, death all but certain. It had begun when he read about the Alamo in the encyclopedia, the doomed soldiers holding off the Mexican army for as long as possible, knowing they would most certainly die. Edwin did not care to think about this fascination other than to simply acknowledge that there was something wonderful about accepting death and then moving into the unknown, the way this impossible action made you invincible.

For hours at a time, he would roll around his room, firing at the invisible army, dodging bullets, before leaning against the wall, his only protection, taking a deep breath, and then firing again, uselessly, into the crowd of oncoming soldiers. It was not important that he kill a single enemy, only that he manage to stay alive for as long as possible. All around him, his comrades would fall, riddled with bullets, slashed open by bayonets. Finally, when Edwin was the only one left, he would allow himself to be overtaken by the enemy, the destiny he had known all along, his body convulsing with each shot, now using his unloaded rifle as a club. He fell to his knees, felt the life shake itself out of his frame, and collapsed in a heap, still holding his rifle.

When the game was over, he would simply begin anew, changing the parameters of the scenario just slightly to account for variations in his doomed circumstances. He would die, over and over again, until it was time for dinner.

The next week at Mass, Edwin sat beside his mother in a pew seven rows from the altar. When it came time for the consecration, the congregation kneeling, Edwin's mother leaned close to him, placing her hand on his back. "Breathe, honey," she said. He nodded and took a deep, lung-expanding breath of air. He took another breath, held it for two seconds, and then exhaled, feeling his heart tingle, and he watched Father Naylon calmly recite the lines that made everything change for the better. As the priest raised the host heavenward, Edwin narrowed his eyes and stared at the round wafer. The bell began to ring, the jangly chime, and his mother again pressed her hand against his back and whispered the word *breathe*. Edwin did as he was told, took his eyes off the host, and felt giddy to be in this moment, just after the ringing bells had faded, to be awake and whole and ready for what came next.

When Mass had ended, Edwin walked with his mother to the entrance of the church, where Father Naylon was waiting for them. He gave Edwin a thumbs-up gesture and smiled. "I have to admit that I was thinking about you, Edwin," the priest said, his hands itching themselves in anticipation of his next cigarette. "I'm glad that you made it through Mass unscathed."

"He just needed to breathe, Father," Edwin's mother said, and the priest nodded thoughtfully.

"That is good advice for all of us, Ms. Rutherford. I have to remind myself of that very thing from time to time."

"You are very kind, Father Naylon," Edwin's mother replied, smiling with such warmth that Edwin wondered, for just a second, if she was in love with the priest. He decided that his mother appreciated being around another person who had forgone companionship, that there would be no trace of pity in their interactions.

Father Naylon shook Edwin's hand and said that he hoped to see Edwin serving Mass once again in the near future. Edwin merely nodded, feeling as if he had lost a specific power but become more of a real person in the process. God had determined that he was not special, and Edwin decided that this was a benediction that he would, in the long run, appreciate.

Three days later, Edwin had finished his homework and his reward was to be killed once again by an unjust but overwhelmingly large army. He had rug burn on both of his knees and moved in hiccups, having lost an alarming amount of blood from all his gunshot wounds. When his mother opened the door to his bedroom without knocking, he was kicking at a toppled chair, having run out of ammunition, holding a spent toilet paper roll as if it were a knife. Edwin immediately stopped his violence; he understood that, even if his mother didn't prevent him from his game, she did not entirely approve. Violence in underwear was not for a mother to witness, he was quite sure. He felt like a soldier who had been neglecting his duties just as a sergeant entered the barracks, and he snapped to attention.

"Put some clothes on, honey," she told him. "Father Naylon is visiting us."

It was evening, close to his bedtime, so Edwin struggled to decide on his pajamas or something more formal. He decided to wear a rarely used pair of old-fashioned pajamas, which resembled a suit, and a pair of penny loafers. When he walked into the living room, Father Naylon was sitting on the sofa, his hair no longer pompadoured and pomaded, but hanging over his eyes. He was nervously flipping a cigarette with one hand. When he saw Edwin, the priest waved so imperceptibly that it looked as if his hand had merely twitched. He smiled at Edwin and invited him to sit down. Just before he walked over to Father Naylon, his mother returned to the living room with a cup of coffee and handed it to the priest. He thanked her and took a tentative sip.

"Father Naylon just told me some bad news, Edwin," she said.

Father Naylon turned back to Edwin and said, "I learned this morning that my aunt died, Edwin."

Edwin did not understand what was happening, why the priest was in his living room, why he was having a cup of coffee, why he was telling Edwin and his mother about his aunt.

"I'm sorry," was all Edwin could think to say.

"She raised me," Father Naylon said. "I haven't seen her in a few years, but she was an important person to me."

"We're so sorry for your loss, Father," Edwin's mother said.

Edwin could smell that the coffee had been doctored with alcohol, and he watched as Father Naylon took a long, silent sip from the cup.

"The reason I've come here tonight is that I've requested to perform the service for my aunt. She lives in Adairville, Kentucky, just across the Tennessee border. The church there is tiny, only a few parishioners left, and they rely on a retired priest who works between two different churches in that area. I think it would be best for me to be there."

Edwin's mother agreed with him. "I know she would be so pleased to know that you were there," she said.

Father Naylon winced and then smiled. "I need an altar boy for the service; the church there has no one, and I was hoping that Edwin might come along with me."

Edwin was shocked to hear the request, the idea that he would travel to Kentucky just to serve Mass.

"Are you sure, Father?" his mother asked. "I wonder if Edwin is really the best person for that, considering his"—she paused before she found the right word—"episodes."

Edwin felt his voice squeak into the room. "I'm better now," he said. "I know to breathe now." He wasn't sure why he now wanted to be included in the funeral, other than the fact that Father Naylon had thought of him and he wanted to prove the priest right in his decision.

"I think Edwin is a fine altar boy, very mature for his age. I think it might be good for him, actually. And he'll be paid. Twenty dollars."

"When would this be?" his mother asked.

"We would leave tomorrow afternoon, spend the night, and then the funeral would be early the next morning. We'd be home that evening."

"He would have to miss school," his mother continued. "I don't know if that would be an excused absence."

"I'm sure it would be okay with the school. I can talk to the principal. We would stay at my aunt's home; Edwin would have his own room, and I would take us out for dinner that night. I would like to get there the day before the funeral so that I can look over some of my aunt's papers and begin to get her affairs in order."

"What do you think, Edwin?" his mother asked him. Edwin looked down at his penny loafers. The only time he had served at a funeral, back when Father Lucius had been the priest at St. Rose of Lima, Edwin had been overcome with the desire to cry, even though he had never known the deceased. He had fought off the tears with great difficulty and made it through the service, its extra, complicated steps: incense, holy water, candles. He had been given ten dollars at the end of the service, but Jeremy had taken it from him before he'd even made it out of the church.

He would appreciate having twenty dollars to spend. He would get to miss a day of school. Most of all, Edwin felt the pleasing sensation of being chosen, that Father Naylon wanted him of all people to be present at the funeral.

"I want to do it," Edwin said.

Father Naylon smiled, held out his hand for Edwin to shake, and then finished the cup of coffee. "I'll pick up Edwin after school tomorrow and we'll head to Kentucky. He can call you as often as you'd like while we're there."

"Thank you for coming over, Father, and for thinking of Edwin. He'll be a good boy, I'm sure. And I'm sorry again for your loss."

Father Naylon smiled, but his face looked so tired, drained of emotion. When he left their house, Edwin watched through the windows and saw the red glow of Father Naylon's cigarette as he sat in his car, still parked in the driveway. Edwin's mother looked through the other window to watch the priest as well.

"I never knew anything about his family," she remarked. "Raised by his aunt. I wonder what happened to his mother and father."

"And his uncle," Edwin said. Finally, the priest finished his cigarette and backed out of the driveway.

"Why are you wearing penny loafers?" his mother asked him, and Edwin simply shrugged. "You're a strange boy, Edwin," she said. "A beautiful boy, but strange, too." Edwin's mother noted this often about him, his uniqueness; he wondered if he could ever do anything to convince her that he was normal, or if he could ever do something that would make her believe that he was worse than strange, that there was something wrong with him. He kicked off the penny loafers and carried them into his room.

He decided against playing any more games of doomed soldier, not wanting to take off his pajamas, and instead climbed into bed and read the entry about the Alamo in the encyclopedia. He'd read the short passage more than a hundred times. He lingered on the drawing of the Mexican soldiers bursting into the room where Jim Bowie, relegated to his sickbed, began to fight them off. The encyclopedia commented, in language that Edwin had always found surprising for such a formal source of information, that Jim Bowie had killed several soldiers with his Bowie knife before his "brains were blown out." In bed, the house still and silent, Edwin would sometimes awaken to the strong belief that someone was trying to enter his room and kill him in his exhausted state. Tonight, however, he slept soundly, imagining the car ride with Father Naylon, the funeral mass, the black vestments, the chance to help send someone's spirit to heaven properly.

When Edwin stepped off the school bus, Father Naylon was waiting in the driveway, his car still running. As the bus had pulled up to his house, one of the kids asked if Father Naylon was his dad. Edwin couldn't tell if he was joking or not and so he didn't say a word. Edwin's mother came to the front door with a small duffel bag, filled with dress clothes and pajamas, and walked over to Edwin.

"Are you ready for your adventure?" Father Naylon asked him. Edwin nodded, though *adventure* seemed the wrong word for a funeral mass in a different state. Edwin's mother handed him the duffel bag and, without Father Naylon noticing, a twenty-dollar bill. "This is for emergencies," she whispered to him. "Whatever you don't use, bring back to me, please." Edwin had never been put in charge of such currency and he felt the immediate fear of losing it, not a single cent returning to his mother. Once the charge ran through him, he allowed himself to dream about what he could buy with twenty dollars, not able to think of anything except dozens of candy bars. Father Naylon put his hand on Edwin's shoulder and guided him to the passenger side. He took the duffel bag and placed it in the trunk. Just before he stepped into the car, Father Naylon was embraced by Edwin's mother, who said, softly, that she was praying for him. The priest seemed to go rigid in her arms, his hands clenching and unclenching, and then Edwin's mother released him and waved as the two of them backed out of the driveway and set off on a road trip that would end, Edwin reminded himself, with the empty vessel of a body buried in the ground.

Father Naylon had two cassettes, Bruce Springsteen's *Nebraska* and Steve Earle's *Guitar Town*. When one would end, he would simply put the other one into the tape deck and let it play until both sides were exhausted. The priest, when he needed a new cigarette, would gesture to the cigarette lighter in the car and Edwin would push the knob and wait for it to pop back out, ringed with fire. He liked the feeling of holding the lighter, his hands trembling slightly, to the unlit cigarette wedged in Father Naylon's mouth. He liked the smell of tobacco and smoke, how it swirled around the ceiling of the car and settled in his hair. He liked the music, the rough voices of Earle and Springsteen singing about darkness that Edwin had suspected but never fully seen. An hour into the trip, Father Naylon had not said a word, his hands softly keeping time on the steering wheel, smoke pouring out of his mouth, his face a white sheet without emotion. Edwin wished he'd brought a single textbook from his book bag so as to have something to read. Instead, he watched the car speed over the interstate and took to adding up the numbers on the license plates of the cars they passed. Finally, unable to stand it any longer, Edwin said, "Your aunt raised you," though he wasn't sure if it was a question or a statement and his inflection was flat and trailed off at the end. Father Naylon didn't answer for a few seconds, his eyes squinting against the oncoming sunlight.

"She was charged with raising me, I guess you could say," Father Naylon replied. He stubbed out a half-finished cigarette in the car's ashtray and then fished another out of the pack in his front pocket. He gestured to the lighter and Edwin dutifully pushed it in, as if this was merely another aspect of Mass that the altar boy must attend to. Edwin waited for elaboration but Father Naylon merely drove on in silence.

Edwin did not know what to do with this response. He had grown suspicious of language, the way it always seemed to close in on itself and never expanded the way he hoped it would. He wondered how adults communicated anything with each other, the guarded way that they voiced even the most benign statement. If the priest would not comment further, Edwin decided to offer up something of his own.

"My dad left us when I was three," he said, staring ahead at the road, afraid of how the priest might take this information. His mother had the marriage annulled somehow, but she still did not like anyone knowing this business, especially a priest. "It's just been me and my mom forever."

The lighter popped out and Edwin lit the fresh cigarette, slowly touching the glowing red coil to the tip of the stick of tobacco, watching the way the brown shavings curled at the touch of the fire. Father Naylon looked over at Edwin and smiled, pressed his thumb against Edwin's chin.

"My parents died when I was five years old. It was a car accident; I was the only one who lived. I was sent to live with my uncle, my dad's brother, and his wife. He was the fire chief in

Adairville, a very good man. My aunt, she was not happy to have a child in the house. She was not maternal, you could say, and I can't blame her for that. It was an unfortunate situation. Then my uncle died in a fire when I was eight and then it was just my aunt and me until I turned eighteen. We did not get along. She was unkind to me in many ways that you shouldn't have to hear about."

Edwin had experienced, for as long as he could remember, a distant tenderness from adults when they learned of his father-less circumstances. Edwin could not understand this reaction, having never known a life with his father and having no real desire to experience it. He merely accepted the slightly conde-scending way that people expected him to be damaged by the absence of someone who, though his mother would not speak often of it, was a terrible person. In Father Naylon's case, he could not even comprehend the unhappiness that he had expe-rienced, the true loss and pain that seemed to have surrounded his early life.

"On the other hand," Father Naylon said, smiling for the first time all day, "she's the reason I'm a priest. I'd wanted to be a firefighter, had been so obsessed with it, but after my uncle died, my aunt forbade me from pursuing it. I wanted so badly to fight fires and wear the equipment and drive the fire truck, even into my teens, but I respected her wishes and became a priest instead. Sometimes, I wish I could have done both."

"You could become a firefighter now," Edwin offered, real-izing with a sickening thud that he was speaking to the fact of Father Naylon's now-dead aunt.

Father Naylon laughed, and the cigarette fell from his mouth and landed in his lap. Calmly, without taking his eyes off the road, the priest reached between his legs and retrieved the cigarette, bringing it back to his lips. He turned up Bruce Springsteen and gunned the engine. Edwin was not sure why what he had said made Father Naylon so happy, but he felt the warm and welcome certainty that he was responsible for it and did not ask further questions.

Thirty minutes later, they stopped at a gas station to fill up, and the priest let Edwin pick out a snack. Edwin grabbed a can of NuGrape soda and found a pack of candy cigarettes in the same style as Father Naylon's brand, though these said *Pell Mell* instead of *Pall Mall*. Back in the car, the priest switched cassettes and Edwin placed the thin, white stick of sugar, the tip haphazardly blotched with red dye, in his mouth. He smoked the candy cigarette, rolling his tongue around the stick until it became a sharpened spear. He took it into his hand and probed the meat of his palm, the tiny sensation of pain, until the tip broke in his hands and he ate all of the evidence.

The house was a huge two-story colonial in obvious disrepair. Weeds shattered the paved driveway and the gray paint was peeling from the house in angry blisters. One of the windows was boarded up with a thin sheet of wood. "This used to be the most beautiful house in the county," Father Naylon said. "I imagine this house was too much for her to keep up with." They got out of the car and gathered their things; Edwin hefted his duffel bag and gingerly carried the vestments for the funeral mass, while Father Naylon slung the garment bag over his shoulder and produced a plastic shopping bag, which held his toiletries. They walked around to the back of the house, the

grass nearly up to Edwin's knees, and entered through the unlocked door. Edwin had the temporary, disorienting fear that
they would find Father Naylon's aunt still in the house, her dead
body still tucked into her bed, but he allowed the feeling to swirl
around his body and then vaporize.

The house was dusty, in need of cleaning, but the furniture was sturdy and expensive-looking, and the floors were
bright hardwood. It was cavernous, rooms expanding into
other rooms, the entire upstairs still undiscovered. In the dining room, there was a table that seemed to be the length of a
football field, and Edwin imagined a young Father Naylon and
his aunt eating at opposite ends. "I'm hungry," the priest said.
"Are you hungry, Edwin?" Edwin nodded that he was, though
he was interested in searching through the house, wondering if
he would be allowed to do so. Its dimensions, if he could be left
to his own devices, felt conducive to his war games of impending death. Nevertheless, he returned to the car, though this time
Father Naylon kept the tape player off, and they drove back into
town for something to eat.

The steak house was a world inhabited by retirees and single
men. Edwin was the only child in the restaurant, perhaps the
first to enter its doors since its opening. He realized that he had
never eaten at a restaurant without his mother, and he usually
just ate chicken tenders or grilled cheese, but Father Naylon
kept encouraging him to order whatever he wanted. "We'll need
energy for tomorrow," the priest told him. "We need to feast
tonight." They sat in the smoking section and Father Naylon
ordered a whiskey on the rocks while Edwin asked for, and

received, a Shirley Temple with extra cherries. As he scanned the menu, he knew he could not possibly eat an entire steak; he was still unsure of his knife skills at mealtime, so the sheer effort of cutting the steak seemed problematic. He did not want fish and all the chicken dishes seemed to be covered in wine or some kind of strange sauce. Edwin's face wrinkled with worry as he turned the menu to the back page and was sickened to see no other options.

For the first time on the trip, Father Naylon seemed to understand that, though Edwin was an altar boy who had come to serve the funeral mass, he was also a child in his care. He finished his drink and then leaned across the table of their booth and scanned the menu with Edwin. "What are you going to get?" he asked, and Edwin shrugged.

"Maybe some soup," Edwin offered.

Father Naylon smiled and said, "Do you like steak?" Edwin shook his head. "I wouldn't think so," the priest replied, and then asked, "Do you like hamburgers?" Edwin said yes and Father Naylon opened his arms as if to embrace the boy and the table and the booth and the entire restaurant. "Hamburger steak," he finally said, rubbing his stomach. "You'll love it."

Right then, the waitress came to the table and Father Naylon took over the ordering. He would have a ribeye, medium rare, and Edwin would have a sixteen-ounce hamburger steak with French fries, creamed spinach, Texas toast, and a side of spaghetti and meatballs. Edwin could not eat this much food, but Father Naylon merely winked and continued to converse with the waitress. Five minutes later, the priest had a fresh whiskey, Edwin had six more cherries in his Shirley Temple, and there was a basket of bread so large that it seemed like a biblical miracle.

The food came like a tidal wave and Edwin struggled to keep track of it all. The hamburger steak was, he realized after the first bite, a perfect and grown-up way to eat a hamburger. He doused it with steak sauce and tore into the sides with abandon. With each bite, Father Naylon seemed to grow more and more happy, encouraging Edwin's appetite. On his own plate, the priest had managed to eat the marbled fat from the ribeye, a surgical precision to his work with the knife and fork.

"My aunt used to eat here every Thursday night," Father Naylon said. "Back when it was the fanciest restaurant in the county. She would leave me at home—I could never come with her—and she would eat and drink and then only come back after I had already put myself to sleep. I remember, in the morning, she would make my breakfast with whatever she had brought back in the doggy bag. Sometimes I would have steak with my eggs or she'd reheat the baked potato and crumble scrambled eggs and bacon into the pouch of the potato skin. Sometimes it was just warmed rolls from the night before with bacon and cheese in the middle. It was both a cruel and kind thing to do. This is actually the first time I've eaten in this restaurant."

Father Naylon looked with bemusement at the surroundings and worked a piece of gristle with his teeth before he finally finished the whiskey. During the entire story, Edwin had listened intently but had never stopped eating. He and his mother almost never went out to eat and, even then, never this much food. He ate and ate and was shocked to discover that, suddenly, there was almost no more food left. As if on cue, the waitress brought them a piece of strawberry shortcake that the two of them shared, the rhythm of their movements easy as they dug bites out of the cake, each taking a turn. It was impossible for

Edwin to resist the urge to imagine Father Naylon as his own father.

When the meal was finished and the check arrived, Edwin reached into his pocket and handed Father Naylon the twenty-dollar bill. "Will this be enough for what I ate?" he asked. The priest looked at the money and Edwin saw the priest smile in a way that Edwin understood quite well, a smile that could, if you let it get away from you, turn into a crying jag. Father Naylon handed the money back to Edwin, gripped the boy's shoulder, and squeezed. "This is all my treat," Father Naylon said to Edwin. "This is all my gift to you," and Edwin nodded his thanks. He could not decide if he was keeping Father Naylon from getting too sad, or if it was the other way around. Edwin decided, now that the check had been paid and the two of them were driving back to the decrepit house, that they were helping each other, and that this was the best way that any life could unfold.

As soon as they returned to the house, Father Naylon told Edwin that he was going to explore a little, look for any important papers or things of interest. Edwin took a bath and prepared for bed, his stomach croaking like a tight sack of frogs. He found a worn packet of Alka-Seltzer in the medicine cabinet, the tablets slightly crushed, and he stoppered the sink and let it fill with water. He dumped the tablets into the water, watched them fizz and hiss, and then Edwin brought his face to the surface of the water and gulped as much as he could, gagging softly on the acidic taste of the tablets. Five minutes later, it seemed to have offered no relief from his stomach pain, but he was so heavy with food at this point that he could barely keep his eyes open.

He could hear Father Naylon banging around in the crawl space of the house, the sandpaper dragging of boxes across the wood floor. Edwin crawled into the bed of the guest room, the sheets damp and slightly moldy, and let himself drift into sleep, missing his mother but feeling safe with the knowledge that a priest was hiding within the walls of this strange house, ready to protect Edwin at the slightest sign of invasion.

Hours later, still pitch-black outside, Edwin woke to the intense and troubling sensation of his stomach expanding long after his last meal. Everything he had eaten for dinner had turned into some kind of stew that simmered within his belly. He was sweating under the covers of the bed, and he kicked them off and stumbled, in the absence of any night-lights, to the bathroom, where he retched and gagged and finally emptied his stomach of whatever he could coax out of his body. He felt instant relief, could not bear to look at the remains of his last meal, feeling guilty that he could not keep down what Father Naylon had paid so much for at the restaurant. As he walked back to his bedroom, he saw light coming from downstairs, and Edwin, now wide awake, felt the humming of discovery and followed the source of the light. In what had once been the library, nearly overflowing with boxes, Father Naylon was sipping from a bottle of George Dickel and holding a black fireman's helmet in his hands, turning it over and over. The priest looked up to see Edwin in the doorway, and he smiled and waved the boy over to him. He was wearing his black pants, but he had removed his shirt and collar and was only wearing an undershirt, stained with sweat. There was a cup of water near the priest's foot, a layer of ash clinging to the surface, an armada of drowned cigarette butts sunk at the bottom.

"Did I wake you?" Father Naylon asked. Edwin said that he had not. "Do you need something?" the priest continued, and Edwin again shook his head. "Would you like to see something interesting?" the priest then asked, and Edwin was happy to finally say yes to something.

He walked over to Father Naylon as the priest reached into a crumpled box and he produced what looked like an old gas mask, a hose hanging down from it. "This is an old respirator," Father Naylon said. "My uncle would wear this during a fire so he could breathe."

Edwin touched the yellowed glass of the mask and then, without warning, the priest slipped the mask onto Edwin's head. Immediately, Edwin could hear his own breathing rattling inside of his brain. He felt as if a thick layer had been placed between him and the rest of the world. He looked up at Father Naylon, who was smiling. "This is how they could stay alive," the priest said. He reached down and held the hose in front of Edwin's limited gaze. "This connected to a filter of some sort; I can't find it in the box, though." Father Naylon then placed the palm of his large hand flat against the hose, cutting off the air to the mask. Edwin felt panic spill out of himself, and his hands gently touched the front of the mask. The priest smiled and then released his palm. "Imagine that, to be in a swirling inferno, your respirator the only thing keeping you alive, and to have it shut off. I had nightmares about these things all the time. A real fire was scarier to me than any story of hell that the nuns would tell us about." Edwin wanted the mask off him, did not want Father Naylon, in this state, in control of his air supply, but he wasn't sure how to go about taking it off. He simply breathed as calmly as he could, unable to imagine himself in any situation except for the one he was currently experiencing. Finally, Father Naylon pulled the respirator off Edwin and then tucked it back into the box.

"I would play for hours with this equipment," Father Naylon continued. "I would put out so many fires in my imagination. And then, sometime after my uncle died, I played a game where I would go into a burning building and then get trapped. My respirator would fail or a piece of the ceiling would come down on me, or the flames would simply spring up around me, and I would go limp, fall to the floor, and let the fire engulf me. It seems strange now, but it was terribly exciting when I was a child."

If there was another person on the planet to whom Father Naylon did not need to explain himself, it was Edwin. Or was this normal? Edwin suddenly wondered, the desire to be dead, or the desire to pretend with such intensity. All Edwin knew with certainty was that he and Father Naylon were alike, and even if the priest had scared him just now, it had staved off the discomfort that had awakened him this night.

Father Naylon reached into the box for a heavy, black coat and then tried it on. "All this equipment fits me now," he said. Edwin watched as the priest stepped into a pair of thick pants with suspenders, then into a pair of boots, still smudged with ash and dirt and dust. He put the helmet on his head and, to Edwin, he looked like a real firefighter. The jittery, tired man Edwin had seen just minutes before took on a different shape in the costume and became rigid and capable.

"Would you like to play a game?" he asked Edwin, and, shocked by the request, to have an adult suggest anything fun, Edwin agreed. "Your house is on fire, Edwin. I'll save you," the priest said. Edwin knew how to pretend. It was one of the few things he was good at doing, to imagine a world and then take up residence there. To have someone else enter into that same world seemed a gift, or, it being so late at night, a dream.

Edwin nodded and then scampered into the kitchen, where he pretended to cook something on the stove, something highly flammable and incorrectly prepared. As the grease spilled onto the burners, he felt the heat of the flames as they touched the drapes and the cabinets. He ran to the phone, pretended to call 911, and then shouted that his house was on fire and that he needed help right away. He coughed into the receiver and heard, from the library, Father Naylon shout that help was on the way and to remain calm, to get out of the house and to stay out.

"I can't get out," Edwin shouted. "The fire is too intense."

"I'm coming," Father Naylon shouted, and Edwin fell to his knees, coughing, his body feverish from either illness or imagination. He lay on the floor, his head tilted back, and he watched the upside-down image of Father Naylon, transformed into a fireman, running into the kitchen. The respirator and helmet obscured his face, but Edwin recognized the priest's hands as Father Naylon scooped him into his arms. He carried Edwin into the hallway, where he gently laid him on the wood floor. The priest ripped off his mask and gently compressed Edwin's chest, restarting his still-beating heart. Edwin smiled, but kept his eyes closed, his body limp. "You're okay," Father Naylon called out, and then he began counting, "one, two, three," forcing the air already in Edwin's lungs out of his body. Finally, the priest's ear resting against Edwin's chest, listening for a sign of life, Edwin began to sputter and flail his arms, coming back to life. It was a thrilling feeling, after so many games where he died, to be resurrected. It was a miracle—Edwin believed this without hesitation—to have another person bring him back from that quiet place where the world ended. He put his arms around Father Naylon and the priest simply smiled. "You're okay," he said again.

Still clothed in the fireman's outfit, Father Naylon led Edwin back up the stairs and into the bedroom. He tucked the boy into bed and said, "Good night, Edwin." Edwin replied, "Good night, Father," and then listened to the satisfying sounds of the priest's heavy footsteps clunking down the stairs, back to the library, where Father Naylon would probably spend the rest of the night.

When Edwin awoke the next morning, his stomach ached in a way that suggested poisoning, a grenade swallowed and detonated within his gut. He had sweated his way out of his pajamas, the sheets twisted in violent shapes around his figure. It had to be the meal from the night before, the toxic way that creamed spinach interacted with tomato sauce. He struggled to his feet and then, as if touched by an electrical current, remembered the night with Father Naylon. It had the distinct elements of a dream, how everything felt real but distorted by strangeness that could not be convincingly explained. He remembered the gas mask, the pretend emergency, Father Naylon performing chest compressions. It was now, in the stark sickness of the morning, entirely possible that it had not actually happened. It was an unsolved mystery that required further investigation, which would commence the minute Edwin followed the sounds of activity in the kitchen and saw Father Naylon again.

The priest was frying bacon and buttering slices of toast. He was shaved, seemingly untroubled by the prospect of the new day, the smell of bacon grease and cigarette smoke heavy in the air, which made Edwin's stomach turn over.

"I let you sleep a little longer, so we have to get moving," the priest told him. "I didn't trust the milk or eggs in this house, so it's just bacon sandwiches. Eat up."

Father Naylon placed a sandwich, filled with nearly burned crisp bacon, in front of Edwin, who had neither the strength nor the inclination to reveal his internal discomfort, and so he took the sandwich and bit into the salt and fat and butter of the sandwich and managed to get it down. The priest wolfed down his own sandwich and then washed the pan in the sink, drinking water from the spigot when he was finished. Edwin slipped the remaining half of his sandwich from the plate and walked back to the bedroom, where he opened a window and tossed the sandwich outside. He could not eat another bite without retching. Father Naylon called out to him as he walked away, "Meet me back here in ten minutes and we'll make our way to the church." Edwin replied that he would be ready, and the priest said, though it didn't seem intended for Edwin, "We'll get through this."

The church was tiny, a stone building with two sets of ten small pews. There were perhaps eight or nine people in attendance, all of them ancient save for the fortyish funeral director who had already rolled the casket to the altar on a cart. "No matter how many people come to a funeral," Father Naylon commented, flipping his spent cigarette into the gravel parking lot, "it always feels like too few."

After they had changed into their vestments, Father Naylon suddenly embraced Edwin, the overpowering smell of tobacco filling the boy's internals, and then said, "We'll do the best we can and only that, okay?" Edwin nodded. He was a servant and he would do exactly what was asked of him, as best as he could, whatever strangeness might await him. He steeled his body against weakness and processed down the aisle, toward the altar, toward the casket, Father Naylon just behind him.

The nausea was so intense that Edwin had trouble following the mass, sometimes needing the instruction of Father Naylon to remember the next step. He was sweating profusely, his skin baking under the heavy garment, his hands clenching and unclenching each time he felt the urge to vomit. He thought of the twenty dollars and then he thought of his mother's disappointment if he ruined this mass. Finally, most effectively, he thought of Father Naylon's words before Mass, how they would help each other, and he knew he could not make things any more difficult than they already were for the priest. He would wait for the miracle of strength and, until that moment, he would find a way to the end of things.

When it was time for the host and wine to be consecrated, Edwin reminded himself, over and over, to breathe, to circulate the air throughout his body. He maintained a steady rhythm, in and out, and when Father Naylon raised the host, Edwin was ready for it, jangled the bells in celebration of transubstantiation, but also, more importantly, his own victory in staying conscious. For the wine, he rang the bells and felt the satisfaction of receiving the very benediction he prayed for. This was the blessing of religion, he decided, the moments when you were rewarded for your faith. Father Naylon smiled weakly at Edwin, the two of them performing rites of great importance for the few people who would bear witness.

Finally, the mass almost ended, Edwin moved to the corner of the altar, where a table held a boat of incense pebbles, red and gray like the gravel in a fish tank, and a box of matches. The thurible was hanging from a stand, and Edwin worked carefully to light the coals inside of the censer. It took five matches before the coals finally began to smoke, the tiny briquettes turning grayish white. The smoke upset Edwin's stomach, and his desire to breathe deeply only pulled more of the smoke into his body. He waddled over to Father Naylon, careful not to let the heat of the thurible touch his garment. The priest took the bowl of incense from Edwin and began to sprinkle the pebbles onto the hot coals. The smell of pine and lemon, of dry wood, wafted across the altar, and Edwin felt the intense nausea rack his stomach. His legs trembled, his grip on the thurible weakened, and he quickly handed the chain to Father Naylon and took two steps backward, trying to get away from the scent. Father Naylon reached for Edwin with his free hand, but it was too late and Edwin felt the lights dim, the buzzing in his head, his stomach gurgling, and he fell forward, right at Father Naylon's feet. He wanted to say he was sorry, but he could not form the words. He felt himself rise up, lifted bodily, and he thought something beautiful was happening, something perfect, and he let himself drift out of consciousness. If it was not a miracle, then Edwin believed there was no such thing as miracles.

When he awoke, he was in the priest's car, moving slowly down the highway. There was a handkerchief in his lap, the fabric splotched red, and he noticed that his nose had been, or perhaps still was, bleeding. He groaned, instantly felt the nausea return to his body, and he leaned toward the AC vent, which poured wind into his face.

"Stay awake, now, Edwin," Father Naylon said, as if this was the fourth or fifth time he'd had to say it.

"What happened?" Edwin responded, hoping that someone had the full story of his circumstances.

"You passed out again, unfortunately; just a flash. You hit your face on the floor and gave yourself a nosebleed. I carried you to the sacristy and finished the mass. Then we walked to the car. I've been keeping you awake, just in case, but I think you're okay. You did manage to give yourself a good bump on your forehead."

"I'm sor—" Edwin began, but the priest cut him off.

"Please don't say it, Edwin," Father Naylon said. "It's not necessary and it's not something I need to hear. It was my fault for bringing you, knowing that you've had problems before. I just thought it might help, to remove you from the situation at Saint Rose. I was wrong, of course."

"It wasn't the same thing," Edwin said, but found he couldn't explain himself the way he felt would result in Father Naylon understanding.

"I'm afraid your mother will be quite angry with me," the priest continued, as if he hadn't heard Edwin.

"It wasn't your fault."

"Someone is always at fault, Edwin. Someone or something is usually responsible for the way things go. Believe me, I know what I'm talking about."

They drove in silence to the cemetery, and, when they finally arrived, the priest instructed him to stay in the car, which was still running, the air conditioner thrumming with effort.

"I'll be back soon," Father Naylon assured him. "I don't have much left to say, honestly."

As soon as the priest disappeared from sight, Edwin cracked open the door and vomited a steady, heavy surge of acid and foam onto the ground. He emptied his stomach, his jaw seeming to unlock to allow for all the poison to spill out of him. He spit and probed his teeth with his tongue when he was finally finished. He felt, almost immediately, as if he needed something to eat. He shut the door and fell asleep until the priest returned.

"Let's go home," Father Naylon said, and Edwin agreed, willing to go anywhere that Father Naylon would take him.

Edwin slept the entire ride back home, his feverish dreams indistinguishable from reality, the trip seemingly without end, his exhaustion without limit. Father Naylon drove in silence, no music, no talking, simply the sound of the tires running over the road. When they finally arrived at Edwin's house, his mother was still at work and had left the key under the doormat. When he felt the car brake and come to a stop, Edwin awoke and then, quickly, pretended that he was still asleep. He was too embarrassed to face Father Naylon, wanted to extend the silence for as long as possible. He kept his eyes shut and did not resist when Father Naylon lifted him into his arms. It was a soothing experience, to be carried into his home by someone strong. He laid his head against the priest's chest and listened for a heartbeat but couldn't hear anything but the jostling of his own body.

Father Naylon stooped to retrieve the key and unlocked the door. He carried Edwin to his bedroom and placed him atop the bed. Edwin pretended to still be asleep, and the priest removed the boy's shoes. Edwin opened his eyes and, when Father Naylon turned to leave, he made sounds of waking, stifling a yawn that turned real just as it began. Father Naylon smiled weakly at the boy and then produced a twenty-dollar bill from his wallet. Edwin shook his head.

"I don't deserve it."

Father Naylon sighed, shook his head, and then placed the money on Edwin's desk. "You deserve this and so much more, Edwin."

"I don't think I can serve Mass anymore," Edwin continued.

"I think that's probably a good idea, unfortunately for me," Father Naylon responded. "Sometimes we're not suited for the very thing that gives us happiness. So much of life is learning to live with what we're capable of doing. Time and time again, you'll have to accept what is available instead of what you actually deserve."

The priest looked around Edwin's room as if he had discovered an unknown land. "God has a plan for all of us, and I can't pretend to know what that is or how it makes sense. So much of what God does, what he puts us through, is beyond me. I only know that there must be something on the other end of this life, something wonderful and true and eternal. If you ever get sad, Edwin, remember that. What comes next will almost always be better than what happened beforehand."

Edwin pulled his knees up to his chest and rolled onto his side, no longer looking at Father Naylon. He could not pretend to understand the priest, other than to know that Father Naylon was an unhappy man who tried to make others happy. It seemed like an impossible task to Edwin, which made him care for the priest even more.

"I love you," Edwin said, hoping the honesty of his words would override the awkwardness of saying them aloud.

The priest did not hesitate to respond. "I love you, Edwin," he said, and then walked out of the room, out of the house, and into his car. Edwin listened for the sound of the motor, but it did not come. He imagined Father Naylon in the car, smoking a cigarette, unwilling to leave Edwin alone. He closed his eyes and felt the safety of having someone watching over him, all the pain of a lifetime kept at bay, and fell into a dream that would ready him for what came next.

Sanders for a Night

She was late. It was twenty minutes since Greg's class had let out for the day and Marta was just now pulling up to the school's entrance. She saw her son sitting on the steps with the principal, Mrs. Chambers, instead of the teacher who usually ran the pickup program. He was staring straight ahead, his wide, blue eyes unblinking, his dark brown hair a tangled mess, as if he was wearing a bird's nest on his head. It was the fifth time she had been late this fall and she knew that Mrs. Chambers was going to be upset. The teacher in charge of pickups had mentioned the issue of her lateness to Marta the last time it happened, and not nicely, either. "We have an after-school program, Mrs. Timbs," she said, "but it costs extra. Perhaps you'd be interested?" She felt so chastised that she didn't even remind the woman that, since the divorce in September, her name was now Mrs. Poltz. Or Ms. Poltz. It was hard to remember even for her. "I'll be on time," Marta had said then, "I promise." Well, she was late again, and now Mrs. Chambers was leaning through the open window of the car. "We need to talk," she said. Mrs.

Chambers's face was pale white, grimacing. She did not address Marta by any name, maiden or otherwise. This was not a good sign.

Greg waited in the car while Marta stood in the hallway of the school building. Mrs. Chambers had gone to get Greg's teacher. "I'm sorry," she whispered, "I'm sorry again," but Mrs. Chambers was already too far down the hallway to hear. Marta was going to be late getting back to the office. She had only started this job in June and they had been nice enough to let her defer her lunch hour every day in order to pick up Greg and take him home. Now she was going to have to stay longer at work to make up for the time she had missed. It was busy at the university right now, all the researchers in her department needing their grants to be prepared, forms that she still wasn't sure she completely understood. She had spent most of this month scrambling to meet deadlines, trying to get everything turned in by the end of October. She had three days left and this was not helping. Nothing seemed to be helping. She had hoped that maybe, finally, things could, if not return to normal, become just a little easier. But now here was Greg's teacher with Mrs. Chambers behind her, both of them saying the same thing. "We need to talk."

But it turned out this talk was not about the late pickups. It was about Halloween. Greg's third-grade teacher, a nice, very young woman just out of college named Ashley, sat in a chair beside Marta in Mrs. Chambers's office while the principal sat behind her own desk.

"Have you and Greg discussed Halloween costumes?" Ashley asked her. Costumes? She was going to have to stay late at work because of costumes?

"No," Marta said, "to be honest, I completely forgot about it. I can grab something at the store, though, so thank you for reminding me." Before she could stand up, Ashley handed her something that Greg had written that day in class.

"I asked them to write about what they were going to dress up as for Halloween," Ashley told Marta with a frown. "I thought we should discuss this." Marta started to read but had to stop at the very first sentence. *I am going to be my brother Sanders for Halloween.* She felt the urge to cry out, but she managed to stop herself just as her mouth opened.

> *I am going to be my brother Sanders for Halloween.*
> *Even though he died and he isn't here anymore, I think*
> *that he would really like this idea.*

"I think you can understand why we wanted to talk to you about this, Ms. Poltz," the principal said. Marta found she couldn't say anything in reply. She stood, still holding the paper, and thanked both of the women, assuring them that she would talk to Greg, that she would handle the situation.

"We have the name of a child psychiatrist," Mrs. Chambers said. "Perhaps Greg might want to talk to him?" But Marta was already walking quickly out of the office, embarrassed that other people always had to be a part of this thing which to her felt so private. When she got to the door of the main office she stopped for a second, then popped her head back into the principal's office. "I won't be late anymore," she said. "I will be on time from now on."

In the car, going home, Marta tried to figure out what to do. She had no idea how to begin a conversation about the Halloween idea, much less prevent it from happening. Greg wasn't forthcoming, either. He rested his head on the window of the passenger side and watched things go by as they moved, quiet as usual. She kept watching him out of the corner of her eye and considered, not for the first time, that he was growing into the same features as Sanders. Big blue eyes, dark curly hair, and a tiny dimple in his chin. It was simply a fact of nature, and though it hurt to be reminded of her dead son, it was to be expected. There would always be reminders, so why not her remaining child? Once Greg grew older than the age Sanders had been when he died, Marta believed it would be easier, the reminders fewer. But that was not for two more years. Many things, Marta knew, could happen in two years.

There was silence until they pulled into the driveway of their duplex, a worn, faded-blue house they shared with a retired couple who no longer needed much space. The Granatos had rented the top half of the house to Marta and her son. It was old and sagging, but the rent was cheap. Also, it felt like a house, or at least a piece of a house, which Marta liked better than a cramped apartment. There was a backyard for Greg to play in, not that he played outside, but still. There was a semblance of normalcy to it. Though it was not like their life before, it hinted at it enough to get by. Greg still rested his head on the window, even after Marta had cut off the engine. She asked him if there was anything he wanted to tell her, about school.

"You were late," he said, "again."

"I talked to your teacher, Greg," she told him. "She told me what you wrote about your Halloween costume." He still would not look at her, but finally he spoke.

"I want to," he whispered.

"But why?" Marta asked. "Do you want to tell me why? Maybe we can discuss it."

"I just do. I want to be Sanders for Halloween."

"Honey, I don't know if the kids or the teachers will understand."

Greg finally looked at her. His face already showed signs of disappointment, a feeling that he would not be allowed the things he wanted. "The kids at this school don't know him. They never met him and they ask me sometimes about him. I just want to show them."

Martha felt tears spring to her eyes but she willed herself to stop crying. There would be time to cry later, there was always time to cry later.

"I just don't think this is a good idea, Greg. And Ms. Ashley doesn't think it's a good idea, either."

"I still want to."

She changed tactics. "What would you do for a costume? How would you do that?"

"I could wear some of his clothes, and get his paddleball game, some of his things. All those things in your closet."

Marta froze, feeling the color drain from her face. "What?"

"You have some of his stuff in your closet. I've seen it."

"Greg . . . well, you shouldn't have gone in there. You have to respect my privacy when I'm not at the house. Anyway, I just can't let you do it, so we need to deal with that."

Greg nodded, as if he expected this response from her, and

pushed open the door of the car, and walked to the house, leaving Marta behind feeling like she never had the time or the exact words to feel satisfied with anything she did. She followed him up the outside stairs to the second floor of the house and unlocked the door for him. She might have to stay even later at work than usual, and so she told him to talk to Mrs. Granato if he needed anything. "We'll talk more about this tonight," she said as she walked back down the stairs. He leaned over the railing of the stairs and, just as Marta was about to get back in the car, said to her, "All the kids get to be whatever they want for one day. I want to be Sanders." Then he went back inside the house. Marta wanted to go after him, to hold her son and say something reassuring, but she was late. She was late and she needed to leave.

It was well past seven and Marta was just finishing up at the office. The work kept her from worrying about Greg; it forced her to stay busy. That was how it worked. You made something else more important than the problem, focused on it, and, before you knew it, time passed and the problem was easier to handle. Sometimes it was actually effective. She knew she would have to talk to Greg again tonight, make sure he understood. But as she sat there mentally rehearsing what she was going to say, she could not think of a single way to explain to him why it was impossible for him to dress as his dead brother for Halloween.

Marta decided to call her ex-husband, Naton. It seemed necessary. Greg was his son, too. He would want to hear this. Mostly, though, she just wanted someone else to know what she was going through. She didn't know if he could help, but she didn't want to be alone with this feeling any longer. She hadn't spoken to Naton since the divorce was finalized, and barely at all in the months before that. He had moved back to Nashville and was living with his father. He wasn't working and was drinking more often, all the things she foresaw when she decided to leave him. When she heard his voice on the other end of the line, it did not sound like the man who had been her husband; it was so quiet, tired. But it was Naton. This was Naton now.

"Yes?" Naton answered, groggy.

She could already tell he was drunk.

"Yes?" he said again.

"It's me, Naton," she said. "I need to talk to you about Greg."

"I don't have a job yet," he told her. "I don't have money right now."

Marta sighed. Why had she thought this would help? "Naton, just listen for a second. I need to talk to you about something. Greg told his teacher at school that he wants to be Sanders for Halloween, that he wants to go dressed as Sanders." There was no answer from Naton, just the sound of his breathing.

"Naton? Hello?"

There was silence.

"I mean, I can't let him. I'm not going to let him, obviously, but he seems determined. I just thought you should know. And I thought, well, I thought you could help me, maybe say something to him."

More silence.

"Naton, please?"

"Let him," Naton said.

"What?"

"Just let him."

"I'm not going to do that," Marta told him firmly. "He absolutely can't do that."

"He just wants one night. I can understand that."

"Obviously it was a mistake to call," Marta said, trying to stay calm but feeling furious. How could he think it would be okay for Greg to go to a Halloween party dressed as his dead brother?

"You don't think about him, do you, Marta?" Naton asked.

She took a deep breath. "I do," she said, "and fuck you."

"I do, too," he said. "I think about him all the time. Just a while ago, I thought about him and it nearly killed me. How Sanders called because he didn't want to stay at that sleepover, and I said he should try to stay. How I didn't think that we should keep picking him up because he was relying on that and was never going to spend the night away from home. I said that. And you said, 'Go get him.' You said that. I was driving, okay, I won't ever forget that, I was in the car with Sanders when it happened. But you told me to go get him. You made me get in that car and get our boy. And now he's gone."

"I'm not talking to you anymore," she yelled into the phone. "Never again." Marta immediately thought of those nights following the accident, when Naton would obsessively list all the different elements that had made the accident happen. The rain. The other car. No air bag on the passenger side. He told her all these things for months after it happened and she listened and listened and finally, somewhere along the way, she stopped listening. And she was not listening now. She was already hanging up the phone. She was already walking to her car. She was already on her way home, to her son, Greg, who was waiting for her.

Greg was in his room when Marta came home, all the lights off in the house except for the band of light coming from underneath his doorway. Marta pressed her hand against the door but did not open it. There was a yellow plastic sign stuck to the door that read PRIVACY in bold, black letters. It had been her idea, the sign. Moving to this new house, in this new town, with this new form of the family, was hard enough, and she wanted Greg to have some things that were under his control. She would let him have this. Marta spoke to the closed door, and Greg behind it, telling him that she had bought fast food, his favorite kind of chicken pieces and milk shake. She went to the kitchen, sorted the mail, and waited for Greg to come out and join her.

Finally, the food cold and the shake reduced to only milk, Greg came to the table. Marta warmed the food in the microwave and they ate quietly. Marta wanted to wait until after dinner, a few minutes of peace, before she returned to the matter that, though she hoped otherwise, was not resolved. To her surprise, however, Greg spoke first.

"I still want to do it," he said, not looking up from his food.

"I know, honey. I understand that. But I also need you to understand that it's just not a good idea."

"There won't be any blood," he said, almost whispering. "I don't want to do anything gross. I just want to be him, like I remember him."

The image of Sanders, bloody, though she had only seen him pale white and cold at the hospital, made her dizzy. She struggled to stay calm in front of Greg and wondered briefly what he pictured Sanders like that last night.

"No," she said. "No and no and no again. I wish you could think about everyone else, Greg, and not just what you want."

"But it would be just this once and then I wouldn't ask again."

"No."

Greg pushed his food away and twisted his face around as if he was going to cry. Marta finally thought of another way to talk to him.

"Greg?"

The boy didn't answer but she continued.

"Greg, I know you want to do this and I know you feel it would be a good thing, but I don't think I could handle it. I think it would make me very sad. It still makes me very sad to think about Sanders. And if you did this, it would hurt me. And so I'm asking you not to do it, for me."

Greg considered this, turned away from her and then back toward the table. Then he stood up, walked out of the kitchen, and went back to his room. Marta cleared away the food, and when she walked past Greg's door, the PRIVACY sign was still facing toward her.

Alone, in her own room, she reached for the box on the top shelf of the closet. It was labeled *Winter Coats,* which she thought would seem innocuous enough to keep Greg from opening it; unfortunately it had not. She knelt down on the floor of the cedar closet, inhaled the sharp smell of the wood, and opened the box, which she could now tell had been opened before, by the clumsy way the top had been folded back into place. There was a large hooded parka on top, which she removed, and beneath that, was what was left of Sanders's things, what she had saved.

A few months after the accident, Marta had read in one of the grief books that she had received from friends and family that it was necessary to cherish your memories of the deceased, including mental images, old pictures, and home movies, but that it was detrimental to recovery to hold on to mundane things that the deceased had owned. And so Marta had boxed up Sanders's sheets and toys and clothes and donated them to the Salvation Army. Naton had been furious. "We could have given those toys to Greg," he had shouted. "He could grow into those clothes." Marta had felt sick at the thought. "We can buy him new toys," she said. "He can have his own clothes."

But she had saved some things, though she had never told Naton, had felt it necessary to keep it from him for some reason. Sanders's favorite shirt, with its navy blue collar and red and blue stripes, a pair of jeans that were worn thin at the knees, a pocket calculator that his teacher had given to all the students, and that he always kept in his pocket. Other things, too, enough to fill the box, and she took all these items out and placed them on the floor, the objects giving off the collected scent of cedar from being stored in the closet. She looked at his baseball mitt, surprised at how it looked exactly the same as when she had placed it in the box two years ago. Though she had done nothing to care for the leather, the simple absence of use had preserved it. She looked at all the items: a toy robot so worn with play that the paint had been scrubbed to the silver metal frame, trading cards with comic book characters, all their faces a serious rictus of effort, a foam fist that, when smacked against a surface, made sounds of breakage and collision. Nothing had changed.

In the morning, during breakfast, Greg said only "Okay." Marta immediately felt that she had the capacity to breathe deeper, that her ability to take in air had improved the moment he had relented.

"Okay?" she said, to make sure.

"I won't do it if it makes you sad," he said. "I just didn't—" He squinted his eyes, seemed puzzled as to how to continue.

"Didn't what?" she said, though already she felt her attention drifting to work, the focus of her mind shifting as difficulties required.

"I just didn't think you still thought about him. I didn't think you still missed him."

There was no malice in it, she could understand that, but she felt the heat rush from her hands and feet, everything moving to the direct center of herself, which needed warmth. "I do," she said, and that was all she could say.

At work, Marta felt things slipping out of her hands. A Ph.D. student had mistakenly provided her with the wrong set of tables for one of the sections of his grant application, and she now had to reenter everything all over again, time-consuming and frustrating and just slightly beyond her comprehension, which Marta felt most surprises ended up being. She had to finish everything by tomorrow, mail it the following day, and she was beginning to realize that it was possible she might not make it. This job, a miracle that she was underqualified to possess, felt like it could vanish with the slightest mistake. Her boss was kind but expected perfection, was already slightly concerned about the fact that Greg occupied a portion of her time. "Children can be such a time suck," he once told her, as if they were a video game or a gambling addiction, something to be kept hidden from the rest of the world.

She was distracted by thoughts of what Greg had said at breakfast. It had stung her, the notion that she did not think of Sanders anymore. Naton had accused her of the same thing during the months leading up to the divorce. "You're in such a hurry to leave me and Sanders behind and start over," he had said. She hated the fact that her grief, because it was quiet, because she worked hard to conceal it, was somehow less genuine. She thought of Naton, drunk, unable to leave his father's house, and she knew that the way she dealt with tragedy was the best way, the one that was necessary to keep going.

She thought about November first, the promise of being done, with the applications, with Halloween, and how the ease of things would come back to her and she could feel calm again. Then she looked at the clock and noticed it was five minutes past three. And she was late again.

When she pulled up to the front of the school, the principal was waiting, Greg sitting by her feet on the steps. Mrs. Chambers walked down to the car and said to Marta, "Greg's teacher said that he was particularly quiet today. Was there a problem last night?" Marta, flustered from having to rush from work and relieved not to be called out for her lateness, answered, "He's probably disappointed that he won't be able to dress up as his original Halloween idea. We discussed it last night, and though he understands, I'm sure he's unhappy about it." Mrs. Chambers waved Greg toward the car, and the boy stood up and began walking to them. "That's fine," said the principal. "This is the reason we like to ensure such a strong parent-to-teacher relationship, to make sure that these kind of . . . these kinds of incidents get addressed before anyone is really hurt." Marta smiled tightly and then Greg slipped by the principal and climbed into the car.

"You were late again," he said, and Marta cast an apologetic glance at the principal, but she was already walking away from the car.

"You okay?" she asked Greg, who nodded and then said, "I need another costume for tomorrow." Marta promised that she would bring something home after work, and when she dropped Greg off at the house, she was so rushed for time that she forgot to tell him that she would be home late, that she would have to work into the evening if she was to stay on top of things, if she was to stay in control.

Marta worked until 10 P.M., the office entirely empty, the doctors and Ph.D. students unconcerned about the grants once they had handed their materials off to her, and though she still had a lot of work left to do, she felt it was possible, that a solid day of work tomorrow would finish it. She was nearly home when she remembered the Halloween costume and had to drive back to Walmart. There wasn't much left, the costumes picked over and the more popular ideas long gone. Marta ended up choosing three costumes, a giant bat, a cartoon character that seemed too young for Greg even as she placed it in the shopping cart, and some strange, almost terrifying outfit that consisted of a navy blue, acrylic business suit and a giant elephant mask. She had no idea what movie or comic book this costume related to, but she was mesmerized by the two parts of it, the mundane suit and the realistic-looking elephant mask. She hoped that Greg would settle for one of them, that her selections would not re-open the discussion. As she passed by the makeup and effects aisle, she picked up a packet of blood capsules, figuring they would increase the costume options: dead bat, wounded cartoon character, Wall Street elephant with a nosebleed. Standing in line to check out, Marta thought about the last Halloween Sanders had dressed up for.

By the time she made it home, Greg was already asleep. Even though the PRIVACY sign was still up, she silently walked into the room, the three costumes draped over her arm. She placed them over the chair next to his desk and then sat down on the bed. He stirred slightly and then fell back to sleep. She watched him for a few moments. He was the only good thing she had left. She could not imagine life without him, felt that if she had to start over alone, without her son, she would have no ties to the person she was before, and the thought terrified her. She did not want to forget about what had happened, only wanted to believe that something just as good as her past life was possible. She stood up, smoothed the indentation she had left on the bed, and went into her room. She opened her closet, took down the box, and was relieved to see that everything was there as she had left it, untouched.

In the morning, the boy came to breakfast wearing the business suit, the elephant mask in his hands. "Good choice," Marta said, smiling. "I thought you would choose that one." Greg only nodded. "So," Marta asked, "do you know who he is? Is he some kind of superhero?" Greg shook his head. "Would you like some fake blood?" she asked, wanting to hear her son's voice, test the tone of it.

"No," he said, "I think he's fine like this. I think he wouldn't like blood on his suit."

At school, she watched her son step out of the car and walk toward the building. She saw Mrs. Chambers watching through the window of her office, and when she caught the principal's eye, they both nodded at each other. Greg turned to wave at Marta and then turned back toward the school, pulling the mask down over his face. "I'll be here on time," she told Greg, who did not respond.

Things moved quickly at work. The sections that, when she had first started the applications, required hours to complete now became more and more routine, and the understanding that she was nearly done allowed her to focus. Her son was at school, disappointed but not angry, and she was amazed at how accurate the phrase "light at the end of the tunnel" actually was, the objects around her gaining clarity as she finished each successive application.

At three o'clock, she was waiting for Greg at school. She had a strange feeling and then realized it was because she was surrounded by other parents, people who were always on time. She felt happy to blend in with them, these men and women who knew enough about her circumstances to be kind but not involved in the actual events so as to be rendered awkward around her. Greg finally walked out of the building with some other children, and when he saw her, he smiled, waved to her, and walked quickly to the car. "You made it," he said. "Did people like your costume?" she asked, and he responded that no one else knew who the elephant was. "Well," Marta said, "no one tonight will care about that. They'll give you candy no matter what."

She dropped Greg off with the promise that she would be back by six, ready to take him trick or treating. He nodded and walked off, stopping to wave to her from the top of the stairs. At work, she managed to finish the applications and avoided the temptation to double-check them, afraid of what she would find. She sealed them into envelopes, addressed them, and dropped them into the box for outgoing mail, assured they would receive a November first postmark the following day.

The sun was setting when she walked inside the house, and Greg was already waiting for her, elephant mask pulled down, his right arm threaded through the rings of a plastic shopping bag. She took a few pictures, though it was hard for him to keep still. "Let's go," he said. "There won't be anything left for me." Marta knelt in front of Greg, put her hands on both of his shoulders, and said, "Greg, I know this hasn't been easy for you. I know you were disappointed. But you see how things can still work out? Things don't always go how you would like them to, but they go anyway and you have to keep up." He pulled away from her grip, just slightly, and said, "I know. I know all that." She gave him a hug and, her face just inches from his neck, smelled the scent of cedar, unmistakable, coming from his costume. She let go of him, nearly pushing him down, and then looked underneath the collar of Greg's costume. It was Sanders's shirt.

"Oh, goddammit, Greg," she shouted, undoing the lace that went around Greg's neck. She pulled the costume down to his ankles and saw Sanders's shirt, his jeans, the calculator sticking out of the pocket.

"I'm sorry," Greg said, his voice cracking, the pitch too high.

"I'll go change right now." He started to walk away, back to his room. Marta grabbed his arm and yanked him back, nearly spinning him around in the process. She knocked the elephant mask from atop his head and held tightly to his arms, unable to do anything else but stare at him.

It was not Sanders. She knew this. It was easy enough to understand that this was not her dead son. And for this reason, the simple fact that Sanders was not in the room with her, Marta was so angry that she was not sure how to proceed. She felt the tears coming, the sickness in her stomach, and for once she finally let it all happen. Greg was now crying, too, and he kept straining toward his room. "I'll go change, Mom," he said. "I'll put all of his stuff back." Marta pulled him even closer to her, holding him tight against her own body.

"No," she said, "I don't want you to go anywhere. Don't you dare leave me." Greg finally went slack and fell into Marta. Though something inside of her kept reminding her that she had to get up off the floor, stop crying, try to fix all this, she just held on to her son, the one who was still alive, and refused to let him go.

No Joke, This Is Going to Be Painful

We called them ice fights. They made things weird for a little while.

I had moved to Coalfield earlier that summer, after I lost my job as a checkout girl at the Bates supermarket in Mount Juliet. It wasn't a huge deal. I was stealing small amounts of money every once in a while and then I got caught and they didn't have any choice but to let me go. If they could have kept me, they would have. It happens.

I was living in a room above my sister and her husband's garage, just my computer, three fans, and a futon we found at a garage sale. For a few weeks, I just sat in that room, nothing but the hum of the fans, no friends, no money, not a thing to do, wishing I was drunk. It was not, truth be told, an uncommon situation for me.

At dinner one night, my sister asked if I'd explored the town and I shook my head. "There's a museum that's not too bad," she said, "and a roller rink that plays good music," and I smiled and felt like I might cry because, although my sister seemed completely oblivious to the kind of person that I was, she wanted me to be happy. I felt like, if I killed someone in front of her, she wouldn't turn me in, even though the guilt would cause her to commit suicide. "Can you drink beer at the roller rink?" I asked, and my sister got excited. "I believe so," she said, and though I never went, it was nice to pretend that I would.

My sister and her husband had a group of close friends, and, in an effort to get me out of the house, they invited me to come along for a barbecue at Henry and Alesha's. After nearly a month of not settling in, I was beginning to think that talking to some capable and attractive and financially secure people might not be such a bad thing. I had devised a theory that if I had some friends, I might not be so quick to want everyone around me to be miserable.

Henry and Alesha had a huge, sprawling yard with a picnic table and a Frisbee that no one even touched and condiments attracting flies while the smoke from the grill got in my hair. These people were nice enough, but they were a little older than me; they talked about TV shows I'd never heard of and drank beer over ice with some lime juice mixed in, which was something that seemed strange and pointless. One of the guys, Eddie, told me when we were alone that my sister had said I was the wild sister and that he had been a little wild in college. "But not anymore?" I asked. He smiled and his face got red and he shook his head. "Not so much," he said, "no."

And then my sister found a fly frozen in an ice cube and plucked it out of her glass. "Gross," she said, holding it between her thumb and middle finger. Everyone was hooting and checking their glass like it was a party game. "Eat it," I said, and everyone stopped laughing. "Gross," my sister said again and frowned at me. Eddie, trying to be wild, said, "Hell, I'll eat it," but my sister shook her head and threw the ice cube in the grass. Wage, whose wife worked with my sister at the high school, said, "I bet you couldn't hit that tree with a piece of ice," pointing toward a dogwood about ten yards away. So far, Wage was the most interesting person in the group. He was cute but he also seemed, at times, to be mildly unstable. For instance, he had talked about a particular comic book character as if he was real. Another time during the party, he had mentioned that he could probably run a marathon this weekend without training, but his wife, Julie, kept saying that he'd never run a day in his life. He just shrugged and looked at me as if to say, *She has no idea what she's talking about.*

Eddie stood up from the picnic table and picked up a piece of ice. "Hell," he said, "I'll do it." He wound up and tossed the ice, missing the tree by a good distance. My sister's husband grabbed another chunk of ice and calmly tossed it at the tree, the ice shattering as it hit the trunk. "Game over," he said, and sat back down. But everyone was getting a little drunk at this point and so the game was most certainly not over. We started winding our arms in big circles, testing our muscles, and then tossing ice into the air, waiting for impact. Wage had hit the tree seven times in a row, each time stepping back a little farther. "I could probably play professional baseball if I wanted," he said, and then he hit the tree for the eighth time. "My hands are cold," Alesha said, but no one stopped playing. Wage hit nine, then ten, then eleven. Everyone else stopped throwing, content to watch Wage continue his streak, twelve, thirteen, fourteen.

My sister's husband had his hand on my sister's ass, rubbing it like a good luck charm. It seemed like it might be a good night after all.

On his nineteenth throw, it was like watching someone put correct change in a Coke machine, and I was getting bored. I fished a piece of half-melted ice from my glass and shook the excess moisture off. Then, as Wage began his windup, I tossed my piece of ice and hit him on the back of his neck. Without stopping his throwing motion, Wage spun around and winged the ice directly at my head. Julie gasped and then yelled, "Wage? Jesus Christ." I ducked and the ice sailed over my head, and then Henry, who was spectacularly drunk by this time, shouted, "Ice fight!" After a few moments of hesitation, people looking around to gauge interest, everyone ran to the cooler, dumped their cups into the ice, and then scattered. Ice was flying from all directions, skittering across the grass as it landed. I could hear the sound of my heart beating in my chest, and I hurled ice at moving targets, rarely hitting anything, but I put every ounce of strength into the throws, as if I was trying to put a hole in someone.

When we finally stopped, the cooler emptied of ice, we were breathing so hard it was like we'd all been fucking for hours. There was the same kind of awkwardness that comes after an orgy, people sheepishly remembering what they'd done and who they'd done it to. Our hands were cold and clammy, wrinkled and pale. But it had been fun for those few minutes. "We should do it again," Wage said, and everyone laughed nervously. "We should," I agreed.

On the ride back home, I sat in the backseat while my sister and her husband sat in front. I had red, puffy welts on my arms that would be bruises by the next day and my throwing arm was already so sore I couldn't lift it above my head. "Eddie really likes you," my sister said, "I can tell." She was trying to be discreet about it, but I could tell she was giving her husband a hand job. "I don't know," I said. "Maybe. What do you think, Sammy?" He caught my eye in the rearview mirror, annoyed, and shrugged his shoulders. "How the fuck should I know?" My sister finished him off and he moaned a little under his breath, and my sister said, "Well, I can tell with these kinds of things."

* * *

Two weeks later, still not looking for a job, I got an e-mail from Wage, which was addressed to all the people who had been at the last party. The subject line read: *Ice Fight, Part II, Revenge of the Cubes, This Time It's Personal, Take No Prisoners*. He was inviting everyone to his and Julie's house for sushi and "more of what you got at Henry and Alesha's." Was he sending this from work? Did he even have a job? I wanted to fuck him so bad, but he seemed so strange that it felt like it would be illegal. I replied to the e-mail and RSVPed. "Watch out," I said, "I'm going to get you bad." Three hours later, he wrote back. "I'm going to bruise you up," he said, and he had made an emoticon that looked like !-), which I think was a face with a black eye. I did a Google search for "ice fight" and found a bunch of videos of hockey players pounding on one another. I wished I had some drugs, but I couldn't decide if I needed to calm down or get excited, so I lay on my futon, all three fans blowing on me, and thought about ice touching skin, how one thing got cold while the other melted.

The party was tense from the minute we arrived. When we first walked in, Julie said, "Wage bought so much ice it's embarrassing. I don't know about this." Sammy said that he might not play because his arm was so sore the last time that he had trouble at work the next day. "Alesha doesn't want to play, either," Julie whispered. I felt my hopes for the night slipping away.

I looked out the window and saw Wage and Eddie in the backyard, placing coolers filled with ice at strategic locations around the yard. There were also little red flags jammed into the earth, though I had no idea what they delineated. Wage and Eddie saw me at the same time and both of them waved. I nodded and they entered the house. "You ready?" Eddie asked, and I said it didn't seem like people were as excited this time. "How much alcohol do you have?" I asked Wage, understanding that whatever he said was going to be too little.

"You're giving them too much time to have second thoughts," I said. "Just let me throw a piece of ice at Sammy and we'll get started right now." Wage shook his head. "I promised Julie we would wait." His face looked like he had only just now realized that maybe Julie was trying to screw him over in regard to the ice fight. "Shit," he said.

Dinner was quiet and awkward; the sushi was a little warm. My sister and her husband told everyone about a complicated movie they had seen the day before. "Someone is bad, but not the one you think," my sister said. Her husband shook his head and said, "Well, I had thought he might be bad, but then I forgot about it after a while." Everyone else just nodded and smiled.

Once the plates were put away, everyone standing dumb and nervous, I finally said, "The ice is melting, I bet. We should probably do something about that." My sister shushed me and looked apologetically around the room. Wage nodded. "It's a lot of ice," he said. "The guy at the gas station said that I must be planning some kind of party, and I told him it was going to be a better party than he'd ever seen in his life." Instead, we were just a bunch of people in a room, calculating our desire for something stupid and senseless. Julie touched Wage on the shoulder and said, "Maybe people would rather sit down in the living room and have some coffee and play a board game."

"Not me," I said, and my sister shushed me again. Wage looked at Julie like she'd just suggested that he put his favorite pet to sleep. "But I bought all that ice," he said. It looked like he might honest to God start crying, and I wanted to punch Julie in the face. If we couldn't have an ice fight, I was thinking, I'd settle for a real fight. But there was my sister and she kept staring at me, her eyes saying, *Be a grown-up; this is how normal people live.* So I said, "Maybe we can vote on it." Wage and Eddie and I raised our hands in favor of an ice fight and the rest of the group voted for coffee and a board game. "Fuck," said Wage, and Julie asked him to come into the kitchen to help her with coffee.

As the rest of us sat in the living room, looking through the board games in one of the cabinets, we could hear them arguing. "This is a little awkward," Henry said, holding an empty glass, afraid to go near the kitchen for a refill. "Well, Wage is always a little awkward," Eddie said, and Alesha and my sister began to giggle. Sammy fiddled with the TV remote but couldn't get it to work. "Sometimes I think that guy's got a screw loose," he said, and again the women resumed giggling. I got red with anger, and without thinking I said, "I guess that explains why I want to fuck him so bad." Then the room got silent and I told my sister I was going to wait in the car until the party was over.

From the backseat of the car, I could just barely see them through the living room window, Henry pretending to ride a bicycle while the others watched with confused looks on their faces. Exasperated, Henry pedaled even harder. I thought about throwing a rock through the window but the desire passed and it was just me in the car, the windows rolled down, too hot for much of anything. And then something hit me in the face, just above my left eye, and I fell back against the seat and moaned, low and heavy, like I'd been kicked in the gut. I'd been kicked in the gut before and it was the exact same sound I'd made then. I looked down and there was a piece of ice in my lap, and then there was Wage's face just outside the car door. "I got you," he said, smiling.

A half inch lower and I'd be blind in that eye, but I grabbed his shirt and pulled him into the car. We made out for a few seconds, his feet hanging out the window, and then he said he had to go. "Julie thinks I'm getting some more coffee," he said, and I told him that Julie was a fucking moron. "She's not so bad," he said. He straightened his clothes, stepped out of the car, and walked back inside the house. I watched the living room window until I saw him standing in front of the rest of the group, his turn to play, pretending to be a robot or maybe someone with stiff joints. My sister shouted something and then she and Sammy exchanged high fives. I got out of the car, ran into the backyard, and knelt over one of the buckets of ice. I jammed my hands as deep as they would go, the ice numbing my skin, and I stayed like that, hidden in the shadows, until I couldn't feel my hands at all.

Back in the car, the night over and everyone going home, my sister turned around in her seat and said, "You probably know this already, but you can't go out with us anymore. And you better not do anything to Wage." I didn't say anything and the rest of the car ride was silent until Sammy said, "If you and Wage had a baby, it would explode the minute it was exposed to air." My sister shushed him, but after a few more seconds of silence, she started to giggle.

Three days later, I got an e-mail from Wage. The subject line read *Ice, Ice, Baby* and the e-mail was short and to the point. "Meet me at the kids' park across from the library. Tonight. 9:30 P.M. I'll be hard to see because I'll be wearing all black but I'll be there, and if you come, I'll be happy."

At dinner, my hands shaking from the anticipation, my sister asked if I'd found a job yet, and I told her that I had not. "You should try harder," Sammy said. "There aren't enough cash register jobs in this town," I said. My sister then spread out four different job applications from places like the Beauty Barn and the Sharp Shopper. "Sammy and I talked about this," she said. "By next week, you need to have a job." Sammy nodded and then looked at me, the first time all night, and said, "Don't tell them you got fired from your last job for stealing." I poured out the rest of my iced tea over his mashed potatoes and left the table with the applications in hand. "I didn't get fired for stealing," I said. "I got fired for not telling them that I was stealing."

I put on a black T-shirt and walked along the empty sidewalk, everyone's house on the block lit up with the glow from TV screens. As I walked past each house, I pressed an imaginary button with my thumb and pretended that everyone inside the house was now dead. I did that until I got bored, which was longer than I had anticipated, and then I was at the park. I didn't see Wage, which was to be expected. I imagined that Wage was the kind of person who put a lot of effort into hiding, so I walked over to a swing and sat down, my feet tracing designs in the dirt.

I heard something shift in the bushes behind me and then there was Wage's voice, whispering, "No joke, this is going to be painful." I turned around and he was holding two bags of ice, bright and sweating in the darkness. "Good," I said.

He dropped one of the bags of ice and then sprinted across the park into the shadows, and I tore open the bag and filled my pockets with ice. A shard winged past my face into the grass, and I tossed a handful of ice in what I believed was his direction. It was so satisfying, the way the ice moved through the air, and how each piece seemed like the physical embodiment of a wish that I was making, hoping that it would connect with Wage and knock him silly. I saw him roll in the grass and then run toward the merry-go-round, and I side-armed a piece of ice. It smacked against his arm and I heard him mutter, "Shit!" I ran back to the bag of ice and reloaded, confident in my aim. I hit him three more times, once in the mouth, the satisfying sound of it clacking against his teeth, and he bounced a piece of ice off my ear, which made me dizzy and nauseated. When the ice had been exhausted, melted into the earth, no trace of our having ever been there, we made out in the bushes, the tips of our fingers like a dead person's, our skin tender and angry. I managed to get his pants down, and though it was thrilling, it wasn't as good as the ice fight. Once it was over, we sheepishly crawled out of the bushes, brushed ourselves off, and sat on either end of a seesaw. We talked in low whispers to avoid detection.

"If a cop comes by," Wage said, "tell him that you just found out you were pregnant and we're trying to decide what to do about it." I decided that Wage was smarter than anyone gave him credit for and I felt smarter for having discovered this.

"I have to get a job," I said. "I want to keep seeing you," he said. We agreed that I would get a job and we would keep seeing each other. He got off the seesaw without warning and I slammed onto the ground. He ran over to me and asked if it hurt and I said that it did not hurt as much as I wanted it to. We made out again, my mouth swollen and tingling, and then we walked away in opposite directions. As I passed by the same houses I had passed before, I pushed an imaginary button that brought everyone inside back to life.

I got a job at the Dixie Freeze, making cones and handling change. I loved the sound of the register making decisions, and I wondered if it was embarrassing to admit that you enjoyed working retail. People don't want you; they want the thing that you're holding, and that makes things so much easier.

I met up with Wage three or four nights a week, different locations, bags of ice weighing him down. We'd throw out our arms and make anonymous bruises on our bodies and then we'd find some hidden place to put ourselves together.

"How can you get away at night?" I asked. "Doesn't Julie get suspicious?" He kept touching my hair, pulling his fingers through it, which normally I don't like but it was okay with him. "We sleep in different rooms," he said. "I go out my window and she doesn't even know I'm gone."

"You sleep in different rooms?" I said.

"I talk in my sleep," he said, not really paying attention to the conversation. "It freaks Julie out."

One night, hiding up in the branches of a tree, dogs circling suspiciously beneath us, Wage asked me to tell him something strange. "It doesn't matter what," he said. "Just something that you don't tell other people." My legs were going numb from being in one position for so long, but I ignored it and tried to think of what I should tell him.

"When I was a sophomore in high school," I finally said, "I got invited by some big-shot senior to go to prom. My sister was a senior and she didn't get asked so it was kind of weird for the whole week leading up to it. That night, I got really drunk and got into a fight with the guy, who was an idiot, and so I just came home and everybody was already asleep and the house was dead quiet. I went into the room that my sister and I shared and I could tell she was awake, but she wouldn't say anything. I put my hands under her shirt and I was trying to kiss her and she told me to go to bed. And I don't know why, but I wouldn't stop. I was trying to kiss her and she kept turning her head away, until finally I got into my bed and went to sleep. The next day, she didn't say a word about it, and I thought maybe I had dreamed it all. And I'm still not exactly sure if it really happened. When my sister is on her deathbed, I'm going to ask her about it and maybe then I'll finally find out."

"You tried to kiss your sister?" he asked, and I nodded.

"I tried to kiss your sister, too," he said, as if it was confusing to him that we had both done something similar.

"When?" I asked, genuinely intrigued, the idea of his mouth against my sister's.

"Some party at Eddie's house, I think," he said. "We were in the kitchen and it was late and I tried to kiss her and she giggled and pushed me away."

"Are you sure that it really happened?"

"Yeah, because she told Sammy about it and he told me that he would kick the shit out of me if I tried it again."

We threw acorns at the dogs below us until they scattered, and then we went our separate ways.

* * *

Of course, everyone in town found out about us and everyone in town hated us and everyone in town hated me a little more than they hated Wage. That's the way it works, I guess. At dinner with my sister and Sammy, there was nothing but the clanging of silverware against plates.

"What?" I finally said. "Did you not expect this?" My sister shook her head. "You steal everything," she said. "You just take things and it doesn't matter if you really want them. You just take them to see what it feels like in your hands." She pushed away from the table and walked off. I looked at Sammy, who was focused on his food.

"Wage tried to kiss her, you know," I told him, and he nodded. "I know," he said. "So you're not his first choice." He finished his meal and walked away from the table, and, with a wide motion of my arms, I swept all the dishes onto the floor, the glass and ceramic shattering and splintering at my feet. I waited for someone to come running into the room, to see the mess I had made, but no one came. I figured it was time that I found somewhere else to live.

Julie made Wage move out and so he got a tiny apartment in the town square. I grabbed my computer and one of the fans and walked awkwardly through town until I was at his door. Suddenly, we were together and there was no point in meeting in the middle of the night in public places.

I made cones and took people's money and Wage stayed at the apartment and typed on his computer. It turns out he wrote original content for some website about electronic gadgets. It turns out they paid him a lot of money to do this. "I could buy a lot of things that I don't need," he said. We bought bags of ice and left tiny dents in the walls of the apartment, pools of water on the floor. My arm was nearly paralyzed from throwing and Wage had chipped a tooth that he did not bother to fix. When we went outside, we carried ice in our pockets, which melted and left our pants embarrassingly damp, though we did not care. We took a clock radio apart and made it look like a bomb and left it in front of the county courthouse. The next day, we checked the newspapers and there was no mention of it. We began to get the impression that people, if asked, did not take us seriously.

On my days off, Wage got irritated with me, sitting in front of my fan, wishing I had a joint to smoke. "You breathe so loud," he said. "It's distracting. Julie did not breathe at all when we were together." I told him that this was impossible and he said, "It sounds impossible when I say it out loud, but that doesn't mean it's not true." He took his computer into the closet and shut the door behind him.

In bed, after we had fucked and we finally fell asleep, Wage made tiny yelps, without interruption, for the entire night. It sounded like he was being bitten by small animals in his dreams, and I found that I could not sleep beside him without imagining that, in his dreams, it was me who was biting him.

"I thought you said you talked in your sleep," I asked him in the morning.

"I do," he said. I asked him what language he thought those sounds were, and he said, "A language that you do not understand." For a split second, I thought about kicking him in the gut and leaving him on the floor, but then I realized I had nowhere else to go. Instead, I bent his finger back at an awkward angle and, as he yelped in pain, I kissed him with so much force that our teeth clacked together. I felt him get hard at the same time that his legs turned to rubber. "Do you understand that?" I asked. He smiled and then nodded. "Yes," he answered, "I understand."

Julie and my sister came by the Dixie Freeze and I instinctively reached for something heavy, expecting a fight. "We just want to talk," they said, and I told them to give me five dollars each, and when they did, I pocketed it and told my manager I was taking a fifteen-minute break.

"I miss him," Julie said. I nodded and looked at her like, *That's not going to get you your five dollars back.* My sister touched my arm and motioned toward the sky or maybe some building in the distance. "This is just some place for you to pass the time," she said. "We live here and we'll still be living here when you move on." I shook my head. I wasn't allowed to be happy, just because I didn't have a place of my own to live?

"That's not it," Julie said, "but do you have to make other people miserable in order for you to be happy?" I stood up and walked back to my register. "You were miserable long before I ever showed up," I said. Julie started to cry and my sister put her arms around her. I made myself a cone of soft-serve and went into the employee bathroom. I smeared the ice cream all over my face and hoped that in a few minutes I would not want to kill some-one nearly as much as I did at that moment. When it had passed, I washed my face, and when I walked out of the bathroom, my sister and Julie were gone. I went back to my register and touched the buttons to add up numbers too large to mean anything.

It wasn't more than a few days later that Wage decided he was going back to Julie. "I think if we stay together," he said, "we might end up doing something that would get us in a lot of trouble." I grabbed his shoes out of the closet and tied the shoelaces together in complicated knots to slow him down. He packed up his computer and some clothes, ashamed to look at me, and I took out an ice tray from the freezer and emptied the cubes into the sink. I threw one of the cubes and it landed flush against the back of Wage's head. He shrugged from the pain of it but kept on packing. I threw another piece and it missed and cracked the mirror in the bedroom. I threw another piece, and then another, and by the time the sink was emptied of ice, Wage's nose was bleeding, and I thought it wouldn't be so bad if I was dead.

"The rent for the apartment is paid up for the rest of the month," he said. "You can stay." I guessed this was what it felt like to love something, wanting to kill it for leaving you, and I kissed him so hard that my mouth was smeared with his blood.

"I'm already wishing I wasn't leaving," he said, and then he left. I ran to the freezer and took two more cubes of ice and held one in each hand, my fist squeezing them into diamonds. I squeezed until the thing that I held had disappeared and then I lay flat on the ground and stared up at the ceiling.

I thought about that night after the prom, how I'd forced myself on my sister, wanted so badly to be against her. I remembered how she had said, almost crying, "You're going to hate yourself so much for doing this." I pulled away from her, stunned, and I whispered, "You think I don't know that?" I felt the anger become dense inside of my chest and then I walked over to my own bed and crawled under the sheets. I kept my back to my sister's bed, but my eyes were wide open. I lay there and waited for her to come over to my bed, to place her hands on me, and to make me feel happy. The entire night, I lay there and waited, but she never came, and I wished that I had only tried harder, had made myself so necessary that I could not be refused.

Baby, You're Gonna Be Mine

Gina received a call from Adam, her only child, at 3 A.M., more than two months since she'd last heard from him. In the dreamlike moments after she answered the phone, listening to him talk over a gaggle of voices in the background, she struggled to remember what he even looked like. She sketched and resketched her memory of his face, his dark, curly hair that framed his huge brown eyes and his costume-big nose that, even as a child, dominated his face as if he were a Muppet, and his mouth, always held in the slightest suggestion of a frown. There he was, finally, her son, in her mind, and she listened as he informed her that his band, Dead Finches, was breaking up, this very moment, and he needed to stay with her for three months.

"All of our equipment got stolen, Mom," he told her. "All three of my guitars, the entire drum kit, even the fucking tambourine. Right out of the goddamn trailer while we ate some dinner. We don't have the kind of money to get new stuff. We're just starting the tour, day two of the fucking tour. We're done."

One of the voices in the background, which she recognized

as Marty, Adam's best friend since grade school, said, "We're not done, man. Don't say that."

"We're done," Adam said to his mother, who had not said a single word during this entire phone call. His voice sounded far away for a second as he must have turned to Marty. "Sorry, dude, we're done. I'm done. And if *I'm* done, yeah, *we're* done."

Finally, Gina spoke, her voice scratchy from sleep, sounding bitchier than she had intended. "Adam, why do you need to stay with me?"

"Because, Jesus, Mom, I'm subletting my apartment to these two European dudes while I was supposed to be on tour, and I can't go back for another three months. We signed a contract and everything, so I'm kind of stuck."

"Can't you stay with Marty?" she asked, the desperation in her voice so clear that she didn't even try to excuse it.

"Mom, I can't be around these guys right now. It's over. We're dead. I wanna be dead by myself, or with you, I guess. Just for three months."

"Okay, then," she said, trying to keep him from the ragged anger that she knew was right on the surface of his entire adult life. "You can come."

"I'm in Portland," he said. "Can you get me a plane ticket to Tennessee?"

"Oh, God, Adam, that's going to be expensive."

"I'll pay you back," he whined, and she heard the drummer, Jody, say, "Get off the fucking phone, Adam. We have to talk about this."

"I'll buy one," she said. "For tomorrow. I'll e-mail you the details in the morning."

"I love you, Mom," he said.

"I love you, too, Peanut," she replied, but he had maybe already hung up. She called out, "Adam?" and it was clear that he was gone.

Two hundred and eighty-five dollars later, she e-mailed her son the plane ticket and realized that, in less than a day, he would be in front of her, his shoulders slumped with heavy bags filled with wrinkled clothes, guitarless. She walked into the room that had once been his, which she had turned into her office. She went through the room, collecting any important papers or financial records, and then shuffled them together and walked back to her bedroom. She opened up the gun safe that her husband, three years dead from cancer, had filled with all manner of rifles and handguns, firearms that he had never once, to her knowledge, fired.

She had taken the guns to the police department the day after the funeral, and she remembered how Adam had yelled at her for doing it. "I didn't feel safe having those guns in the house without your father keeping watch over them," she had told him, but he angrily muttered obscenities and then said, "Those were my birthright," without a hint of self-awareness. Adam, she knew from the earliest age, could not be trusted with anything that had the potential to ruin a life. "At the very least," he said, finally coming to the truth, "we could have sold them. Split it fifty-fifty."

Now, the gun safe was empty save for some jewelry, a thousand dollars in cash, and some photo albums. She placed the papers into the safe, like dropping a rock into a black hole, and closed it.

Gina took some sheets from the closet and went back into the office. She unfolded the sleeper sofa and made a bed for Adam. Unable to sleep, she sat down at the desk and booted up her computer. She went onto YouTube and typed in "Dead Finches." And what came back to her, from her simple request, were hundreds of little squares of images, many of them featuring her son's dark eyes staring back at her.

Dead Finches had formed when Adam was in high school, and Gina could remember driving the entire band to Nashville for all-ages shows at Lucy's Record Shop, waiting in the van until they were done. She remembered the smell of sweat coming off the boys in jagged waves, almost overpowering her, making her swerve the van if she wasn't careful. She would listen to them excitedly talk about the songs that worked and the ones that didn't. She watched, in her rearview mirror, her son smiling, his face as open and as happy as she'd ever seen it before or since.

Adam decided against college, which drove his father absolutely crazy and did not surprise Gina in the slightest, and the band released two albums on their own nonexistent label and toured nonstop, Adam returning from the road looking twenty pounds lighter, his hands shaking, until Sub Pop miraculously signed them. They got more and more popular, as popular as any indie band could get, enough that people her own age had heard of the band. And then one of their songs, "Baby, You're Gonna Be Mine," was used in a beer commercial that played during the Super Bowl and subsequently made it to number seven on the Top 40, which made Adam and his friends an obscene amount of money. And it made Gina so happy, to see her son, if not happy, at least rewarded for his intense belief that he deserved attention. Adam visited when he had time or the inclination, which was almost never, but she would play his CDs on her stereo while she made dinner and she would hear the weird time capsule that kept his voice perfect and wonderful, as smooth as an R&B singer's that could instantly turn sharp and punk rock.

The rest of the story went poorly, and Gina tried not to think of it, her husband constantly asking Adam why he needed to borrow money when the kid had a huge apartment in Portland and wore clothes so thin and plain that they had to cost hundreds of dollars to achieve that kind of simplicity. "Where did those millions go, son?" he would ask, and Adam would shake his head, so angry, and say, "It was never millions. You always think it was millions. It was just hundreds of thousands of dollars. And it's gone. It's all gone."

No one bought albums any longer, no one paid for music, and so the only money left was in licensing and touring. So Adam toured, nonstop, putting out albums only as an excuse to get back on the road. And this had been going on for nearly a decade, less and less money, Adam singing songs that sounded like things he would have thrown away when the band first started. Their last album had a song called "Baby, You Are Also Gonna Be Mine," and Gina always skipped right past it when it was cued up on her iPod, had never once listened to it.

Now, in her office, she clicked on the music video for "Baby, You're Gonna Be Mine," and she watched her son strum his guitar and then sing, in that dreamlike, smooth voice, "Baby, you're gonna be mine / We can leave all this sadness behind / Baby, you're gonna be mine / Until the end, the end, the end, of time." He had on a baby-blue T-shirt that had the word *Gina* in black, block letters printed upside down. "Where'd you get that shirt?" she had asked him the first time she'd seen the video. "I had it made," he said. "I spent my own money to have it made."

"Why?" she asked him.

"'Cause I love you; 'cause it's a secret just for you," he said, smiling.

As she watched the video again, the sun now rising, she stared at her son and slowly turned him upside down in her mind, until her name was in front of her, the message received.

At the airport, she watched Adam descend the escalator; he was clicking away on his phone, not even bothering to look for her. He took three steps off the escalator, following the traffic, and she called for him, touched his arm. He put his phone away and hugged her, smiling.

"How was your flight?" she asked.

"Okay, considering my life is over," he said. "It's actually kind of nice to fly without having to deal with carrying on a fucking guitar."

"Well, that's looking on the bright side," she admitted.

"It's what I do best," he said.

At baggage claim, they waited for his duffel bag, olive green and stuffed so full that it seemed like his entire apartment would explode from the bag, all four walls included. Adam hefted the bag with some difficulty. "Getting old," he grunted, and they walked to the parking garage and loaded the bag into Gina's car.

They settled into their seats, buckled up, and just before Gina started the engine, she turned to Adam to ask about lunch options and noticed that he was crying. "Adam?" she asked, but now he was shaking, sobbing, unapologetically breaking down. She reached for him. "Peanut?" she said.

"Could you just get me home?" he asked, turning away from her.

"Sure, Peanut," she said, and she pulled out of the garage with some haste. When she paid the attendant, the man looked past her at Adam, still crying so loudly, and then raised his eyebrows, which seemed unprofessional to Gina.

"His band just broke up," she said, and the man raised his hands as if he was being mugged but he wasn't entirely convinced.

For the entire hour-and-a-half drive home, Adam cried, stuttering sobs; at times it seemed that he had calmed, his moans drying out and normalizing, before he would start up again. It seemed to Gina, from having watched a few movies on the topic, that he was trying to kick a heroin habit, the way he contorted his body, still belted to his seat, into so many different positions. Was it withdrawal or loss that was causing him such unhappiness? She only knew that, if she had lost the one thing that had mattered to her, she might react the same way. But no, she admitted, probably not this extravagant grief. Not her.

When they finally made it home, idling in the driveway, Gina unbuckled her seat belt and leaned over to Adam. "Peanut," she said, hugging him, rubbing his back. "We're home. You're home, and it'll all be okay."

He looked at her finally, his face so blotchy that it looked like he was deathly allergic to his own sadness. "I think I should sleep," he said. "I'm really tired is all."

"You're not hungry?" she asked.

"I'm more tired than I am hungry," he said. He unbuckled his seat belt, adjusted his neck with several deliberate movements, and then stepped out of the car, already walking to the front door. His gait suggested that he was sleepwalking and could not be disturbed, so Gina awkwardly hopped out of the car, fumbling with her keys, and ran ahead of him to unlock the front door, which she pushed open just in time so that Adam didn't even have to break stride.

"I turned your room into my office, Peanut," she said, calling to him as he ascended the stairs. "But there's a sofa bed and a closet for your stuff. I made it all up for you."

He raised his hand, like he was pledging an oath, his back still to her, still rising to the top floor, and Gina leaned against the frame of the front door. She watched him shuffle into the office, quietly shut the door, and Gina waited for a few minutes to make sure that nothing was going wrong, listened carefully for more crying. Finding only silence, she remembered his bag in the car. She went back to the trunk, struggled with the bag, the awkward, sharp bulges banging against her legs, and finally deposited it at the foot of the steps. She was breathing hard, the tenseness of the situation finally overwhelming her. Though she never napped, she walked to her own bedroom, pulled down the sheets, and climbed, fully clothed, into the bed and fell into a dreamless, deep sleep.

When she awoke, it was six in the evening, and she listened to the sound of activity downstairs, which startled her. She walked into the kitchen to find Adam moving from the stove back to the kitchen counter, a whirl of activity. The air smelled of rosemary and rendered fat.

"Mom!" Adam shouted over the sound of sizzling meat. "I'm making dinner. Sit down. It's almost ready."

Still dazed from sleeping the day away, Gina went to the dining room table, where she could watch as Adam took a flank steak, which had been in her freezer that morning, and expertly sliced it into thin strips. He then used a bread knife to cut open several dinner rolls and then slathered them with some kind of mustard sauce before topping it with spinach.

"When did you learn to cook?" she called out to him.

"I mostly watch cooking shows," he said. "It calms me to watch people make food. I pick stuff up now and again. This is flank steak, marinated in olive oil and rosemary, with a mustard-tarragon sauce and arugula on a baguette. But you didn't have any tarragon or arugula or baguette, so I improvised."

"I don't keep that kind of stuff on hand," she said.

"It's okay. We can stock up tomorrow," he answered as he plated and served the meal, which apparently was only going to be these steak sandwiches and some potato chips that he had taken out of the freezer, where Gina kept them to make sure they stayed fresh. Adam was watching her, smiling broadly, waiting for her to try it, so she took a bite of the sandwich and was amazed by how good it was. The steak was perfectly cooked and the rosemary made it taste much fancier than anything she would have made.

"It's wonderful, Peanut," she said, and he shrugged, still smiling.

"It's that British chef's recipe," he said.

"The mean one?" she asked.

"No, not him. The young one. He's real handsome."

"I don't know any handsome British chefs," she replied, but Adam seemed not to hear her. He was trembling, not touching his sandwich, twisting his head from side to side as if trying to assuage a crick in his neck.

"Are you okay, Peanut?" she asked, and he again seemed not to hear. She took another bite of her sandwich, which was still delicious, and ate a handful of cold potato chips. Finally, Adam turned to her and said, "Did you say something?"

"I asked if you were okay."

"I am. I'm fine. I'm happy. I . . . never mind."

"No, what?" Gina asked.

"I found some coke in my bag that I didn't even know I had, just a tiny amount, but I took it and it's made me feel a lot better."

"Oh, Peanut, you can't be doing that here," she said.

"I don't do coke," he said, as if she didn't understand, never understood. "That's why it was so weird to find it. I mean, I used to do it a lot, but I'd stopped a while back, but it just turned up in my bag. It's good that the airport guys didn't find it, huh? Actually, it gives me some reservations about the thoroughness of their work, if they can't find drugs in people's bags. What else are they missing, you know?"

"You can't do drugs in my house. I can't have you doing that to yourself," she said, knowing that, if he refused or promised but then backslid, there was little that she would actually do to punish him. He was an adult. What could she do? She'd taken him back into her home. It seemed impossible to send him back out.

He might, she now realized, never leave.

"I won't. I promise. It's gone now, the coke. I just needed something to get over the trauma of the band breaking up.

These three months are going to be therapeutic, I think. I can get my life in order and then, when I go back to Portland, I'll be ready for what comes next."

The thought of Adam going through her kitchen, turning her nights into days, forever present in a house that she had gotten used to being alone in, once again made her nervous. She had not considered the physical presence of him, his body always arranged on a piece of furniture with such apathy and sloth that it seemed barely able to hold his liquid form.

"I do want you to rest, to get yourself back in a good frame of mind," Gina said, already prepared for the rest of the evening to be ruined. "But I think three months is long enough that you should look for work."

Adam paused, considering his mother's advice, and then picked up his sandwich. He took a small bite, nodded his approval, and then set the sandwich back down. "What now?" he said.

"A job, maybe?" she asked.

"Well, I just took that coke, so I won't pass any drug tests for a while. Maybe in a month or so I can look. I'll check online."

"Well, I know Martha Morgan's son runs a landscaping company. I don't think, if I asked her to tell him that you need work, that he'd make you do a drug test. He runs it all himself. I don't think he's set up for drug testing."

"Landscaping," Adam said, nodding. He did not seem able to blink. "Maybe. Sure, maybe."

This was as much as Gina could ask for on the first day of Adam's return home. He was no longer crying uncontrollably. He was considering work. He had made dinner. Gina would accept this with gratitude.

The next day, Gina let Adam sleep as long as he wanted, and she started to return to her daily routine. She realized, with some embarrassment, that there was little that anchored her to the world. She ate and kept her house cleaned. She watched some TV. She played card games on the computer, though Adam's presence in the office now kept her from that particular pleasure. She had never had many friends; her husband was her closest confidant, and even he was sometimes so distant from her. But somehow, someway, she had made a life for herself without her husband, without her son, and she had carefully cultivated it. Now, with Adam in the house, his twisted form snoring beneath thin sheets in his old bedroom, she realized how sad her life might seem to him. Then she realized that Adam, in his state of grief, would probably not notice the particulars of her routine. She was safe from scrutiny, an unintended benefit of her son's self-absorption.

She wiped down the kitchen counter and rearranged the pantry; at half past one, she heard Adam making noise upstairs. He was excavating, searching, she could tell by the sound of objects being precariously lifted and dropped. A few minutes later, she heard the strumming of a guitar, and she took it as a cue to check on him.

When she opened the door, Adam reacted as if he had been abusing himself. The reverberation of the last plucked string echoed in the silence between them. Finally, Adam said, "I found my old guitar." He held it up, a child's model, comically small in Adam's giant hands.

"I see. I'm glad I kept it," she replied. "What was that you were playing?"

"Nothing much," he said, blushing. "It's just a slowed-down

version of 'Girls Just Want to Have Fun.' I find it helps calm me down."

"Cyndi Lauper?" Gina asked, feeling confident that she had it right.

Adam nodded, though Gina could not tell if he was happy or sad that she knew the song. Then, like a funeral dirge, Adam began to strum the guitar again and sing, "I come home, in the morning light, my mother says *when you gonna live your life right,*" his voice so clean and sad that it made Gina want to cry.

Adam then stopped playing, considered something, and plucked a tune that was jangly and fast, fingerpicking without effort. "Bob Dylan," he said to his mother, and then he sang, "It don't even matter to me where you're wakin' up tomorrow / But, Mama, you're just on my mind."

"You know a lot of mother songs," she remarked.

"Well," he said, continuing to play the guitar, "I don't think that's his biological mother that he's referring to." He played a little longer, then nodded. "Maybe, though. Interesting enough."

"I like Bob Dylan," she offered.

"That's what I should have done from the beginning," he said. "Solo. Just me and my guitar. It would have been so much easier. I wouldn't have to split the money. Wouldn't have to share the women. Wouldn't have to drive around in some beat-up van with people I hate. Wouldn't have to share the spot-light."

Gina thought that Adam had rarely shared the spotlight, even in a band. She could not imagine what his life would have been like if it had been only him in the music videos. Though she allowed that he had always deserved the attention, had been the unique talent in the band.

"So," Adam finally said, putting the guitar on the bed. "How is this going to work?"

"How is what going to work?" she asked.

"This," he said, gesturing to the walls of the room. "You and me in the house together. Do we divide up the chores? Do you give me an allowance? Do I have a curfew? Do we watch TV together every night?"

"You're an adult now, Peanut," she replied. "I'm happy to have you here for the time being. But I'm on a fixed income. I can't give you much money. I think it's best if you look for a job, something to keep you busy, so you're not just stuck in the house all day. And you'll have some spending money while you figure out what you're going to do next."

"I bet if I played a few solo concerts in Nashville, I could make some good money," he said, eyeing the old, child-sized guitar, wondering if it would hold up to a performance or two.

"I think you need to take a little break from music. Just get things in order so that, when it's time to go back to your place in Portland, you're mentally prepared for your new life."

"I don't have any other skills, Mom," he said, defiantly. "I've played music since I was a teenager. I don't have a college diploma. I haven't had a nine-to-five job ever."

"Well, I know you could get this landscaping job. You used to cut our grass," she offered.

"Fuck," Adam said softly, shaking his head. It was clear to Gina that he thought she didn't understand his particular unhappiness, but he was wrong. She understood exactly what was happening, that he had devoted his life to something that had ended before he was ready. And now he was alone. She knew this. She knew what it felt like. She also knew there was nothing to be done for it. You simply picked something else and lived with it.

"You'll be outside, working with your hands. You'll make some money. You'll be tired at the end of the day and you'll sleep well."

"It sounds so awful," he admitted, "but, fine, okay, I'll do it."

"Good," she said. Now she would call an old friend that she did not know very well anymore and beg for a job for her son. It would be humiliating, to ask the favor, to admit that her son was in need of some kind of structure. But it would clear up the space in the house, would reduce the amount of time that they were together, wondering where they went wrong.

"Can I have an advance on my pay?" Adam asked. "I'd like to buy some beer today."

Gina went to find her purse, and she heard Adam again playing that pressed-wood guitar, exorcising sounds from it that were so carelessly perfect.

Three days later, Gina packed a lunch for Adam as he waited on the front porch for his ride to work. He wore a pair of hiking shorts and a stained gray T-shirt that said JESSE JACKSON FOR PRESIDENT in red letters. He had covered himself in so much sunscreen that he looked like some kind of cave-dwelling creature, unused to light.

"I'm nervous," he admitted, when Gina brought him the minicooler, fruit, bologna sandwiches, two bags of chips, some granola bars, a bottle of Gatorade. "I feel like the technology of lawn care has gone right past me and I won't be able to keep up with the other guys. I haven't mowed a lawn since I was a teenager. I can just see all the other guys showing me how to use the weedeater and laughing behind my back."

Staring at him in his tiny shorts, his legs so pale and, strangely, hairless, Gina felt the stabbing pain of not being able to control the life of your child. It was like he was five years old, waiting for the bus to take him to kindergarten. He had that same lost, faraway look on his face, trying so hard to reassure Gina that he wasn't terrified. She wanted to hug him. So she did. She leaned down and kissed his cheek, holding him for as long as he would allow. "You'll be fine," she said.

"I better be," Adam said, softly.

It had been a huge embarrassment, calling Martha Morgan, asking for charity. "Well, Tyler is always looking for good help," Martha had said cautiously, after expressing surprise at hearing from Gina. "But is Adam really interested in this kind of work? Shouldn't he be producing music or doing jingles for an advertising company?"

"He wants to do something physical," Gina lied. "He wants to work with his hands."

"That's great," Martha said. "Not enough men are willing to get dirty, to really work for their money."

"That's so true," Gina replied, hating herself.

Her own husband had spent his entire adult life hating work, saving money for retirement, dying almost immediately after he stopped working. "Only fools work hard for their money," he would say, defeated. "Rich people, the money just comes to them." Like Adam, she had thought at the time, cashing residual checks so large that it seemed obscene. But what happened when the money stopped coming to you? What then?

A few minutes later, a huge truck, pulling a trailer filled with all manner of lawn care equipment, a bit of overkill it seemed to Gina, parked in front of the house. Gina heard her son gulp, the action so loud it seemed comical. She knew not to touch him, to show affection. Martha Morgan's son, Tyler, so confident that his chest seemed puffed up to a ridiculous level, strode toward Adam, who quickly picked up his cooler and ran over to the truck. Tyler waved to Gina, who waved back, and then he shook Adam's hand. He pointed to Adam's shirt, shaking his head, and then snapped his fingers. From the truck, which was filled with middle-aged Hispanic men, an orange T-shirt flew out the window and Tyler caught it without looking. He handed it to Adam, who looked back toward his mom and then, after a slight hesitation, took off his Jesse Jackson shirt, revealing his pale, concave chest, and pulled the orange T-shirt, which read MORGAN'S LANDSCAPING, over his head. It was a size or two larger than it should be, but Adam did not complain. One of the men in the truck got out and levered the seat so that Adam could climb into the back, which took some effort. As the truck drove off, Gina waved but could not see Adam clearly enough to know if he waved back.

She spent the rest of the day sitting at her dining room table, waiting for Adam to call, to tell her to come pick him up, that he had quit or been fired. When five o'clock came and went, she worried that something had happened to him. At 6:30, she heard the rattling equipment in the trailer, and she ran to the porch to find the truck coming to a stop in front of her house. Adam crawled out of the truck, shook hands with one of the other men, and then stood on the sidewalk while Tyler strode with great purpose toward him. Tyler counted out a handful of money and gave it over to Adam, who immediately folded it and put it in the pocket of his shorts. Tyler clapped Adam on the back, which made Adam recoil from the impact, his shoulders rising up to his ears, and then he carried his cooler to the front porch, right past Gina. Tyler waved again to Gina, who only nodded, walking inside and closing the door behind her.

"How was it?" she asked, almost crying.

"Fine," he said. "Really hard work. Lots of carrying stuff from place to place. I'm going to be sore tomorrow, I'm sure. The other guys were nice, though. None of them really speak much English, so that might have been why I think they're nice. One of them gave me a cigarette during a water break. Tyler told them that I was a rock star, which was humiliating, but they had no idea what he was talking about."

"Do you want dinner?" she asked.

"I'm just going to drink a beer and sit in the bathtub and take some Advil and go to bed. I gotta be ready to go again tomorrow." He fished a beer from the fridge and then slowly trudged upstairs. He stopped halfway up and then walked back down. He reached into his pocket and produced the money. He took one of the twenties and handed it to Gina. "This is to pay back the money you loaned me for that beer," he said. Gina accepted it, though she didn't want the money. Then he hugged her; he smelled so musky, so earthy.

"I love you, Mom," he said.

"I love you, too, Peanut," she replied.

Thirty minutes later, after Adam had run a bath in which he was still soaking, Gina ate her dinner and watched a TV show; suddenly, she heard Adam upstairs, that loud, jagged crying, bouncing around the tile of the bathroom. He cried for nearly forty-five minutes, long enough that he turned the water back on to heat up the tub again, but Gina let it happen, knew not to disturb him. He was coming to terms with something, and it would not help to make herself known. When there was silence, she turned off the TV, slowly crept up the stairs, and slipped into her own bedroom, realizing that she had been holding her breath the whole time.

After a few days of stability, Adam finding landscaping to be a fairly straightforward job that suited his focus, he called Gina to say that he was going out for drinks with the other guys. "But they don't speak English, right? What are you going to talk about?" she asked, not wanting him to be drinking out in the larger world, preferring that he have a few beers in the bathtub and cry himself into exhaustion. That, she reasoned, was manageable. She could locate him, could understand him. The thought of him at some bar, holding on to the money he had just earned, made her nervous.

"They know enough English. They know more English than I know Spanish, right? They asked me. That's good. It means that they accept me. I'm going to just have a few drinks."

"Okay, Peanut. I'll leave the light on in the hallway. Don't stay out too long."

At eleven o'clock, no shows left to watch, nothing left to clean, still no sign of Adam, she considered getting in her car and driving around until she found him. She had called his cell six times, always going straight to voice mail but she was hip enough to know not to leave a message; she imagined him rolling his eyes as he listened to the first few words of each message, her voice growing more and more quavery with each call.

Still, she was worried, paced the kitchen, snacked on some candied bacon that Adam had made on a lark the day before. She thought that the other men might have tricked him, taken him to some kind of underground fighting club and stolen his money. And then she realized that it was only eleven o'clock, late for her but not for a man who mowed grass all day and drank beer all night. She would have to adjust her expectations to accommodate her son's new circumstances.

She went to her bedroom, and, as she prepared for sleep, she listened to the debut Dead Finches album, her son's voice reassuring her that he would return. By the time she had fallen asleep, she had forgotten that her son was anywhere other than inside her own head.

She awoke to the sound of conversation coming from downstairs, whispery voices that were much louder than whispers should be. Drunk whispering, she understood it to be. She recognized Adam's voice and almost walked out to the hallway to check on him, but then she made out the other voice, a woman's, and she pulled the covers up to her chin. The woman was laughing, and Gina heard the fridge open, beer bottles clinking, and then her drunk son and this drunk woman climbed the stairs, giggling the whole way up. Gina was frozen in place, knew she should go back to sleep, but instead she stared at the clock, counting the hours until Adam had to be back at work, finding the number so small that it seemed pointless to do anything. A few minutes later, Gina heard, to her own horror, the sound of the sofa bed creaking with effort, the woman moaning. It went on and on, grunting and creaking, for what felt like hours, and Gina turned on the TV in her bedroom, flipped to a cooking show featuring an impossibly attractive celebrity chef, and turned the volume as loud as necessary to drown out the sound coming from her office. But she could still hear them, impossible not to.

When it was over, some more laughing, whispers, Gina turned off the TV. She wondered if she could sleep but found that the stress of the situation had exhausted her. She needed to use the restroom, but she closed her eyes and waited for the morning. Just before she drifted off, she heard her son's voice and the strumming of that goddamned kid guitar.

"Baby, you're gonna be mine," he sang, and Gina swore under her breath and placed a pillow over her head.

At 6:30 the next morning, nothing left but to grit her teeth and do this thing, Gina knocked on her son's door.

"Yes," the unknown woman answered through the closed door.

"Is Adam in there?" Gina asked, as politely as she could.

"He's asleep."

"Could you wake him?" Gina asked.

"He's out cold," the woman said.

"Are you dressed?" Gina asked, waiting for the moment that she didn't have to ask another question.

"Sort of," the woman replied.

Gina opened the door and found Adam lying on his back, his mouth open like a cat could crawl into it and live there. The woman was shockingly young, her face so plain and unlined that it momentarily stole Gina's breath.

"How old are you?" she asked, fearing the police, all kinds of unpleasant charges, but the woman replied, "Twenty-one, as of last night."

"Oh, thank God," Gina replied.

"It was a big birthday party," the girl admitted, smiling, as if she and Gina would become good friends with enough time.

"Do you know how old Adam is?" Gina asked, feeling mean.

"Thirty?" the girl guessed.

"He's thirty-six," Gina replied, but the girl did not seem shocked.

"I knew he was older, the stuff he talked about," she said. "My mom has his album. She's gonna freak."

"He has to go to work," Gina said. "They'll be here any minute now."

She nudged Adam, who moaned and then flipped over and pulled the covers over his head. "Not now," he groaned.

"Adam," Gina said. "You have to go to work, right now."

"I'm going to take a sick day," he said.

"You can't take a sick day, Peanut," she said, instantly feeling embarrassed, remembering that this woman was right there. "It doesn't work like that."

"I quit, then," he said.

"Adam," Gina said, wanting so badly to shake her son until his teeth fell out of his mouth, "I begged Martha Morgan, a woman that I don't really like all that much, for her son to hire you. You cannot quit. You have to get up and go to work."

"I'm not going to work, Mom," he said, finally pulling down the sheets, sitting up and wincing at the light and the hour. "I'm not going."

"You are," she said.

"I'm a fucking rock star, Mom. I am not going to push a wheelbarrow around in ninety-degree heat."

"You are not a rock star, Peanut," Gina said, almost shouting. "You're not a rock star anymore. Not for a long time. You are someone who does manual labor and lives with his mother."

"Mom, please," he said, holding his head.

The truck idled at the sidewalk; the horn honked twice.

"Please, Adam. I'm begging you. Go to work."

Adam finally sat up. He stared at his mother with genuine disgust, great fury. He took a deep breath. "Okay," he said.

He stood, put on the clothes from the night before, that bright orange T-shirt, and walked out of the room. He turned to his mother and said, "What you just said was very cruel. It hurt my feelings."

Gina felt her knees weaken. She felt the lifetime frustration of never giving her child what he wanted, of never giving anyone what they wanted. "I'm so sorry," she said, but Adam was already walking down the stairs. He slammed the door shut, and Gina was about to cry when she realized that the woman was still in the room. She looked over at the girl, wearing only a neon-green tank top and rainbow panties, who shrugged and said, "Tough love, you know?"

"Do you want some breakfast?" Gina asked suddenly, not wanting to be alone.

"I would love breakfast," the girl said, raising her arms in the air like she'd just won an election.

The woman, her name was Tina, strangely enough, made coffee, while Gina cooked some scrambled eggs, adding rosemary because she now added rosemary to everything in order to seem fancy, having learned from her son that things like rosemary and tarragon and sea salt and saffron made regular things special.

Tina was taking a break from college, had actually been made to take a semester off after a violation of the honor code. She tried to explain the particulars, involving copying notes for a test, but Gina could not keep up. Still, she was a sweet girl, had big plans for the future involving graphic design, and Gina felt that Tina might be good for her son while also realizing that her son would not be good for Tina.

"How did Adam seem last night?" Gina asked. "When you met him?"

"At first he was really standoffish. He was drinking with these guys from the lawn care place, and I kept flirting with him, trying to get him to open up and have fun. All my friends are at school, and it was my birthday so I just got drunk and tried to make my own friends, but Adam wasn't having it. He said he was really tired, that he worked manual labor, had been doing it for years, and he just wanted to drink."

"He said he'd been doing manual labor for years?" Gina asked.

"Yeah," Tina said, suddenly realizing the lie. "That's right.

And later, when he wouldn't stop talking about how he was a rock star and had just left the band to start a solo career, I didn't even call him on it. Shit. Anyways, I went to sing karaoke and I was really bad, and the crowd started booing me, and that seemed to make him take notice, take pity. He walked up to join me and he sang this Coldplay song perfectly, even better than the Coldplay guy."

Gina knew, from having heard it many times, that Adam hated Coldplay. He hated all British pop singers, for some arbitrary reason.

"That's when he started talking about how he was a rock star, and how he'd hit a rough patch, that he wasn't inspired. He said he was living with his mother, which was kind of an honest thing to admit, kind of baller, actually. I respected that kind of honesty. I'm living with my mom, too. He said you were trying your best, but he felt bad for being here, for disappointing you. Then we started making out and we came back here."

"I *am* trying my best," Gina replied.

"I can tell," Tina said. "My mom always walks into the living room or kitchen and I'm already there and I can just see it on her face that she can't believe this is happening, that I'm not at school, that I'm watching reality TV on her sofa. It's real quick, but I can see how sad she is about it. That's why I like going out at night, to stay away until she's asleep and we don't have to be in the same place."

Gina knew she made this same face when she found Adam, his front half hidden by the open fridge door, digging around for food. She made this face when she walked into her office and found him looking at expensive sneakers on eBay. But she thought that maybe she was better than Tina's mother at hiding this expression of disappointment. She thought that Adam had not noticed because he was so intensely focused on his own unhappiness.

Tina took her plate to the sink and washed it, putting it in the dish rack. "Thanks for breakfast," she said.

"Thank you, Tina," Gina replied.

"I probably won't see you again," Tina admitted. "This was kind of a onetime birthday thing."

"I understand," Gina said.

"Tell Adam good-bye for me," Tina said, and then she walked to her car, parked in Gina's driveway, and drove off, leaving Gina alone, waiting for Adam to return.

That evening, Gina heard the truck rumble to a stop in front of the house, but she stayed at the kitchen counter, working on a cross-word puzzle. After their fight, she knew enough to give Adam his space, the way his body expanded to take on so many edges that, if jostled, sent him into a rage. She heard the door open, and Adam walked into the kitchen. Gina looked up, but Adam walked past her, to the fridge for a beer. She noticed a cut on his leg, the skin around it angry and purple, and she stood up, alarmed.

"Adam," she said, "your leg."

"It's nothing," he said, the words nearly vibrating with frustration. "I cut it on a trimmer. I wasn't concentrating. It's fine."

Without saying another word, he went upstairs to his room. Gina took some comfort in the fact that he did not slam the door shut. A few minutes later, she heard him playing his guitar, lazy cowboy music, and she started gathering the ingredients for a simple dinner. The entire time that she cooked, Adam played guitar, singing in a deep, cartoonish voice. She made out the words *lonesome* and *traveled this whole world* and *orphan*.

"Dinner?" Gina called up to Adam, just loud enough to be heard, her voice bending it into a question, as if Gina wasn't sure what she was offering her son. There was no response.

"Adam?" she said. When there was still no reply, she said, "I'm so sorry about this morning. I'm sorry that I hurt you. I never want to make you feel bad."

She carried the plate upstairs and set it in front of his door. "I love you, Peanut," she said. She took a shower and then got into bed, when she heard Adam's door open slowly, softly creaking, and then close just as quickly.

She and her husband had almost never fought, hardly an unkind word between them, though rarely was the absence of anger filled with anything resembling affection. When they did argue, it was always over Adam, what he was doing with his life, how responsible they were for the person he had become, what they should have done differently.

Her husband would always bring up a single event, when Adam was four. He had found a hammer in the toolbox in the hallway closet and then climbed onto the dresser in their bedroom to remove a small, oval mirror from the wall. He then tap-tap-tapped until the mirror was shattered. Gina had been making dinner and her husband was reading a magazine in the den, and Adam called out for them to come quickly. When they got to the bedroom, Adam was smiling. He placed the hammer on the dresser and then gestured to the broken shards of the mirror, which had belonged to her husband's mother. Before Gina could say anything, her husband ran over to Adam and yanked his arm, which made Adam howl. "You son of a bitch," he shouted at Adam. Gina wedged herself between them and was about to comfort Adam, when the boy took one of the shards of the mirror and dragged it slowly across his cheek, the violence so calmly produced that both Gina and her husband were too stunned to prevent it. A thin line of blood formed on Adam's cheek, and Gina finally picked him up, held him against her, the blood smearing her own face.

Behind her, her husband said angrily, "He did that on purpose, to keep us from punishing him."

"Well," Gina said, kissing Adam, who squirmed in her arms, "it worked."

Early the next morning, Gina looked down the hall to find the plate, now empty of food, nothing but crumbs, sitting outside the door of Adam's room. She smiled, then crept back into bed. Adam soon began his morning routine, getting ready for the day. When the truck pulled up, Gina stayed in her room. She heard the front door open and there was a moment of silence before Adam called up to her, "Bye, Mom," and Gina shouted back, perhaps too loudly, "Bye, Peanut."

After he left, Gina got dressed and went to the supermarket, buying all manner of spices and produce, even some fairly expensive ribeyes. Tomorrow was Sunday, Adam's one day off for the week, so Gina imagined a quiet day at home. Perhaps, in the afternoon, they could visit her husband's grave. She imagined Adam driving the car, the windows down, a Dead Finches song playing on the stereo.

Back at home, she cleaned the bathroom and put fresh sheets on Adam's pull-out bed. She took the pile of his dirty clothes and washed them. In a pocket of one of his pairs of shorts, she found an empty baggie that smelled of pot, but she simply threw it in the trash and did not think of it again. If she had asked him about it, he would say that he had been holding it for one of the other guys in the crew, or that he had found it on the ground while mowing and placed it in his pocket to throw away later. Or, the more she considered it, Adam would simply say that he was just so shocked that weed was this cheap in Tennessee compared with Portland and it had been crazy not to buy some while he was here. And with any of these scenarios, her response would be the same, silence and acceptance.

When Adam returned home from work, he pushed open the door, yelling for her to come quickly.

"What is it?" she said, immediately worried, all the anxiety rushing back to her.

"It's good," he said, holding up his phone, the screen too small for Gina to see what he was talking about. "Come upstairs and I'll show you."

They went to the office and Adam sat down and woke the computer from its sleep mode. "Marty's been e-mailing me ever since I got back here, but I stopped reading them. It was, like, the past, you know, so I didn't want to get caught up in it. But today he called and left a voice mail, and I was driving home with the guys and I checked it."

"What did he say?" she asked.

"Something amazing," he said. He typed an address into

the web browser and then turned the screen so she could see it. "Look."

Save the Dead Finches, the website said. Beside it was a box that read *$42,377.*

"What is this?" she asked. "What does that mean?"

"Marty set up this crowdfunding thing, like donations, I guess. He wrote about how we got all our stuff stolen and couldn't afford to keep the band together. He set up all these incentives for people to donate, like signed CDs and personalized thank-you cards or some such nonsense. Someone paid $5,000 alone for us to play a house show for them and ten of their friends. But it's only been up for four days and already we've got more than $40,000. It's insane. And it's still going. He's been talking to venues and rebooking shows."

"So you're not quitting the band?" she asked.

"Not if we can still make this kind of money. We can still do a tour. We can buy new instruments, better ones."

"That's amazing, Peanut," she said, amazed at how much people were willing to pay to keep her son happy, having thought she was the only one.

"Look," he said, almost jumping out of his seat. He had reloaded the page. "$43,101 now! It won't stop!"

That night, Adam grilled the steaks and made an Argentinian chimichurri. They opened a bottle of merlot that had probably been in the house for more than a decade. Every few minutes, Adam reloaded the crowdfunding page on his cell phone and smiled.

"I thought tomorrow we could go by your father's grave," she said. "Say a prayer. Take flowers."

"Hmm?" he said, staring at his screen, chewing loudly on a piece of steak. "Oh, Mom, I gotta get back to Portland. Marty says that I can stay with him. We gotta practice and all that, get ready for a new tour. I don't think I can stay here."

"You're going to leave tomorrow?" she asked.

"Well, not immediately, but I've got to get myself situated. I'll call Tyler tomorrow to let him know that I can't stay on. That's the right thing to do. The other guys will be bummed, for sure. But they'll understand. They'll be happy for me."

"I hope this makes you see how you need to stay positive, how things work out sometimes," she reminded him.

He nodded, looking back at his phone. "It does. Things do seem to work out for me. It's like, things get really bad, but somehow it always works out."

"Just remember this the next time things get difficult," she said.

"I will," he promised. "I'll remember."

"I liked having you home," she said.

"It was nice," he said. "You've always taken care of me."

"You're my son," she said, as if each time that she asserted this, it became more and more true.

"And you're my mom," he said, holding up his glass of wine.

Three days later, Adam was back in Portland, and Gina had the house all to herself again, almost no trace of Adam to remind her that he had even been there. He had even taken the guitar back home with him, saying that he really loved the tone of the instrument, thought it would make for some good songs. She still had his MORGAN'S LANDSCAPING T-shirt, kept it folded on the dresser in her room, but she regretted laundering it because now it smelled of detergent instead of him.

It was eleven o'clock at night, but she couldn't sleep. She checked the crowdfunding page and saw that the number was even higher than it had been the day before. Several news websites had written about the stunt. One had interviewed Adam and he stated, "It's nice, you know, to remember that you are loved."

Gina went to YouTube and typed in "Dead Finches." All the same videos came up and she scrolled through them. Then she typed a new search phrase, "Dead Finches Bitch, Your Dumb Ass Is Mine," and it brought her to a grainy video of concert footage. She clicked on it and watched the video slowly gain focus as her son stood onstage, tuning an acoustic guitar. The rest of the band had left the stage, only Adam remaining for the final song of the encore. "This is a new song I've been working on. Brand-new, actually," he said, never looking up from his guitar.

Slowly, in a voice so beautiful that it broke her heart every single time, Adam softly sang, "Bitch, your dumb ass is mine." The crowd hooted and hollered but Adam remained intensely focused, gripping the guitar tightly as he strummed. "Don't bother sending a Valentine. Bitch, your dumb ass is mine. Until the end. The end. The end of time."

This was what had become their hit song, only after Adam, with Marty's help, sanded down the original until it was saccharine and hummable and impossible to forget. The faster it got, the happier it sounded, the more popular it became. But Gina had always preferred this version, could hear her son so clearly in the song. It was meant to be slow, rumbling, uncertain. She heard all the anger and frustration in his voice, and yet, underneath that, his singing was so beautiful, so hypnotic, that you believed it truly was a love song. You knew that he was only saying these things because he could not articulate what he truly meant, that kindness always mutated just slightly inside of him and came out wrong. But Gina knew what was in his heart. Her son.

She went back a few seconds in the song and listened to her son sing to a crowd of people, but really to her. "The end," he sang. "The end. The end of time," and Gina knew it was true.

The Horror We Made

The slumber party turned into a horror film and Jess wanted no part of it. As soon as Lanie mentioned the idea, their very own movie, shot overnight, Jess asked if she could handle the camera work. She decided very quickly that life would be easier if there was no trace of her involvement in the footage. Jess had enough smarts to know that slumber parties led to a very specific kind of embarrassment.

"Let me ask Wolfgang," Lanie said, and then she tapped out a text message to her twenty-five-year-old brother, the only source of adult supervision, since Lanie's parents were in Colonial Williamsburg for the weekend. Wolfgang was upstairs in his room listening to sludge metal at such a low volume that it sounded, from Jess's position in the living room, like whales dying. The girls had begged Wolfgang to go somewhere else during the filming, but he had flatly refused. He even confiscated a small portion of their weed in exchange for not telling Lanie's parents what the girls did at the slumber party.

Lanie's phone hummed. "He says no," she said. "He says it's

his camera and it's really expensive and so he's the only one who can touch it." As soon as she finished reading the text, another came through. "He says you can be the monster." The other girls giggled, but Jess thought about it for a second and then said, "Can I wear a mask?" Lanie asked her brother, who responded, "A kind of mask. Sure." Seeing no way out of this, all of them so jumpy from the Adderall they'd snorted earlier in the night, Jess agreed. If she was going to be in a movie, she decided, she'd at least like to be the one holding the knife.

They had been planning the slumber party for weeks. They thought it might be hard to get permission to stay in the house without Lanie's parents to watch over them, but their parents agreed without any reservations, seemed shocked to remember that they had daughters in the first place. The girls' first thought was to have a house party with kegs and loud music and no concept of the consequences of their actions. But Jess and Lanie and Mary Beth and Heather and Wallis were not popular kids. They saw how quickly they would be shuffled into the corner of their own party, overpowered by other sixteen-year-olds who did this kind of thing regularly. The girls decided they would be better off scoring some low-level drugs and watching horror movies all night. These girls, and they always thought of themselves collectively, like a dues-paying club, weren't athletic or exceptionally studious or overly attractive. But they weren't overweight and they weren't Goth and they weren't special ed. They did drugs, but always together and never in a place where someone would take advantage of them. Their grades were good enough to keep their parents happy but not invite the attention of well-meaning teachers. They existed in a no-man's-land where the kinds of boys they wanted to kiss would forget them instantly and treat them like shit around their own friends, and the kinds of boys who wanted to kiss them were too terrified to ask; so they made do with what they had. And what they had was one another and the weird ideas that sat unchallenged in their brains.

The girls went into the kitchen and made radioactive nachos and drank some Mountain Dew Code Red while they planned out the movie. Lanie said the first thing, before a single shot was filmed, was to figure out the deaths. "They need to be, you know, as real as possible. It needs to look like we really got killed and then the Internet will get sued because it's online." Mary Beth and Heather, who were twins and therefore really spooky to look at when they were tweaking because their head tics were in unison, agreed. "We know how to make blood," they said. "We learned it in home ec once when Mrs. Jolly was drunk and said we could pick the lesson for that day." While Lanie wrote things like "blood" and "balloon heads" on a dry-erase board, Wallis made a fake knife with cardboard, aluminum foil, and electrical tape. It took her about ten minutes and looked, according to Lanie, "real as shit." Lanie handed it to Jess, who tested the weight of the weapon in her hand and made a few lame jabbing motions. She was still finding the necessary emotion to play a remorseless killer. She nodded her approval to Lanie, who turned back to Wallis and said, "Make, like, ten more of them. We're gonna need a lot of knives."

After a few more text exchanges between Lanie and her brother, each punctuated by the other girls imploring Lanie to not involve him, Wolfgang had come down the stairs, movie camera in tow, and stood over the girls in a way that did evil things to their buzz. "So you guys want to make a movie," he said, and it was creepy enough that Jess hoped someone would say, "No, actually, we do not." No one did, however, and now he was going to share their space, intrude on the weird things they wanted to do on their own.

Jess did not know Wolfgang very well, had only seen him a few times in her life, even though Lanie was her best friend. He was attractive in that sexy elf, *Lord of the Rings* kind of way, high cheekbones and pale, perfect skin. He covered up this beauty with a layer of grime and scruff that, for Jess, made him handsome. She'd heard all the stories from Lanie, who seemed impressed by her brother's fucked-up-ness. He'd been expelled from high school for drugs, checked into a very posh rehab clinic, then went to some alternative ranch college where he got all muscular and tough, and then he went to film school, but had just been kicked out for either drugs or absenteeism or stalking one of the girls in his classes. He was the kind of person whose future Jess could see without wanting to, a sad accidental death at an age not young enough to be tragic and the awkward funeral where everyone acted like it was a surprise. His camera, though, Jess had to admit, was top-of-the-line.

"You kids keep saying movie, but this is barely going to be a short film," said Wolfgang, his eyes so red from pot smoke that he looked like he should be the monster. "Shut up, Wolf," Lanie said. "Just shoot what we tell you to shoot." Wolfgang shook the hair out of his face and looked aggrieved. "I'll have some say in how this gets made," he said, his voice rising for no good reason. "I'm a part of this movie now." Jess, without even thinking about it, corrected him. "You mean *short film*," she said. His eyes narrowed and he looked in her direction. "She's going to be difficult," he told his sister, pointing at Jess.

"If you want to finish this by morning," Wolfgang continued, "we don't have time to come up with a backstory for Jess. She's just, you know, real fucking crazy and violent."

"Maybe we ganged up on her in the locker room and made her show us her bush," said Heather, "and now she's out for revenge."

"If that helps, then you can use that backstory to get into character," Wolfgang allowed.

"So we're having a slumber party," Lanie said, testing the viscosity of the fake blood that the twins had made, "and Jess sneaks in and she kills us one at a time. The end."

"Shouldn't one of us live?" Wallis asked.

"No," Lanie said, as if she'd been thinking about this for years and it wasn't just some revved-up nightmare she'd made up on the spot. "Everybody dies and the monster gets away."

Lanie was obviously the director, and Jess found it hard to do anything but what she wanted. They set up for the first scene and Jess watched as Lanie demonstrated the part of the killer. She stepped out of the house, having turned on the floodlights so she could be seen starkly against the dark night, and pressed her face so forcefully against the glass window of the back door that they could see her canines, bared and vicious. Loud, so that she could be heard, she told Jess to punch out the window and then unlock the door. "I'll cut open my hand," Jess said, and Lanie frowned, exasperated, and then came back inside. She grabbed a green towel from a hook beside the fridge and handed it to Jess. "Use this," she said. Jess did not want to break the window, had some inkling, despite the Adderall's insistence that this moment was the only thing that mattered, that they would be punished for this vandalism. But Lanie's eyes were doing that dilated thing where it seemed like her internal organs had gone radioactive.

Instead, Jess thought in terms of the movie, the only thing that now mattered to Lanie. "Wouldn't the killer want to get inside without the girls' knowing she was there?" she said, and the other girls, and thank God even Wolfgang, nodded in agreement. "Fine," Lanie said, defeated, her brain already recalibrating the scene, three steps ahead of everyone else. "There's a sound outside and I go investigate. I open the door and call out, but nothing's there. Then I turn around and you're standing in the floodlights. You push open the door because I forgot to lock it." As Lanie moved on to the next thing, Jess had the feeling that she had talked someone out of murdering a person who deserved it.

Jess still needed a mask. Wolfgang, getting into the spirit suddenly, the weed wearing off and his own weirdness starting to seep out of his pores, ran upstairs and came back with a white T-shirt with yellowed stains under the arms. He dipped his hand into the bucket of fake blood and flicked, then smeared, unknowable patterns across the fabric. "Put your hair in a ponytail," he commanded, and Jess was unnerved by how his forcefulness, and her inability to refuse, reminded her of Lanie. She gathered her hair in a rubber band and then Wolfgang, with unexpected gentleness, placed the T-shirt over her head, pulling the ponytail through the neck of the shirt, so that the chest covered her face. He took off the shirt and then cut eye slits where they were needed and placed it back on her head. "That looks creepy," he said. He tightened the mask so that it looked more ominous. "Creepy and beautiful," he said, and Jess knew what he was doing, the stupid ways that boys thought they were clever.

"You look like a psycho killer," Mary Beth said with the kind of admiration that was typically reserved for moments that were not this one.

The other girls stood behind Wolfgang, as if he would protect them from Jess's knife. "Action," Wolfgang and Lanie said at the same time, both of them making strange faces of irritation in the aftermath, but the moment had started and there was nothing to do but move forward. Jess, already realizing how hard it was to breathe in the mask, which reeked of Wolfgang's bad decisions, crept into the house, following the track made by Wolfgang's camera movements, and flashed her aluminum foil knife and then the shot was done. Next, Wolfgang filmed Lanie ("I just want to die first so I can focus on the rest of the movie," she said) standing in front of the open refrigerator, swigging from a freezing-cold bottle of vodka, slipping her other hand into a bag of shredded cheese.

"Cut," Lanie yelled, and Wolfgang set the camera on the kitchen counter and then leaned into Jess, whose face was sweating from her own hot breath.

"Kill her good," Wolfgang said, his voice a cloud of pot smoke, and he rubbed the back of her neck with his clammy hand.

Jess felt the sick certainty that, not tonight but sometime

before he died, she would fuck him. He would be her first and nothing would ever be that weird and awful again. Her future turned crystalline and assured and then it retracted and she was back in her body. She pushed Wolfgang away from her, holding the knife like it was real and could protect her from her own desires.

Before the first murder, the girls went into the bathroom and took some more Adderall, which prevented them from growing bored and going back to watching slasher movies on the computer. Jess had decided to leave the mask on, because it was a pain to take it on and off, so she rested her head in Wallis's lap while they watched Lanie perfect the special effects that would accompany her own death. Lanie hacked a wedge of vanilla ice cream from the container and dumped it into a blender. Then she added as much of the fake blood as would fit and let it all spin until it was ice cold and frothing. "We get one shot at this," Lanie said. She chugged the concoction as quickly as she could, her throat making sounds like she was eating an entire world.

"Goddamn, brain freeze," she coughed once she'd finished, her mouth foaming. She wiped her face clean and took her place, steps unsteady, in front of the fridge. "Action," she shouted.

Wolfgang followed Jess as she crept behind Lanie with her knife featured prominently. Jess could not tell if it was better to inhabit the role and think like a psycho killer for whom Lanie was just an irritating light that needed to be extinguished or if she should stay in reality, however obscured by drugs it was, and hold on to the strange feeling of killing her best friend while everyone watched. Before she could decide, Jess's hand touched Lanie's relaxed shoulder and she spun her friend around and jabbed the knife, which crumpled upon impact, into her stomach. Lanie's eyes grew wide and she clutched at the wound, crushing the plastic bag filled with blood that was hidden in her shirt. Then, right on cue, she projectile-vomited the mess of blood and ice cream, her body having rejected the ice-cold monstrosity. She sprayed the counters and floor with an unending stream of blood, gurgling and moaning until she'd purged the milk shake from her body, and then she fell into a heap on the floor and went still.

"Cut," Lanie said, her voice weak with exertion. "That fucking ruled," Mary Beth and Heather said at the same time, and the rest of them, even Jess, agreed. The only way it could have been grander was if Lanie had actually died. Wolfgang wiped a spray of blood from the lens of his camera. "You die good, sis," he told her, and Jess knew for a fact that it was the sweetest thing he'd ever said to his younger sister.

I feel like I should be in the movie, too," Wolfgang said as they prepared for the next scene. "I want Jess to kill me." Jess refused to look at him, but she was pleased to hear each of her friends, with great emphasis on the word, say, "No!" Lanie touched Jess's hand and pulled her toward the bathroom, shouting over her shoulder, "This is just for girls, what we're doing," and Jess didn't know if she meant the movie or whatever was waiting for them.

From one of the bathroom drawers, Lanie produced a fancy box of chocolate truffles. "My mom hides these in here and eats them when she gets sad," she said. She handed one to Jess, a work of art, a sugared, purple flower sitting atop the chocolate. Jess lifted the mask up so that her mouth was exposed and ate the truffle in one bite. Lanie did the same. For the second chocolate, Jess took her time, let the filling melt in her mouth and coat her teeth.

They lay in the bathtub, which was as large as a wading pool, though they fit themselves closely together. They were shoulder to shoulder, pressed against each other, their legs tangled up so that Jess kept flexing her toes to differentiate between what was hers and what was Lanie's. The intimacy of their arrangement, if they were not best friends, would have taken up eight diary pages to explain.

It always amazed Jess that she was friends with Lanie, someone so rich it couldn't be quantified by the teenage brain. She could not understand why, with all this money, Lanie wasn't more popular. The only reason, which Jess kept coming back to, was that Lanie did not want to be popular. She wanted to be as strange as the money and her parents' lack of interest allowed.

"I think my brother is falling in love with you," Lanie said to Jess, who could feel her friend's breath on her cheek. She wanted to look at Lanie's face, to see her expression, but it would require too much effort to reposition herself.

"I don't know anything about that," Jess replied.

They were silent for a few seconds, sharing another truffle, when Lanie finally said, "Please don't let him ruin you. I know that sounds melodramatic, but don't do something with him that would make you feel weird."

"Sometimes I like feeling weird," Jess said.

"There's good weird, like you and me in this bathtub," Lanie said, "and then there's bad weird, which is whatever my brother would do to you."

Jess felt like this was the best chance she would ever have to make out with Lanie, and yet she knew it would be an effort that would turn toxic over time. It would complicate their relationship in ways Jess could not quite see to the end of. She felt like she was in the ocean and a massive wave was building up behind her. If she just paddled hard enough, made herself a part of it, she could ride it all the way back to dry land. She had maybe four more seconds to decide how she wanted to remember this night, and, as usual, the moment passed and Jess's mouth was wide open and dumb.

"I feel like I threw up my soul down in the kitchen," Lanie said. She stood up in the tub and then stepped out. "Come on," she said, "you have a lot of killing left to do."

What were you doing in there with my sister?" Wolfgang asked, cornering Jess while Wallis and Mary Beth and Heather each went over their upcoming deaths with Lanie, who was showing them what it was like to die.

"None of your business," Jess said. She loved this mask, the way it obscured her emotions and made her stronger. She would be taking it home with her in the morning, that was for sure.

"Don't turn her lesbian, okay? Lanie has a hard enough time as it is," Wolfgang said.

"We're not lesbians," Jess said, though she didn't feel indignant at the accusation or even certain of her reply. "We're best friends."

"Fuck," Wolfgang said, almost in a whisper. "I can't tell the difference with girls." He tried to look into her eyes, but Jess knew the eye slits were throwing him off. "Okay, forget I said anything," Wolfgang said, and then stalked over to Lanie to prepare for the next scene.

At first, Mary Beth and Heather wanted to die in the bathtub, with the whirlpool jets spreading their blood around the water, but Lanie said they'd have to get naked for it to make sense. Instead, the twins brushed their teeth and Jess jumped from behind the shower stall and stabbed them, a fake knife in each hand.

In the first and only take, Jess stabbed them each in the neck and blood spilled out of the twins' mouths, mixing with the toothpaste foam and spurting against the mirror. Jess then shoved them into the bathtub, where they would bleed out. Heather lost her balance and hit her head on one of the knobs and got a huge goose egg on her forehead, already red and angry as she wobbled out of the tub. "Fuck," said Heather, touching the bump like it might explode, inspecting herself in the mirror. "I always get hurt when we're fucking around." Wolfgang came back from the kitchen with a box of frozen canapés and placed it delicately against her head. "You're sweet," Heather said, and Jess was jealous for exactly one second.

They took a break and smoked some pot and watched videos of cheerleader accidents on YouTube. Wolfgang went back to his room to check his e-mail and probably do something unsavory.

It was now three in the morning and the girls were finding it hard to reclaim the initial rush of making something so stupid and violent. They were out of Adderall and the pot, as always, made inactivity seductive. Mary Beth held Jess's mask up so that Jess could take another hit from the pipe, pulling calmness down into her lungs. On the computer, a cheerleader did a backflip right into the face of another cheerleader. "I'm so fucking hungry," Wallis said. Only Lanie, her own desires burning the pot right out of her system on impact, kept her focus on the movie.

"It's the ending that needs to be perfect," she said. "We're gonna kill Wallis and then . . . what?"

Jess, almost asleep, said, "And then the killer just disappears into the night, off to who knows where."

Lanie nodded, but wasn't satisfied. "Of course that's the easy ending. I want something better than that."

"I'm thinking maybe I don't want to be killed anymore," Wallis said.

"Okay, fuck," Lanie said, closing the Internet window on the computer and clapping her hands together furiously. "Everybody just hold on for another hour and we'll be done."

"Let's just eat some popcorn and go to bed," Mary Beth said.

Lanie grunted and then disappeared from the room. She came back with a prescription bottle and dumped the pills onto her math textbook. She put her civics textbook on top and jumped up and down on the books until the pills were reduced to a fine powder. "These are my mom's weird fucking diet pills that some shady doctor gives her. They are pretty much speed, I think. We're going to snort this and then finish the movie and then we're going to collapse in bed together like a big litter of newborn kittens."

"Ugh," Wallis said. "Fine." The other girls gave their grudging consent and bent over the lines that Lanie was cutting up.

The girls were not used to so many drugs, though they tried to pretend it was no big deal, like they were teenagers in a bad movie and all they ever thought about was getting high and having sex. Truth be told, they smoked small amounts of pot on a weekly basis, to make the world tolerable, and then they took Adderall when they really needed to not fail an exam. Real drugs were too much trouble to keep circulating through their bodies. Now, however, the drugs stacking in their systems, their bodies confused by the irregular gorging on junk food, they were wired and glossy in a way that felt very dangerous, even in the safety of this empty house. Wolfgang, who demanded he get some of the diet pills, was starting to become a tangible threat, the way he no longer cared about their personal space, forcing himself into their circle as if he were one of them. He started filming them in random moments, which he said was for "behind the scenes" footage. He was so lanky and petulant and doofy, however, that her increased caution around him was perhaps more paranoia than good instincts on Jess's part. Or perhaps the threat lay not entirely with Wolfgang, but within herself, the things she might allow herself to do. Her body had built up an excess of static electricity that had seemingly nowhere to go.

"He shouldn't be doing drugs, right?" Jess asked Lanie as they watched the twins take the brunt of Wolfgang's non sequiturs and vague come-ons. "With the rehab and everything?"

"That was a while ago," Lanie said. "I don't think it matters much now. He does what he wants."

Wallis was to die on the stairs. Lanie filled a plastic shopping bag with fake blood, tied the handles shut as best she could, and, after they had filmed Jess stabbing Wallis, shoved the bag under Wallis's shirt. Lanie poked a hole in the bag and Wolfgang filmed Wallis as she crawled up the staircase, a river of blood trailing her movements. Halfway up, Wallis slumped on the stairs and slid down to the bottom before crawling up again. When she reached the top, she shuddered and died.

The other girls clapped in appreciation of her fantastic death. For the first time in a while, Jess felt unambiguously happy as she watched Wallis smile, blood smeared across her face and neck. Then Jess realized that Wallis wasn't so much smiling as she was grinding her teeth. Still, she hugged Wallis and they sat on the stairs and watched the blood pool and collect, a huge mess that they would not even consider cleaning up. Wallis had been a track star in junior high but quit before high school for reasons no more mysterious than boredom. Still, she had that straightforward dullness in her eyes that Jess recognized in athletes and was pretty in a boyish way that suggested she could leave them behind if she wanted to.

"Are you having a good time?" Jess asked her.

"Every time I think I might not be friends with you guys anymore," Wallis confessed, "I remember that I love shit like this and no one else would do it with me."

It made Jess happy to hear this admission, as if their friendship had been secretly tested and found to be strong enough to withstand it. It was their weirdness, she realized, that kept them together, and though she imagined this would burn out over time, she was grateful for it now.

Lanie had given up on an ending, settling for the killer slipping away in the night, leaving carnage behind. From a storytelling standpoint, Wolfgang said, this made the most sense. Jess was amazed that, even with his truncated experience in film school, Wolfgang had a very limited vocabulary when it came to making movies. Or maybe he was just really high, she realized.

"I have an idea," Jess said.

"Let's hear it," Lanie replied.

"I just stay in the house," Jess offered. "I don't leave."

"Maybe," Heather said, getting excited, "it was her house all along."

"Ooh, I like that," Mary Beth said.

"Maybe," Wallis added, "she killed all her sisters and now it's just her."

"I like that," Wolfgang said. "It's a nice twist ending."

Jess felt certain of herself, a rare occasion, but she still waited for Lanie to weigh in.

"It's perfect," Lanie finally said. "You're not some killer. You're just some girl."

"Or," Jess said, "I'm just some girl who's also a killer."

They set up the shot quickly. Wolfgang following Jess as she climbed the stairs, walked into Lanie's bedroom, and pulled off her mask. She shook out her hair. Going on instinct, she walked over to the nightstand and rubbed some moisturizer on her face. Then, without thinking too much about it, not caring that

Wolfgang and the other girls were watching her, she stripped off her sweatpants and T-shirt. In just her bra and panties, she slipped into Lanie's bed and turned off the bedside lamp.

"Cut," Lanie said, her voice ragged and chewed up.

It was dark enough that Jess could not discern where Wolfgang and the girls stood in the room. It was silent now, no one moving or speaking, and Jess lingered in the bed, holding on to the moment, the movie finished, before she would have to pull back the covers and join her friends again.

She had made this moment happen, surprised by the power of her own desires. She had killed everyone around her and created a place just for herself. She lay in the bed, breathing softly, and she heard Lanie say, "Jess," her voice pitched slightly higher than normal, worry having crept in. But Jess didn't respond. She stretched her body and felt her muscles, which had been so tense throughout the night, relax just enough that it felt like a new drug in her system. "Jess?" Lanie said again, and finally Jess replied, "I'm okay." The lights came on and everyone was staring at her, half smiles on their faces. She threw off the covers and smiled back at them, even Wolfgang, and stepped out of the bed. It was six in the morning, the sun just beginning to rise, every single disaster in the house softer in the daylight.

Now that it was all over, every fake knife broken into uselessness, Wolfgang uploaded the footage to his laptop and they watched it with the detachment of a fever dream. Wolfgang promised that he would edit it into something perfect and they could upload it on Vimeo and the entire world could see it. "This feels like something viral," Lanie said. Jess, who had wanted to be invisible, suddenly realized that a lot of people would watch her in her bra and panties, but it seemed silly to mention this worry now. Perhaps this was how bad decisions worked, she considered. They happened so quickly and felt so unreal that you didn't really care about the repercussions until it was too late. But a thing probably happened whether you wanted it to or not, good and bad, and you either allowed it to happen, or you fought it off long enough that you felt absolved of the eventual outcome.

Framed like the ending to an entirely different horror movie, their bodies were scattered around the room. Wolfgang had fallen asleep on the floor, wedged between Mary Beth and Heather, who hadn't bothered to change out of their blood-stained clothes. Wallis was curled up on a beanbag chair and snoring so loudly that it seemed fake. Only Lanie and Jess remained awake, still giddy, though their excitement was tinged with the sadness that the night was over, that they would never be able to conjure those exact feelings again.

They did not bother to clean up the blood that covered the floors and walls of the house. They left that horror to the parents' return the next day. In order to escape the morning sun, now filling the house with unwanted light, Lanie and Jess hid under the covers of Lanie's bed. Half afraid that if they let go they would fade, ghostlike, into this atmosphere, they wrapped their arms around each other tightly until every last bit of the drugs wore off, but not the thrill of making a truly wonderful disaster.

The Lost Baby

1.

The baby was so beautiful, so perfect, that Meggy constantly allowed herself the fantasy of eating her baby, of consuming him until the baby was housed entirely inside of her own body. "You are so beautiful," she whispered to the baby.

After the baby was gone, she thought of how often she imagined the pleasure of devouring him, knowing that she would never actually do it. How would she, in reality? And what struck her now, in the baby's absence, was that the baby, without a care in the world, swallowed Meggy whole.

The baby was so beautiful, so perfect, that Paul could not imagine the baby's future. To imagine an adult with his son's name, to imagine a future where the boy did not entirely need Paul, it was impossible.

After the baby was gone, he thought of how simpleminded he had been, the way he perpetually placed the baby's future self in a kind of stylized fog. And what struck him now, in the baby's absence, was that he could not conjure, no matter how hard he tried, an image of the child as it must now be, out in the world, separate from Paul.

2.

Meggy and Paul passed a crudely made coupon offering one night of free babysitting between the two of them, each one examining the simple piece of paper as if there was hidden fine print. The baby was eight and a half months old, gurgling and happy, lying on his back. In those eight and a half months, Meggy and Paul had not spent a single moment alone outside of the house. They were, though they told no one, not even their best friends, on the verge of a breakup. They loved the baby more than anything they'd ever loved before, more than, they were surprised to learn, each other. They could not yet determine if this was natural, or if it spoke to previously unexplored problems between them. Or maybe they were simply exhausted and prone to overthinking things. They still loved each other, felt the intensity of their longing when the other was away. They simply loved the baby more. Or, maybe, they suspected, the other person didn't love the baby with the same intensity as they did and held it against them. Or perhaps they didn't love the baby as much as the other person and were being judged for this. They were so tired, did not realize that love and exhaustion could cause such mania.

Paul taught fiction at a tiny liberal arts college in the middle of nowhere. Up until eight months ago, Meggy taught poetry workshops at the same college. But Meggy was now on maternity leave. And she would be taking a leave of absence for at least a year after her maternity leave ended. Paul would keep teaching, it was decided jointly, to keep a steady paycheck, for him to continue to move toward tenure. Meggy's job was always more tenuous, simply a visiting professor gig, tied to Paul's own position. Paul told Meggy that this would work out, that she could "focus on her poetry" during the leave of absence, and she wanted to take her fingernail and drag it deeply down the side of his face. When would she write poetry, when she was changing diapers full of shit? When she was rocking the baby at three in the morning, reminding herself with great effort not to rock the baby so hard that it died? When the baby was napping? If he said, *when the baby is napping,* she would drag that fingernail down the other side of his face. He shrugged. He knew about the imbalance of gender roles when it came to parenting. He was a college professor. But he was never a great student; he didn't pay enough attention when he should have, so he made most of it up as he went along. Like when he suggested that, if she didn't get a lot of writing done, perhaps she would get a lot of reading done, which could also be really instructive and helpful.

And Paul thought about how, when he would return from a day of teaching, he would sometimes, often, find Meggy sitting alone in the living room while the baby wailed in its crib. "Sometimes I want to stab myself in the stomach with a knife," she once told him, seconds after he walked into the house, and he said that she was a great mother, that it was going to be okay, and she replied, "That's not why I want to do it." He would hold the baby while he did his best to make dinner, nothing more than a protein and a vegetable, sometimes both roasted in the same pan. He would bathe the baby while Meggy watched a TV show or napped, and then he would wait until everything was quiet, his son and his wife asleep, and he would go into their shared study to grade and plan his lessons. And when he fell asleep, he slept so deeply that he had no idea what went on during the rest of the night, and he was always shocked to hear how many times Meggy had to tend to the baby, how little sleep she had gotten. "I had no idea," he told her as he made breakfast. "Didn't you?" she asked him.

Both knew that the other was doing their best. They just weren't sure that this was enough to stay together.

What they now held in their hands was a coupon. Their next-door neighbors, the Shibayamas, gave them the coupon at the baby shower, a time so far in the past that they could not quite remember it. They had invited the Shibayamas, Jameson and Mindy, because it seemed awkward not to, because they lived in the adjacent house and they were aware of the impending baby. Paul and Meggy barely knew them, simple small talk when they were caught outside with them. And then they had invited the couple and it was clear from the Shibayamas' reaction that it was a kind of intimacy that they were unprepared for.

Mindy was a lawyer, her specific area of expertise unknown to them, though she was beloved by the people of the town for her community work. Jameson wrote science fiction novels and developed tabletop RPGs. He had given his most well-known novel, *The Silver Corsair*, to Paul and Meggy, signed, "With gratitude for your interest in this world I've created." Paul read the first one hundred and fifty pages but gave up, unable to understand the vagaries of galactic treaties, the particulars of the underlying tensions between alien races, the oftentimes blatant misogyny of the titular Corsair. When he next saw Jameson, Paul commented on how much he had enjoyed the novel. "What specifically?" Jameson asked him, and Paul, dumbfounded, worked his way toward an answer, smiling the entire time. "Well, I loved the way you pulled everything together by the end," he finally said, and Jameson nodded, pleased. "But I also left quite a bit up in the air," he said. "That, too," Paul admitted. "There's a sequel," Jameson said, "but you'll have to buy that one. Only one free book per family." That night, Paul ordered the sequel from a website that specialized in out-of-print books, and he left the book out in case Jameson ever happened to come inside their house.

At the party, the Shibayamas spoke only to Meggy's brother-in-law, would not leave him alone for reasons that Paul and Meggy could not decipher, and then they said that they had to leave early and gave Paul and Meggy an envelope. "Open it later," Mindy told them, and it wasn't until two days later that Meggy remembered the envelope, which had been bundled together with all the greeting cards that they had accumulated. When they opened the envelope, they found a single index card with this written in black marker: "This coupon entitles the bearer to one free night of babysitting."

"What the hell is this?" Paul asked, holding it up for Meggy to read.

"I guess they'll watch the baby one night," Meggy said, shrugging.

"Why?" Paul asked. "We don't even know them."

"I wonder if they just assumed that we'd never ask them."

"That is kind of shrewd," Paul admitted.

And they had forgotten the card, hidden in a drawer in the kitchen, until this very night, five minutes after their babysitter had canceled, the dinner reservations already made.

"Are we going to do this?" Meggy asked her husband. The baby continued to gurgle, as if delighted by their anxiety.

"Why not?" Paul asked.

"They don't have any kids," Meggy said. "Do they even know what to do?"

"The baby will be asleep the entire time," Paul said. "They just have to sit in the living room and wait until we get home."

"Is this okay?" Meggy asked again, almost crying.

"Goddammit," Paul said. "I want to have a night alone with you."

"Well," Meggy said, her voice rising, "I want to have a night alone with you."

"Well," Paul replied. "Then what's the problem?"

They both looked at the baby, who had stopped gurgling and was now watching them in that curious way that made both of them intensely feel different things. For Meggy, the baby's calm, searching gaze made her flush, made her want to straddle someone and slowly grind on them. Not the baby, God, but Paul or someone like Paul. For Paul, it made him feel like he had not been a good person in his early life, that he was not capable of taking care of a child, but it made him, each time the baby looked at him in this way, resolve to be worthy of the baby.

They looked at each other, nodded, and then looked at the baby one last time before they finally decided.

While Meggy fed the baby and rocked it to sleep, Paul sat downstairs with the Shibayamas. Mindy had brought a huge basket of yarn and was already knitting. Jameson was looking at the list of instructions and numbers and tips that, single-spaced, filled up two pages. Their dinner reservations were in twenty minutes and the restaurant was twenty minutes away. Jameson placed the instructions on the coffee table and then smiled at Paul. "You know," he said, "we never thought you'd actually use the coupon." Paul blushed; he could not tell if Jameson was mad about this or simply surprised.

"We trust you guys," Paul said. "And we really appreciate it."

"It's necessary," Mindy said, not looking up from her knitting. "You put too much of yourselves into raising a kid, you have nothing left over for each other."

"It's true," Jameson offered.

"Oh, do you two have children?" Paul asked, and instantly regretted it.

"One," Jameson said. "She died when she was seven. Cancer." Mindy didn't look up from her knitting, didn't seem to have even heard. Jameson gave him the weakest of smiles.

"Oh, God," Paul said. "I'm sorr—"

"He's finally asleep," Meggy said over Paul's apology; she was softly walking down the stairs, putting on her coat.

"We'll take good care of him," Mindy said, still knitting. Whatever she was making, Paul believed, did not require this much concentration.

"You have our number?" Meggy asked.

Jameson held up the sheets of paper. "We have all the numbers," he said.

"Have fun," Mindy said as Paul and Meggy walked out of the house.

"We will," Meggy called back, but it sounded, to Paul, like a question.

They immediately ordered a drink when they arrived at the restaurant. Paul gave his order to the hostess as they were being led to the table, who merely smiled and said, "Your waitress will get that for you."

Meggy ordered a whiskey, neat, a drink that she had never ordered before; she wanted something brown that tasted of wood and caramel. She wanted it to work quickly. When she ordered, Paul smiled at her, but she knew that he was trying to remember what the rules were for a breastfeeding mother. He knew it was okay, but he could never remember *how* okay, and she already understood that there would be awkwardness when she ordered her second.

Still, they were happy to be together, though they both felt so sleepy, like they had stepped into an egg-shaped space filled with warm blue light. They were without the baby. They never knew quite how this would happen. They both ordered steaks.

"I love you," Paul said, smiling.

"Duh," Meggy said. "I love you, too."

"We're doing okay," he then said, and she wanted him to stop talking. He was trying to construct a narrative for her, to show her that he could write a story where they were happy. She didn't care about stories, not the way that he did. She liked a single line, perfectly rendered, one that echoed and did not immediately satisfy. She felt the lingering guilt of having left the baby. She was used to being apart from him, but she was not used to the fact that, if the baby needed her, he would not be at arm's length.

Paul sipped his Paloma and wondered which of the Shibayamas would attend to the baby if it awakened. He imagined that Mindy would have finished her knitting by then and simply draped the finished blanket over the crying baby. But the baby wouldn't wake up. That was not his style. He slept like a rock until midnight, and only then were all bets off.

One of his students had turned in a story for workshop that week, and he told Meggy about it. In it, a woman finds a box on her doorstep. There are three kittens in the box, just born. The woman does not want the kittens and walks two houses down to leave the box on her neighbor's doorstep. But the neighbor sees her doing this. She takes the kittens back to her house and she feeds them milk with a dropper and lets them sleep on her bed.

"Do you like the story?" she asked him.

"I think so. I don't know. I have to read it again. I might be missing something."

"I thought for sure that she was going to kill the kittens," Meggy admitted.

"Why?" he asked.

"I don't know. I just thought that was where it was going."

"You think most stories end up in violence," he said, smiling, but Meggy was annoyed by this. She finished her whiskey and ordered another, but with Coke in it this time. She needed sweetness now, just a little, to cut the sharpness.

The steaks came to their table, and there was a huge dollop of butter atop the ribeyes, already melting and pooling around the steak. Meggy felt slightly queasy, but she cut into the steak and it was amazing. Then the phone rang, their own home phone showing up on the caller ID. Her knife and fork clattered against the plate and she answered.

"What's wrong?" Paul asked, but Meggy shushed him.

He watched her face blush so deeply red, burning her cheeks. "What the fuck is wrong?" Paul asked, and the couple at the adjacent table turned to look at them.

"We need to go," Meggy said, putting the phone in her purse. Her hands were shaking.

"What's wrong," Paul asked again, but Meggy was already up, pushing away from the table.

"The baby is gone," she finally said, her voice rising.

They ran out of the restaurant. They left without paying, but it would be weeks before either of them remembered this fact.

3.

There were three police officers in the house when Paul and Meggy returned home. The Shibayamas were nowhere to be found. The initial officer, who seemed to be in charge of things, asked them to sit on the couch, but Meggy was getting hysterical. "Where is my baby?" she shouted.

The police officer looked somber. He was squat and round,

with a bristly mustache. Paul remembered that one time he was speeding and this particular officer simply gestured for Paul to slow down instead of pulling him over. The officer's son was the star running back on the high school football team. It was a tiny town. It was easy to know these things, whether you wanted to or not.

"Ma'am," the officer said, "your child is missing."

"Where the fuck is he?" Meggy said.

"She's had a drink," Paul said, apologizing, though he knew instantly that this was a mistake.

"Fuck you," Meggy said to him, her voice so deep, not even looking at Paul. Months from now, when he looked back on this night, it was hard for Paul not to imagine that this was the exact moment that their marriage fell apart.

"I need to ask you some questions," the officer said.

"Is he dead?" Paul asked.

"Where are Jameson and Mindy?" Meggy asked. "What did they do?"

"Just sit down here on the sofa," the officer said. He had a sorry little pen and a notepad. Paul felt, in that moment, that his son was dead and nothing that this officer wrote down would change that. He sank into the sofa, so tired he could barely keep his eyes open. He felt as Meggy reached for his hand and squeezed it so hard that he almost told her to ease up. Instead, he held on to her hand, as if the intensity of their anxiety would be lessened the longer they touched. As the officer talked to them, asked them questions, it was hard not to imagine that their son was simply upstairs in his crib, sound asleep. If Meggy or Paul simply stood up and ran to their son's room, he would be there. But they could not move. They held on to each other and told the officer what he wanted to know, information that would not bring their son back to them.

4.

Paul slept, and Meggy was amazed (and angered and, yes, envious) at how quickly he could shut his body and mind down. They were in a hotel room in the next town over, had checked in at four in the morning. The police were still going over the house. Meggy had wanted to check every door, look under every piece of furniture, but they wouldn't let her search. It was forty-five degrees outside. There were a group of people, some of them their neighbors (though not the Shibayamas) who had been walking around the woods near their house, sweeping the beams of their flashlights across the ground, listening for the sound of their crying baby. There wasn't much else to do. The town was so small. There was barely a police force. There was no mobile command unit or elite squad. There was no ice-queen special agent who had experienced her own tragedy years before but who used complicated methods of deduction to find missing people. There was nothing but the expansive nature of the universe and her son, her baby, lost in it.

Her throat ached from crying; her muscles felt shredded, little raggedy bits of herself floating around in her body. She took a pen and some hotel stationery and tried to organize the facts as she knew them. She wrote and she wrote. She imagined that when she was done writing, she could give the list to every person she had ever known and they would not have to ask her a single question. They could immediately join the search and they could help her find her baby.

Her breasts ached and her nipples were leaking milk. She had forgotten the pump; what an odd thing if she had remembered, to leave her house, her baby missing, toting the pump, which she hated so fucking much. She imagined the looks on the faces of the police officers, all of them men, as they watched her carry the pump to the car.

She put down her pen in frustration and walked into the bathroom and washed her hands. She undid her dress and her bra and then cupped her right breast and squeezed until a few drops appeared. She applied more pressure, ignoring the discomfort, and the milk started to dribble onto her hands, dripping into the sink. She wondered if she should store the milk, pull the stopper on the sink and let it collect, but she was too tired to do anything about it. She expressed as much milk as she could from both breasts. She looked at the milk as it ran down the bowl of the sink, where it had dribbled on the counter. She didn't clean it. She put her bra back on, pulled up her dress, and went back to the desk.

Paul roused and sat up in bed, still in his clothes. "What's going on?" he asked.

"I'm working."

"The baby . . ." he said, and started crying.

"I know," she said. She knew that she should get into the bed with him, hold him, but this was more important. The baby was missing. They would comfort each other later.

"How long have I been asleep?" he asked.

"I have no idea, really," she replied.

"What can I do?" he asked, and she was relieved to have an answer for him.

"Nothing," she said. "Go back to sleep."
And he did.

5.

The list looked like this:

* Paul and I left the baby in his crib at 7:15. Mindy and Jameson Shibayama were in the living room when we left.
* Jameson said he checked on the baby around 8:00 and it was asleep. Mindy was knitting.
* At 8:30, Mindy and Jameson both went to check on the baby and discovered that he was not in his crib. They turned on the lights, checked the entire room, but found no sign of the baby. They checked the hallway and the adjacent rooms. They went back to the baby's bedroom and checked the windows, which were latched shut.
* There had been no sound save for the white noise of the machine. They heard no crying or sounds of disturbance over the baby monitor.
* They called me and Paul and then called 911.
* The police questioned Jameson and Mindy and then searched the entire house. They called in an Amber Alert and asked for assistance from the neighboring town to set up checkpoints.
* The police searched the area around the house and then searched the Shibayamas' home and yard.

* Two police dogs from the neighboring town searched
   the woods around the house.
* I was questioned for forty-five minutes about the baby
   and the circumstances of our last interaction. Paul
   was taken into another room and questioned.
* No signs of a struggle or any blood was found in or
   near the house.
* A command post was set up at the Shibayamas' house
   next door. Police from the entire county are now
   working in unison. The Shibayamas have not spoken
   to us since the initial phone call. I do not know where
   they are.
* Our baby is still missing.

When it was finished, she woke up Paul and asked him to
read it. She watched his face as he silently read the list. He nodded several times. "This is good," he said.

"Thank you," she said. Now that the list was complete, she
could sleep, felt exhaustion take over her entire body. She curled
against Paul, pulled the sheets around her body.

Even though she was tired, even though she felt shattered in
ways that she knew, no matter what happened, she would never
recover from, if Paul had tried to have sex with her in that moment, she would have let him. She would have let him slide himself into her and she would have asked him to go real slow at
first and then harder once she'd gotten used to him. She would
have done this because sex, when it was good, felt so obliterat-
ing. The world was entirely vaporized around you and it took
so long afterward for the mist to coalesce into reality again. She
eased herself against him, pressing against his dick, which be-

gan to harden. He rubbed her ass, and then she fell asleep before anything else could happen. She did not dream about the baby and, in the morning, she was so angry that she had not conjured the image of her child in those moments when everything was quiet.

6.

The baby had vanished. There were no signs of him, not a single clue that offered any explanation for where the baby had gone. Paul and Meggy had purchased jogging suits from Walmart, toiletries. They could not go back to their house yet. They received hourly updates from the police, but they were told not to watch the news, not to check the Internet, and not to talk to any reporters. Paul checked his e-mail and there were nearly fifty e-mails waiting for him. He realized that he had a class that afternoon, but he had no energy for dealing with this fact. Someone else would take care of it.

The Shibayamas, they learned, were staying at a hotel in the town beyond the town where Paul and Meggy were staying.

The police called and said that they needed Paul and Meggy to come to the station, that there was no news, but they had some questions that might help them in their search. Paul drove and Meggy stared out the window. "Where do you think he is?" she asked him as they drove the twenty minutes to the police station.

"I don't know," he replied, because he truly had no idea.

"I guess I mean . . . do you think he's dead?" she asked.

"I don't know," he said.

"I think he is," she finally replied.

"He's not," he corrected her.

"You just said that you didn't know."

"Well, I guess now I do. He's not dead," he said, stumbling over his words, trying to sound certain.

"What would be worse," she then asked, "if he's dead or if he's disappeared and we'll never find him?"

"Both are really bad," he admitted; he was starting to cry again.

"Maybe we never had a baby," she said, her voice empty of emotion. "Maybe this is all a dream."

"I don't think so," he said, and they drove the rest of the way in silence.

The police took them into separate rooms. They weren't interrogation rooms, just offices. Paul wasn't even sure if the local police had interrogation rooms. Were there even jail cells here? What did the police do besides give tickets to students who were speeding around town?

The police chief, a woman in her sixties, walked into the room. She had short, nearly buzzed gray hair and dark brown eyes set deeply in her face. She looked like she had been at the first Woodstock, had the air of a faded hippie, even in her police uniform. He knew little about her. She was kind of a legend in the town; in the only violence that anyone could remember in the last twenty years, she shot and killed a local man who was trying to abduct a young woman. Now she sat opposite Paul and smiled.

"I'm so sorry, Mr. Lincoln," she said.

"Me, too," he said. He wasn't yet used to this sentiment, did not know how to respond to it. He would, eventually. He would get it right.

"This is unlike anything I've ever encountered," she admitted. "I will not say that I am ill-equipped to handle this, because I honestly don't know anyone, man or woman, young or old, who would know what to do with this case. It's utterly confounding, which I'm sure you don't want to hear, seeing as how we're trying to find your baby."

"It doesn't make sense," Paul said, as if the very next thing that the police chief said would make sense.

"I have one question that I want to ask you, Mr. Lincoln, and I know this is difficult. When your wife left the house with you that night, after she had put the baby down, what was her mood?"

"She was tired," Paul said. He was certain of this.

"Agitated?" the police chief asked. "Depressed?"

"No," Paul said. "Just tired. But excited for the night out."

"And let me ask you this. When the two of you left the house, do you remember what your wife was carrying with her?"

"Her purse?" Paul asked, like he was on a game show.

"Are you certain?" she asked.

"She needed her ID to get a drink, so she had her purse with her," he said, this time with more certainty, though he honestly could not remember. He was working with the clues that he had.

"How big was the purse?" she asked.

"Normal size, I guess," he responded, shrugging.

"I'm going to ask you this and I want you to try your best not to get upset. Did you two stop anywhere on the way to the restaurant? A gas station? The drugstore?"

Paul wasn't sure why he was expected to be upset about this question. "No. We were trying to get to the restaurant on time.".

"And when you got to the restaurant, did your wife head to the bathroom when you got there?" the police chief asked.

Paul figured it out. He was slow; he had always been slow, but he always got where he was going. "Do you think my wife killed our son?" he asked her.

She held up her hands as if to defend herself. "I'm trying to figure this out."

"The Shibayamas were the last ones to see the baby, so there's no way Meggy could have taken the baby with her."

The police chief paused, thinking this over. "Well, that's the issue here. As of today, Jameson Shibayama states that he actually did not go into the room to check on the baby. The door was closed. He listened at the door and then went back downstairs. It wasn't until later that evening that they checked the room, at which point your baby was gone."

"That seems awfully convenient for him to remember now," Paul offered.

"He says that he was embarrassed that he hadn't actually checked, as if you two would judge him for that oversight."

"Nevertheless," Paul said.

"Believe me, Mr. Lincoln. No one is under more scrutiny than the Shibayamas. But so far there is nothing to indicate foul play. That leaves us with your wife."

"She did not get rid of our baby," Paul said, and he was certain of this. He was not the kind of husband in a bad TV movie who let doubt lead him astray.

"Was your wife unhappy? Was she experiencing postpartum depression?" the police chief then asked, as if this would do anything to Paul.

"You know that's . . . that's not really any of your business," Paul then said, and he stood up, which felt too dramatic and so he sat back down. "Where is Meggy?" he asked.

"She's being questioned right now. It shouldn't be much longer."

"Do we need a lawyer?" he asked her. For whatever reason, he trusted that what she told him would be correct.

The police chief looked away for a brief moment. She seemed, to Paul, like someone who wanted to smoke a cigarette but could not. "I would get one," she then said, and she let him wait in the reception area until Meggy returned, crying, shaking her head, empty of something important.

7.

Meggy's sister took over. She was a lawyer, obscenely wealthy, a life so far removed from Meggy that they rarely talked to each other, as if there was no way for the other to understand. Diana was married to a nice-enough, nearly mute man who did something with finance, and they had no plans for children. "Kids freak me out," Diana had told Meggy immediately after Meggy had told her that she was pregnant. They lived in a mansion in Atlanta, ran marathons, went to galas, and sat on boards. Meggy still had student debt, a book of poems with a small press, and she listened to cloud rap. But Meggy had donated a kidney to Diana when her own kidneys had failed in college, and so Meggy always had the sense that Diana resented the fact that Meggy had something over her older sister. The missing baby seemed Diana's chance to even things out.

"I have the best lawyer for this kind of thing," Diana said.

"What kind of person specializes in this kind of thing?" Meggy said, her voice listless and thick from the Xanax.

"I'm paying for all of it," Diana continued, as if Meggy hadn't spoken. "And I'll do all the talking. You guys take care of each other and don't talk to anyone. You're traumatized. You don't need to deal with anything except thinking good thoughts for the baby."

"Thank you," Meggy offered.

"And I'll handle information. I'll let you know what's going on, and update you. Do not get on the Internet. Don't look at all."

They did check their e-mail, which was now flooded with requests for comments and offerings of grief or accusation. They were easy enough to delete. Paul had stopped responding to e-mails from his students, his colleagues, his dean. He just marked all unread e-mails and deleted them in bulk. It was so disconcerting how easy it was, to have everything vanish without any effort.

One time, Meggy and Paul checked news stories on their baby, each one with the same photo that they had provided to the authorities, the baby almost smiling, probably just gassy, wearing a fuzzy zip-up that made him look like a tiger. The articles offered little of substance, the same information over and over, just the number of days since their baby had disappeared changing. The comments, on the other hand, were a cesspool. Half the people assumed they had killed their own child. The other half assumed that the Shibayamas had killed their child, but that Meggy and Paul were ultimately responsible for putting their child in the care of such people. And the blame was not equal. Paul was rarely mentioned. It was Meggy who was at fault. It was her lack of care, of mothering instincts, that led to this. Or it was her depression (how did they know about her depression?) that had pushed her to such an extreme act.

They closed the browser window and looked at each other. "If he comes back," Meggy asked, so empty of tears, her voice ragged, not her own, "will they even let us have him?"

8.

Paul's first and only novel, *The Cross,* had to go into another printing. It wasn't enough to get on the bestseller's list ("Not yet!" offered his agent by e-mail), but there was definitely an uptick in sales that was directly related to the disappearance of their baby. Meggy's book of poems was already out of print, three years after it came out. A few weeks after the vanishing, someone sent a copy of Meggy's poetry collection by mail, asking for her to sign it and return it in the SASE that had been provided. Meggy threw the envelope away and spent the morning rereading her poems, which had all been about the natural world and humanity's insignificant place in it. One poem, about the time that Meggy had spent a month in Iceland, glaciers and volcanic rock, ended with the line "A baby? It means nothing to the ice." She hiccuped with sobs, and Paul found her holding the book. He took it from her, found a random spot in the bookcase, and slid it safely away from sight.

9.

"I miss him so much," Meggy said to Paul one night in bed. Her milk had dried up months ago. She kept the door to his room locked. For hours, she would sit on the sofa and watch slide-shows of the baby, the hypnotic way each image solidified his presence in her heart.

"I do, too," Paul replied.

They held each other, and Meggy could feel how hot Paul's breath was on her face. She reached down for him, stroked him until he was hard. She turned away from him, and he pulled down her panties and, with some effort, slid inside of her. They took turns moving, one letting the other do all the work until they tired and then the other would take over. It felt plea-surable at the same time that it felt like nothing. "I love you," Paul said, but Meggy pretended that she hadn't heard, grinded against him.

When it was over, she tried, in the dark, to find her panties, and finally had to turn on the light. She looked over and saw that Paul was watching her.

"What?" she asked.

"I think it would be easier if we just knew. It'd be better if he were dead and we knew for certain. This is worse, don't you think?"

"It's bad in a different way," she admitted.

"How long do you think we can live like this?" he asked.

"Not long," she said.

He turned away from her and settled himself for sleep. "I wonder," he said, but she didn't respond.

10.

"I don't know how it took this long to find out, honestly," Diana said to Meggy and Paul over the speakerphone. "As far as optics go, it puts the burden back on them."

Jameson Shibayama had once been James Fry, son of an esteemed Texas politician. In 1972, he married a woman, Camilla Thursby, the heir to an oil fortune. On their honeymoon, James, an accomplished sailor, had taken his new wife on a voyage to Central America in the sailboat, an Amel Kirk 36, that his wife's family had purchased for them as a wedding gift. Only a few days aboard the boat, James radioed early one morning that his wife had disappeared and was nowhere to be seen. He stated to the authorities that they had gone to sleep that night and, when he awoke, Camilla was gone. Ultimately, he was not charged with any crime. Her death was ruled a suicide. Camilla's diaries had revealed that she had battled depression for years and had not wanted to marry James, but her family had insisted. The incident produced a true-crime book in 1975, *Honeymoon Disappearance: Foul Play on the High Seas,* long out of print. Two years later, Fry legally changed his name to Jameson Shibayama.

"Why Shibayama?" Paul asked, and then felt foolish, as if the whole story was undone by this one mystery.

"I don't know, Paul," Diana said, annoyed. "It doesn't matter."

"So he's not even Japanese?" he asked.

"I don't think so," Diana said.

"He didn't look Japanese," Meggy said.

"The point is that Jameson Shibayama has been a primary suspect in two mysterious disappearances," Diana continued. "The police will redouble their efforts, dig deeper into his past. Public opinion is entirely on your side now. We're getting closer to the truth."

The Shibayamas had moved out of their house, were living with Mindy's ancient mother in Nashville, and the house now sat empty. It wasn't clear if they still owned it or if no one else had bought it. There was no sign in the yard.

"And they had a daughter that died young," Paul offered. "It was cancer, but maybe that wasn't actually the case. That's got to put suspicion on them as well."

"What?" asked Meggy. "No."

"That's not right," Diana replied. "They've never had any kids."

"No," Paul said, starting to stammer. "They told me that they had a daughter that died when she was, like, seven or eight or something like that."

"When did they tell you that?" Meggy asked.

"The night all this happened," Paul said.

"I think you're misremembering, maybe," Diana said.

"No, I'm not," Paul said. "Ask them about it."

"They never had any children," Diana said, as if that settled everything.

"Well . . ." Paul said, but now couldn't remember with certainty, everything about that night both intensely vivid and yet so far in the past that it was difficult to remember what was a dream and what was real.

"What's the end result at this point?" Meggy asked.

"What do you mean?" Diana asked. She had appeared on several talk shows. She had set up a foundation in the baby's name. She was becoming famous.

Meggy and Paul sat in their house and tried to write. The university had given Paul a year's paid leave. They were stuck in this space where their child was not with them, and they had no idea how to open it back up. They were left with words, and they did nothing, offered nothing.

"I mean, he's dead. Right? Jameson killed him or he didn't, but he's gone," Meggy said to Diana.

"That's not true, Meggy," Diana said. "You can't give up hope."

"Then where the fuck is he?" Meggy yelled.

There was a long pause before Diana said, "Jameson could have given him to someone else. He could have sold him."

"Jesus, Diana," Paul said, his voice rising.

"I'm sorry," Diana said immediately. "I'm just saying . . . I'm just saying that you can't give up hope."

"But I don't know why," Meggy said, so listless and tired that she wanted to go back to sleep except for the fact that she had just woken up.

"You will see your baby again," Diana finally said. "I know this. Somehow. Someway. In this world or the next—"

Paul reached for the button and turned off the speaker-phone. The silence felt crackly, as if Diana at any moment would come back on the phone and keep talking.

Paul and Meggy stared at each other.

THE LOST BABY 261

"I wrote a poem about him," Meggy said.

"I started writing a story about him," Paul admitted.

They were quiet for a long moment. "Would you like me to read your poem?" Paul asked her, and Meggy shook her head.

"No," she said. "I don't want anyone to read it."

11.

A year had passed. Nothing had changed. Or perhaps so much had changed that it was impossible to tell what their new lives were. Meggy and Paul were dumbfounded that no one had been arrested. It was infuriating, the way the police simply seemed to shrug and then wait for something to break. They had stopped calling with updates. There were none.

At times, Meggy wished that the police would charge her with the death of her baby, just so that she could move into a new identity, could move out of this stasis of half mourning. It seemed so obvious to her and Paul. Something had happened to their baby and the Shibayamas, if not directly responsible, knew more than they had admitted. Where was a no-nonsense, old-school detective who would get Jameson Shibayama in a locked room and hit him with a rubber hose until he confessed? How did this person not exist? What if Meggy borrowed a million dollars from Diana and then offered it to Jameson in exchange for the truth? Even if she promised that he would suffer no repercussions, would he tell them?

Paul opened the mail one afternoon and found a letter with no return address. Inside the envelope was a greeting card with

an image of a cartoon cat wearing a sailor's outfit. *Bon Voyage!*
it said. Paul showed it to Meggy, who opened it to read aloud
what was in the card, written in the tiniest handwriting, so precise that it seemed like a robot had done it. "You will find your
baby buried under the bench at the dog park." She dropped the
card, then picked it back up, then held it by her thumb and index finger. "Should we put this in a plastic bag?" she said. She
was shaking. "For evidence?"

"It's a joke," Paul said. "It's a really fucking cruel joke."

"What if it's not?" Meggy said.

"Then we'll give it to the police and they can decide."

"No," Meggy said.

"Then what?" Paul said. It seemed, in the past month, unless they were fucking, they could not stand to be in the same
room as the other. It wasn't that they hated each other. It was
just that their grief was such that it could not touch against the
other's without turning toxic. In five weeks, Paul would go back
to teaching. Diana had invited Meggy to live with her for a few
months, to get out of town, but Meggy refused. "I want to be
home," she had told Diana.

"In case he comes back?" Diana guessed, and Meggy didn't
answer.

Now, holding the card, Meggy looked at Paul. "Let us do
this. Just you and me."

That night, they sat in the car across from the dog park. It was
two in the morning. They finally walked to the enclosed park,
each carrying a trowel. They stopped at the only bench in the
dog park and knelt as if they were about to pray.

The ground showed no signs of wear. It looked like the rest of the ground in the dog park.

"There's nothing here," Paul said.

"Okay," Meggy replied.

"God," Paul said. "There cannot be anything here, please."

"Let's just dig," Meggy said, and she jabbed her trowel into the earth.

Thirty minutes later, the digging harder than they had imagined, Meggy's shovel hit something metal. She felt her breathing become so rapid that she had to lie on her back. Paul placed his hand on her chest. "It's okay," he said. "We can go home right now."

Meggy sat up and then leaned over the hole. She picked up the trowel and cleared away the dirt. Paul shone the flashlight into the hole, and Meggy pulled out a small tin box. It was rusted.

"I don't want you to open it," Paul said.

"I'm going to open it," Meggy said.

"It's not him," he told her.

"I know," she said. "But I don't know for sure."

"Please, Meggy," he said.

She opened the box and there were eight birthday candles, burned halfway down, a clear plastic bracelet, and a tiny plastic baby, the kind that you would find inside a king cake.

Meggy closed the box. She then felt the intense sensation of being watched. She stood up quickly and looked around. There was nothing, nothing that she could see.

"He's gone," Paul finally said.

"I know," Meggy said. "I guess I know that."

"I love you," Paul said.

"Not right now," she replied. "Please."

They each sat on the ground, leaning against the bench. They looked up at the sky, but there were no stars visible.

"I'm going to go live with Diana," Meggy said after ten or fifteen minutes of silence.

"Don't do that," Paul said.

"Just for a little while," she said.

"We could try again," Paul offered.

"Let's go home," Meggy said. She knew it was pointless to reply. They both knew that they could not go through this again.

Meggy placed the box back in the hole and covered it with dirt. On the walk back to the car, they held hands.

12.

Three years later, Meggy lived in Decatur, Georgia, near Atlanta, in an apartment that her sister paid for. Diana also gave her a monthly stipend that was generous enough that Meggy didn't have to work. Instead, she wrote poems. They were about the relationship between a mother and a son, spanning nearly forty years of their lives. She had published most of them in prestigious journals, all under a pen name, so as not to arouse suspicion or to make the poems into something that they weren't. Of course the poems were exactly that, but she didn't need anyone else knowing it.

Paul was denied tenure. He had expected this. His teaching had become atrocious, the bare minimum to get through the semester. He hadn't published anything since his first novel. Also, people wondered if he had murdered his own baby. He waited out his time and then he had to go somewhere else. He found a job teaching composition at a community college in Atlanta. He was eight hundred pages into a novel about a baby who disappears and the husband and wife who never stop searching for the baby. He expected that it would take at least another eight hundred pages before it was finished, and he already knew that there would be no resolution.

His apartment was fifteen minutes from Meggy's, and they saw each other often. They would meet at a coffee shop and share a table, reading or writing. They rarely spoke to each other, simply shared the same space. They were still married, legally. They still fucked in those sad moments when they needed it. They were together and apart, and it made perfect sense to them.

After Mindy Shibayama's mother died, Jameson and Mindy sold her house and, according to Diana, moved to Mexico. They disappeared so easily because of course it was that easy. Who was stopping a single person in this world from vanishing without a trace? How hard was it to step out of your life and into something that not another person knew?

Paul and Meggy had long given up on closure. It seemed such a privileged thing to expect, answers in light of such a mystery. They knew that their baby was dead and was also alive. They knew that nothing would ever change that.

13.

Seven years after the disappearance of their baby, Meggy walked into the DeKalb County Public Library to see a poetry reading at the Georgia Center for the Book. It was a quarter after five in the afternoon. She sat on a bench outside the restrooms, waiting until six, when the event would begin. She was reading another fifty-page chunk of Paul's novel, which was now more than fifteen hundred pages long. It was, she had to admit, completely engrossing, though she wondered if anyone else would think so.

Her own book, *Motherson,* written under the pen name S. R. Swann, had been published by Four Way Books, and it had been a finalist for the National Book Critics Circle Award. She did no readings, no book tour. There was no author photo on the back of the book, the briefest of bios. Her sister had worked with another lawyer to set it all up, to ensure that no one else knew the author. This mystery had created enough interest that Meggy sometimes imagined that the acclaim for the book was partly based on the sheer fact that people wanted to know the truth. And she knew that she would never give it to them. For as long as she lived, they would never know.

While she sat on the bench, she felt the presence of someone hovering in front of her. She looked away from the manuscript pages and stared into the face of her own son.

"Hello," he said, smiling. He was older, seven or eight, wearing a pair of camouflage shorts and a white T-shirt. He was chubby, his hair cut severely. But she could see her son in this boy. His eyes, his expression, whatever light was inside of him, this was her son. She could not breathe. She wanted to reach out and touch his face, but she held back. She had to be sure.

She said the name of her baby, and the boy smiled. She said it again, and the boy nodded. "Hi," he said.

"Can I kiss you?" she asked her son, and he nodded. She

kissed him on the lips, which were so soft. He smelled like grape bubble gum. He was missing one of his teeth.

"Can I take you home?" she asked. Her son nodded. "I have a backpack with clothes in it," he said, growing excited. "I have some books, too. I checked them out."

She stood, her entire body electrified. She could not make her arms and legs do what she needed them to do. Her son seemed to understand. He took her hand, it fit so easily into his, and he led her through the hallway, out the doors of the library, and onto the street.

"My car is over there," she said, and the boy walked with her. She unlocked the door and he slid into the backseat. She got into the car and started it. The radio was playing, and she quickly turned it off. She waited for someone, anyone, to stop her, to tell her that this was not real, that it was all a dream. She waited for someone to come and take her son out of her car. But a minute, maybe two, passed, and nothing had changed. She looked in the rearview mirror and there was her son, still smiling. She pulled out of the parking lot, onto the street, and started driving.

"Where are we going?" her son asked.

"Home," she said.

14.

"I'm hungry," her son said once they were back at her apartment, and Meggy asked him what he liked to eat. "Pizza," he said. "I love pizza." She had frozen pizzas in the fridge. She would learn everything that he loved, everything about him. She turned on the oven and then she sat at the kitchen table beside him. She ran her fingers through his hair. "That tickles a little," he said, giggling.

There was a knock on the door. She had called Paul from the car, had told him only that she had found their son and did not stay on the line long enough to have to explain. She stood and walked to the door, but she paused before opening it. She knew that he might not believe her, that he could try to make her give their son back. Right now, it was just her and her son and no one else in the world. It was so thrilling to keep it this way. But Paul deserved a part in this. He had been through it just the same as her. Just the same as their son. She opened the door.

Paul pushed past her and stood over the boy.

"Hi," the boy said. Paul said the name of his son. The boy nodded. Paul knelt beside the boy and stared at him. After a few seconds, he looked over at Meggy. "It's him, isn't it?" he asked. She nodded. Paul hugged the boy tightly.

"Is the pizza ready yet?" their son asked, and Paul and Meggy both laughed.

After dinner, night coming on, the three of them climbed into Meggy's queen-size bed, their son between Paul and Meggy.

"Are you happy?" Meggy asked her son.

"I am," he said. "I'm so happy."

"We never stopped thinking about you," Paul said.

"Good," their son said. "That's good."

"We love you so much," Meggy said.

"I love you, too," their son replied, so easily that it broke their hearts into a million pieces.

Meggy's cell phone, which was on the dresser, was vibrating. Paul's own phone was playing a soft ditty under the pile of his clothes on the floor. Then the room grew silent, nothing in the entire universe except the sound of the three of them breathing. And when the phones sounded again, and then again, and then again, never stopping, Paul and Meggy simply held on to their son, the thing between them, that held them together, that they had lost and somehow found. They had found him, and they would never ever lose him again.

ACKNOWLEDGMENTS

Thanks to the following:

Julie Barer and everyone at the Book Group, especially Nicole Cunningham.

Zack Wagman and Ecco, with special mention to Allison Saltzman and Emma Janaskie.

Kelly and Debbie Wilson; Kristen, Wes, and Kellan Huffman; Mary Couch; John, Meredith, Warren, Laura, Morgan, and Philip James; and the Wilson, Fuselier, and Baltz families.

St. Mary's Sewanee, for the use of the Hermitage, where I wrote several of these stories.

Sewanee: The University of the South.

My friends Ann Patchett, Leah Stewart, Matt O'Keefe, Sam Esquith, Cecily Parks, Isabel Galbraith, Lucy Corin, Lee Conell, Claire Vaye Watkins, David Syler, Heidi Syler, Jason Griffey, Betsy Sandlin, Manuel Chinchilla, Lauryl Tucker, Kelly Malone, Elizabeth Grammer, Katie McGhee, Matt Schrader, and Caki Wilkinson.

Finally and most emphatically:

Griffith Fodder-Wing Wilson and Patchett Halcomb Wilson.

Leigh Anne Couch.